HER REBEL HEART

ALISON STUART

Oportet Publishing

Her Rebel Heart

Text Copyright © 2015 by Alison Stuart

ISBN: 9780995434226

This edition: Oportet Publishing 2018

Editor: Annie Seaton

Cover Design: Fiona Jayde

Formatting: Ebony McKenna

Discover other titles by Alison Stuart at www.alisonstuart.com

Praise for Alison Stuart

"...BY THE SWORD was one of the most moving and powerful books I have read in a very long time...This book pulls at your heart strings and you hold your breath until the very end praying for these two characters." *5 CUPS:Coffee Time Romance*

"...THE KING'S MAN is an absolutely terrific historical I just couldn't put down! Alison Stuart is a master storyteller who has written a story that's fast-paced, enthralling, passionate and absolutely impossible to resist..." *Ecataromance*

"GATHER THE BONES is breathtakingly romantic. This moving and dramatic love story will haunt you long after you turn the last page..." *Anna Campbell, best selling author*.

Herefordshire, England 1643

As the English Civil War divides England, pitting brother against brother and father against son, in a county loyal to the King, tiny Kinton Lacey castle is one of the brave few loyal to the roundhead cause.

With her father away, Deliverance Felton will do whatever it takes to defend her family home against the royalist forces ranged against it. She can shoot and wield a sword as well as any man and anything she needs to know about siege warfare she has learned from a book...but no book can prepare her for what is to come.

Captain Luke Collyer, soldier of fortune and a man with his own reasons for loyalty to the parliamentary cause, is sent to relieve the castle. Everything he knows about siege warfare in general and women in particular he has learned from experience, but when it comes to Deliverance Felton has he met his match?

Deliverance will not give up her command lightly and Luke will have to face a challenge to his authority as fierce as the cavalier foe outside the walls. He will do whatever it takes to win Deliverance's trust but will he run the risk of losing his own, well guarded, heart?

Alison Stuart

HER REBEL HEART

A romance of the English Civil War

This book is dedicated to the love of my life, DJB.

We met doing officer training in the military and, like Luke and Deliverance we have enjoyed many interesting discussions about the correct placement of defensive works and the siting of guns — just like any normal couple really!

Chapter One

Kinton Lacey Castle, Herefordshire,
July 25, 1643

Startled out of an uneasy doze by the crackle of musket fire, Deliverance sent books and papers flying as she rummaged through the detritus on the table in her search for the flint. As the candle sputtered into life, the door opened and her steward, Melchior Blakelocke, stood outlined in the doorway, holding a covered lantern.

"Are we being attacked?" Deliverance asked.

"I don't think so," Melchior replied. "In fact, my lady, I think it is our besiegers who are being attacked."

Hope sprang in Deliverance's heart. "Is it Father? Has he come to relieve us?"

She reached for the elegant French Wheelock musket her father used for hunting, running her hand over the well-polished wood of the stock. It had a kick that threatened to dislocate her shoulder every time she used it, but she took pride in her mastery of the weapon.

Outside, the entire garrison of Kinton Lacey Castle had deployed along the walls, but to her relief, the firing and shouts came from beyond the crumbling walls of the old castle. She took her now accustomed vantage point on the northern tower of the bastion gate and squinted into the darkness and confusion.

Smoke and flame from burning outbuildings lent a surreal light to the melee of men that whirled and danced in the shadows as if re-enacting some ancient pagan ceremony. Only the clash of steel instead of cymbals brought home the grim purpose of the bizarre pageant.

Two men on horseback appeared out of the smoke and cantered towards the castle. Backlit by the fires, they could have been a pair of vengeful spirits.

Her heart pounding, Deliverance raised her musket and fired, cursing in a most unladylike manner as the musket ball skimmed past the two men, taking the taller man's hat. His horse, startled by its rider's jerk of alarm, reared up depositing the soldier on the ground. For a moment he lay still, before rising to his hands and knees. Shaking his head, he rose slowly to his feet, casting an upwards glance in the direction of the castle, as he dusted off his hat and remounted his horse.

Melchior cleared his throat. "While that is excellent shooting, I think you will find they are friends not foes."

Deliverance's stomach lurched. "How can you tell?"

"They wear the orange sash of the parliamentary forces, my lady."

Deliverance leaned the musket against the wall, clenching and unclenching her hand in an effort to disguise her shaking fingers. Nausea rose in her throat. It was the first time she had fired the weapon intending to kill and she had nearly killed one of their own relieving force.

She took a deep breath, struggling to regain her composure as the two men came to a halt at the bridge over the castle's defensive ditch. Facing them were the stout oaken gates to the castle that Deliverance had shut on her foe two weeks earlier.

"Hold your fire." The man she had shot at called up to the defenders. "We are sent by Sir John Felton to relieve this castle."

Deliverance picked up her musket and drew back to a vantage point where she could see without being seen. "You answer, Melchior."

Melchior cast her a sidelong glance and stepped forward to the battlements. "Your name, sir?" "Captain Luke Collyer."

"How do we know they've come from Father?" Deliverance prompted her steward. "How do I know you are sent by his lordship?" Melchior demanded.

The man who had identified himself as Captain Luke Collyer produced a paper from his jacket and waved it at the wall.

"These are my orders. While I don't wish to appear churlish, sir, we have no great desire to remain outside these walls when those knaves could be back at any moment."

"What do you mean?" Melchior asked, leaning further over the ramparts.

"We appear to have seen off your besiegers for the moment." The man's voice rose to make himself heard by all on the castle wall.

Deliverance drew a sharp intake of breath as relief flooded through her. The siege was over but she still had to be careful. She put no trust in Farrington not to try and gull her in this fashion.

"Very well, Melchior, let them in, but I want every man with a weapon to have it trained on them." She tapped a fingernail on the stock of her musket. "I will meet them in the Great Hall."

"May I suggest a change of dress, madam?"

She looked down at her breeches. "Demure and ladylike?"

Melchior nodded. "Demure and ladylike."

"Well, this is a warm welcome," Luke said, as he and his comrade, Ned Barrett, rode under the gatehouse into the courtyard beneath a bristling bank of muskets. "First I'm shot at and now this. Hardly what I would have expected."

He turned to Sergeant Hale, who had followed them in on foot. "Clear the village, Hale. Make sure none of the blackguards are left to bother us for the time being."

"Sir!" Hale saluted smartly and turned back through the castle gate.

A tall, thin man with wispy, greying hair and a lugubrious expression waited on the steps of what would have once been the castle keep, but now more closely resembled a comfortable manor house, with mullioned windows knocked through its sturdy walls. Roses grew around the stonework. A few well aimed cannonballs would reduce it to rubble.

"My lady will receive you in the Great Hall," the man announced, gesturing at the open door. Fingering the hole in his hat, Luke, with Ned beside him, followed the man up the wide stone stairs toward the front entrance.

Despite its façade of tall walls, a tower at each corner and a solid gatehouse, even in the dark, he could see some of the walls had crumbled. The years had turned Kinton Lacey from one of Edward III's ring of stout Marches castles to a family home that would be hard to defend.

They were shown through an ornately carved wooden screen into the Great Hall. A branch of candles on the long, oak table cast a thin light in the cavernous room. In keeping with rest of the castle, it appeared to have been modernised to provide such comforts as fireplaces, glazed windows and wooden panelling. Another tribute to more peaceful times.

In the shadows of the lofty ceiling, faded, dusty standards hung from poles and rows of hooks on the walls, indicating the places where ancient weapons had once been displayed. These, Luke assumed with amusement, probably now armed the garrison.

"Are you the men who saved us?"

Both men turned back to face the screen. A woman walked toward them across the flagged floor. Luke's blood stirred as she came into the light thrown by the candles. This girl was a beauty. Soft, fair curls framed a serene oval face and azure-blue eyes held his gaze from beneath long lashes. Her perfect rose- coloured lips parted in a smile of delight as she looked from one to the other.

"Mistress Felton." Luke gave her the benefit of his most courtly bow before prodding Ned to do the same. He could see from the idiotic smile on Ned's face that he had fallen instantly in love. He just hoped Sir John Felton's assertions concerning his daughter's ability to defend her honor were not misplaced.

"You must be so brave," the young woman enthused. "There were so many of them."

"Captain Collyer?" Another woman's voice, clipped and businesslike, cut across Ned's stammered protestations of how simple the job had been.

Both men looked away from the fair-haired beauty. Another woman strode across the floor toward them.

"I see you've already met my sister, Penitence," she said as she reached them. "I am Deliverance Felton."

Luke stared. If this was Deliverance Felton, she could not have been more different from her sister. As dark as Penitence was fair, she was at least four fingers shorter, with a strong jawline, a long nose. Her saving grace were her eyes, large light blue eyes, the colour of the sky in summer. Where Penitence's hair hung in carefully coiffed curls, Deliverance's attempt at a similar style resembled bedraggled rats' tails.

"Deliverance Felton?" Luke enquired with a trace of uncertainty in his voice. "Yes," she replied curtly, holding out her hand. "Your orders, Captain Collyer?" Luke fumbled in his jacket, presenting her with the crumpled and stained paper. "My orders," he said with an inclination of his head.

Deliverance Felton turned the paper over and broke the seal. A second, neatly sealed letter fell to the floor. She stooped and picked it up, turning it over to peer at the seal, before tucking the packet away in her skirts.

She looked at Luke. "I thought my father might have come himself."

Luke spread his hands. "He sends his apologies, Mistress Felton. The defence of Gloucester commands his full attention."

"How is he?" Penitence asked.

"Well," Luke replied. "Yes, very well, when I last saw him. In fine voice..." Ned's elbow pressed into his side.

Sir John Felton had only let them out of Gloucester after an hour long lecture on how to conduct themselves. They were both in disgrace. A few long nights in one of the inns and the complaints of several good burghers of Gloucester had brought them to Sir John's attention. He had judged their behaviour unfitting for the forces of the godly parliamentarians and the affronted citizenry of Gloucester and had sent them to the relief of Kinton Lacey.

"I see you have orders to reinforce the garrison here." Deliverance looked up, cutting in on his reverie. "How many men did you bring with you?" "Forty-five," Luke replied.

Her eyes widened and the corners of her mouth turned down at the corners. "Only forty-five?" "How many do you have in the garrison at present?" he asked, with a sense of foreboding. "Twenty-three," she said.

Luke glanced at Ned. "Colonel Felton led us to believe the garrison numbered over fifty."

"It did," Deliverance replied. "But Father took the able-bodied men and those left behind returned to their fields and to defend their own homes, particularly once Sir Richard Farrington started to send out raiding parties."

"Sir Richard Farrington?" Ned asked. "The local royalist commander."

"An odious man, even before the war began." Deliverance shuddered. "Always thought himself superior to us. It is his men who have been camped outside our walls for the last weeks."

Luke smiled. "You do not seem particularly worse the wear for the inconvenience."

Deliverance met his eyes with a smile of satisfaction. "That is because we were well prepared, Captain Collyer. We could withstand a siege of some months if need be."

"I see." Luke looked up at the bare walls. "And your weapons?"

She followed his gaze and a little colour stained her cheeks. "Ah...you guess rightly, Captain Collyer. We're not well armed."

"We've brought fresh arms and powder and a couple of small cannonade," Ned said.

Deliverance Felton beamed, the smile transforming her face. "Oh, that is wonderful news." Her eyes gleamed in the candlelight. "Cannonade—"

Luke cleared his throat. "Are there other Parliamentary garrisons in the area?"

"This is a county that holds strongly for the King, Captain Collyer, but there is a small garrison held for Parliament at Byton Castle, five miles north." Deliverance sighed. "Other than that, we find ourselves in the midst of very unfriendly neighbours."

Luke considered the odds as she had presented them: Two tiny outposts of parliamentary sympathy in a county professing itself loyal to the King. Did Felton really think he could hold Kinton Lacey? This Farrington, whoever he was, would have greater resources to draw on, and would return to swat this annoying little insect of a garrison at the earliest possibility.

He looked down at Deliverance.

She watched him, with the same bright, intelligent gaze as her father.

"I have the plans for the defence of the castle in my father's library. I just haven't had the men to do the work. Of course, now you're here...Come this way gentlemen."

She set off across the hall, leaving the two men scurrying to catch up with her. At the screen, the tall man stopped them, inclining his head to Luke.

"Your sergeant tells me the town is clear of the malignants," he said.

"Excellent," Luke said, allowing himself a small instant of self satisfaction. There would be precious few such moments in the weeks to come he suspected.

Deliverance regarded him from beneath her dark fringe, her hands on her hips.

"Captain Collyer, I am impressed. With less than fifty men you have seen off a force of three times that number?"

Luke smiled and inclined his head. "It would seem so. Darkness and a little subterfuge, madam." Deliverance turned to her man. "Melchior, I was just taking Captain Collyer and..." She looked at Ned. "I'm sorry, what was your name?"

"Ned Barrett, ma'am," Ned replied. "Your servant."

"This is Melchior Blakelocke, our steward and my second-in-command."

"Your steward is your second-in-command?" Luke asked, the ill-concealed disbelief colouring his tone.

Deliverance cast him a frowning glance of disapproval. "Melchior saw service with my father on the continent, Captain Collyer."

Luke glanced at Blakelocke and then back at his mistress. "I didn't mean to imply—" She cut him short with a wave of her hand.

"People are not always what they seem, Captain Collyer." She turned to a set of stairs, pausing to look back at the two men. "Are you coming?

Deliverance opened the door to the pleasant room that served her father as a library, when he was at home. In his absence she had taken it over, and it had become her sanctuary from the world. The familiar scent of dust, beeswax polish and musty books greeted her.

The papers she had dislodged in her haste to get to the walls, still littered the floor and the large table in the centre of the room could not be seen beneath the piles of books which were stacked haphazardly around a drawing of the castle and its surrounds. She had spent hours preparing this plan for the defence of her home.

Captain Collyer picked up a much-thumbed copy of *The Exercise of Armes* from one of the piles on the desk, and she caught the quick glance he exchanged with his colleague.

Heat rose in Deliverance's face. "I am afraid all my learning is from my father's books."

She didn't add that those books she had not found in her father's collection had been secretly

ordered from her longsuffering book seller in Ludlow.

"Well, it's an excellent book," Luke Collyer said, setting it back on the table. The quirk of his lips into a quickly suppressed smile did not escape her notice. Her skin prickled at the condescension in his tone.

She pulled the plan of the castle from beneath the tomes. "I've had ample time in the last two weeks to consider the defence of the castle." She flattened the creases from the paper. "Now, I think if we put a redoubt in here..." She stabbed at the paper with her forefinger. "And a defensive ditch, along here."

When her remarks were met with silence, she looked up. Both men stared at her as if she had walked into the room stark naked.

"Is there a problem?"

Luke cleared his throat. "With respect, madam, but your father... Sir John Felton... has placed me in command of this garrison and I—"

"Do you not think me capable of having an opinion on how to defend my own home?" She fixed him with a well-practiced stare which would make a weaker man quail.

Luke Collyer returned the gaze without blinking. "I respect your opinion, madam, and if... when... I need your advice I shall ask for it."

How dare this man speak to me in that condescending manner. She took a steadying breath and squared her shoulders. She was Deliverance Felton, chatelaine of this castle and this Collyer a mere...a mere...

"And what experience do you have, captain?"

The man's gaze held hers and he too straightened, resting his hand on *The Exercise of Armes*. "I have been a soldier since I was nineteen, madam. I have fought on the continent and in the Scottish wars. Your father chose me for this task with every confidence in my abilities. You can trust me with the protection of this castle, and you can return to more appropriate concerns."

"More appropriate concerns?" Deliverance bridled. "What is more appropriate than the safety of Kinton Lacey?"

Luke Collyer's eyes narrowed. The unusual light grey eyes, at odds with the dark brown hair that framed his lean, tanned face were fixed on her had lost all trace of humour. She saw a hard, uncompromising soldier. "Forgive me, madam, but military matters are not for gently-bred women. All I am saying is that you are free to return to—"

"My embroidery, perhaps?" she said in a tone that dripped ice. "I assure you, Captain Collyer that the defence of my home is of far greater importance to me than its decoration. I have read all these books," she gestured at the table, "and I warrant I know as much of matters military as you, Captain Collyer."

"And I have had years of practical experience, madam," he responded in a tone that matched hers for frigidity.

Melchior cleared his throat. "I think, madam, this is a discussion for the morning. These two gentlemen have ridden from Gloucester and fought a battle, vanquishing our foes. Sirs, you must be tired and hungry. Let me show you to your quarters and see you are fed. In the morning we will all be in a better position to discuss defensive works."

Deliverance shot her steward a quick, angry glance. She did not need or want Melchior's intervention but it had the desired effect, the tension in the room dissipating as if he had opened the window and let in the breeze.

She tossed the paper back on to the table and sniffed. "Very well. If you need me, I shall be in my chamber hard at work... at my embroidery."

"Insufferable man." Deliverance ranted to her sister as she concluded her summation of the discussion with Captain Collyer.

Penitence looked up from her needlework. "He is a man, Liv. Of course he is going to want to take command. What does Father say?"

Deliverance pulled out their father's letter and began to read.

"*Dearest daughter, I trust this letter finds you and your sister in good health. Reports of Sir Richard Farrington's increasing movements in the area of Kinton Lacey has caused me some concern, so I am sending one of my best men to you to reinforce the garrison and command the defences in the event of an attack by the King's men. I trust you to defer to Captain Collyer in all matters military. I feel more certain in my mind knowing you and my beloved Kinton Lacey are in a man's hands.*"

"There you are," Penitence commented. "Father is quite explicit. Your Captain Collyer is here to take command."

Deliverance sniffed and continued, her eyes widening as she silently read the next sentence.

"*Deliverance, daughter, I must warn you that Captain Collyer has something of a reputation and an eye for a pretty face, so I trust you to see to the protection of your sister's honor and to report to me should any indiscretion occur.*

Yr loving father, JF."

Deliverance set the letter down, wounded by the tone of the

letter, particularly her father's last words. Beautiful, gentle and serene Penitence would always be considered the one worthy of protecting, never her.

"What's the matter?" Penitence, always intuitive to her sister's moods, looked up, her brow creased with concern. "What else did Father say?"

Deliverance forced a smile. "Nothing. Just sent us his love." She ran a hand across her forehead. "It has been rather a trying day."

She refolded her father's letter and tucked it into her skirts. "Deliverance?" her sister prompted.

"I should be grateful to Captain Collyer for relieving me of the terrible responsibility of the castle's defence. Grateful? This is my home, my castle..."

As Deliverance paced the floor, Penitence bent her head to her embroidery. Deliverance heard her sister murmur as she stabbed the needle through the cloth. "Poor man."

Chapter Two

T his is quite good," Ned remarked as he bent over the plan of the defences that Deliverance had shown them the night before.

Luke spun the paper to face him. "Hmmph," he agreed grudgingly. "They would be fine if we had unlimited men, supplies and time, but as we lack all three, a little more practicality is called for. Pass me that pen."

"You better not let Deliverance catch you tampering with her plans."

At the sound of a woman's voice, both men looked up. Penitence stood in the doorway, a smile playing at the corner of her luscious lips. Luke cast his friend a quick sidelong glance. Ned's mouth had fallen open as he stared at the lovely Mistress Felton.

"Ned," he said in a low voice. "Remember our conversation with Sir John." Ned's mouth clamped shut.

Luke glanced up at the portrait above the fireplace. The man glared down at him with such severity that he shivered. What Sir John lacked in height he made up for in force of character, and Luke could still feel the painful clench of the supposedly friendly hand the man had lain on his shoulder.

"*Collyer, Barrett,*" he had said, his tone exuding calm and bonhomie. "*I know your reputations. If so much as a whisper reaches my ear that either of my daughters has in any way been compromised by your attentions to them, it will be my personal pleasure to firstly detach you from a certain part of your anatomy with a blunt knife and then hang you from the nearest tree. Do I make myself quite clear?*"

Looking into the man's eyes, Luke knew that Sir John meant every word and gave his solemn oath on the spot.

He shuddered at the memory and bowed respectfully to Sir John's youngest daughter. "Good morning, Mistress Felton."

Penitence responded with a graceful curtsey and an inclination of her head. "I trust you slept well? I am afraid accommodation within the castle is a little short."

As they had been assigned Sir John's own bedchamber, neither man had any complaint about the accommodation.

"Oh, there you are, Pen," Deliverance Felton appeared at the door beside her sister. She looked into the room and scowled. "Good morning, gentlemen," she said, her voice cold.

Luke acknowledged her unenthusiastic greeting with a deep bow.

"And a good morning to you, Mistress Felton. We were just looking at your plans for the defence of the castle." Feeling he may have got off on a bad footing with the formidable Mistress Felton the previous night, he tried to make amends. "Your work is commendable."

Deliverance Felton's face brightened. "So do we start this morning?"

An awkward silence fell on the room as Luke and Deliverance met each other's gaze. "Collyer..." Ned prompted him.

"Yes, of course, we will start this morning," Luke said at last, trying to keep his tone light and pleasant. "However, there will need to be some modifications to your *excellent* plan."

Deliverance crossed to the table and looked down at the paper, now covered in crossing out, and notes written in Luke's impetuous hand. Her back stiffened and she rounded on him, her eyes hot with anger. "What have you done? Do you know how long it took me to prepare that plan?"

"And a fine plan it is, Mistress Felton." Luke sounded condescending even to his own ears. "But, in the circumstances we find ourselves, impractical."

Deliverance picked up one of the books and waved it at him. For a moment Luke wondered if she planned to throw it at him. He tensed in anticipation.

"I followed the principles of defence to the letter," she said.

"And as an academic exercise it cannot be faulted, but I'm sorry, we do not have the men or the resources to do anything more than excavate the ditches on the west wall and put palisades against the north wall. The east wall is well protected by the river. I don't see that as a problem"

"But what about the south wall?" Luke heard Ned draw a quick breath.

What about the south wall? They had debated that point over breakfast after a quick inspection of the castle in daylight.

The woman really did know what she was talking about.

"Mistress Felton, please do not presume to teach me my business," Luke responded. "I've made an assessment of the castle and its surrounds this morning, and I see the major threat being to the east and north walls."

Deliverance drew herself up, and he could see from the cast of her mouth and the determination in her chin that she was not going to meekly walk out of the room and return to her preserves...or embroidery...or whatever she should have been doing.

"Deliverance, please let's not argue among ourselves," her sister said. "That is not what father wants."

Deliverance cast Penitence a quick glance. "Of course, Captain Collyer. You may do as you wish. I would not presume to interfere with the command of your men."

Something about the acquiescent smile and the sudden demure way Deliverance clasped her hands in front of her skirt, filled Luke with a cold premonition of dread.

"Thank you, Mistress Felton. I am glad you agree," he said.

"You have made the position quite clear, Captain Collyer." As she turned to leave the room, she stopped and without turning back, she added. "Of course, my men will continue to answer to me."

Luke clenched his jaw shut and cast an appealing glance at Penitence who merely smiled and shrugged before gliding from the room in her sister's wake.

Deliverance moved the food around her plate with her knife, conscious of the awkward silence around the table. Ned Barrett and Penitence had been chatting brightly but their forced cheerfulness only emphasised the brooding atmosphere between Luke Collyer and herself. Now Penitence and Ned had fallen silent.

Luke cleared his throat. "Perhaps, Mistress Felton, you could tell me a little more about Sir Richard Farrington?"

Penitence looked up, her brow furrowed with undisguised distress at the mention of the Farrington name. Deliverance sent her a warning glance and her sister returned her gase to her plate.

"What do you wish to know?" Deliverance asked. "What manner of man is he?"

"Sir Richard owns Brandon Hall, ten miles to our north. He and my father enjoyed relatively cordial relations before the war and indeed—"

She gave her sister's bent head a quick glance. Luke Collyer did not need to know about Penitence's broken betrothal to Jack Farrington. "He has two sons who serve with him. The eldest, Charles, is a ..." she struggled to find the right words to describe Charles. "He is a bully. Even as a child he could be cruel." She looked up at the high beams of the ceiling, remembering. "On one occasion I saw him kick a puppy to death."

She returned her gaze to Luke and read the understanding in the grey depths of his eyes. She didn't really notice people's eyes, but Luke's eyes were the colour of autumn smoke.

"I see," Luke said "And his other son?"

"Jack is quite different," Deliverance said, avoiding looking at Penitence. "He did not go willingly to war whereas Charles is probably thriving on it."

"Thank you. It is always helpful to know who we are facing," Luke said. "And Sir Richard, what resources does he bring to this affair?"

"Money and the King's ear," Deliverance said with a trace of bitterness in her voice. "He would like to own Kinton Lacey. We have forestry rights and a tin mine that he covets."

Luke raised an eyebrow. "Rich pickings indeed."

Deliverance nodded. "So you see why we must hold our land?"

Luke shrugged. "He probably already has the mine."

"And his men are making free use of the forest. I know this is the fate of war, Captain Collyer. Do you think he will leave us in peace now you are here?"

Luke laughed and took a swig of wine. He set the cup down and shook his head. "You're no fool, Mistress Felton. He can profess to seize your land and assets in the King's name but it is total possession he seeks, and to accomplish that end he must drive you out of Kinton Lacey."

Deliverance looked down at her cold, congealing meal. Silly, girlish tears pricked her eyes. She sniffed them back and set her mouth in a determined line before she looked up again. "Then he takes it over my dead body." Her gaze moved to Penitence. "But Penitence, if you want to go to father in Gloucester—"

Penitence's blue eyes blazed. "Never! As long as you are here, Liv,

I will not leave."

Luke Collyer looked at Penitence and his face softened. An old grievance clawed at her. What was it about Penitence that made the hardest man soft and pliable?

"Your sister is right, Mistress Felton. You may be safer in Gloucester," he said, addressing Penitence. "You use the word 'may', Captain Collyer. I doubt anywhere in England is safe and I am not going to be driven from my home by bullies like Sir Richard and Charles Farrington," Penitence declared. "Well said," Ned raised his cup. "To the defence of Kinton Lacey."

Luke flung his hat on to the table with such force that Ned had to spring to the aid of the ink stand before it toppled over, restoring it to an upright position. Luke scowled down at him.

"What's the problem?" Ned asked. "That...woman..." Luke said in a low growl.

Ned sat back and thoughtfully picked apart the quill feathers of his pen. "Of course," he mused. "What's she done now?"

"Every time I give an order, she countermands it and issues another order. *Her* men will only do what she tells them, and mine are so confused they don't know what to do."

Luke strode over to the window and leaned on the sill looking down into the courtyard where his soldiers, under the redoubtable Sergeant Hale, were occupied in cutting staves of wood to use for the palisade.

"I wouldn't mind, but there are times when what she says makes perfect sense and I curse myself for not thinking of it myself," he admitted.

"Well, she knows this castle well and, to be honest, she is

certainly better read on the subject of defence than you."

Luke turned to look at his friend. "You don't learn to be a soldier from a book, Ned. You know that."

"Perhaps if you stop persisting in treating her like a woman, and started thinking of her as a colleague in arms, you may get further?" Ned ventured. "What do you mean?"

"Luke, I've been your friend through thick and thin for at least six years," Ned set the pen down, "and it is my observation that those women who don't fall at your feet in adoration, are, to your way of thinking, good for only washing your clothes and feeding you."

"That's a little harsh," Luke said indignantly. "I like women."

"And mostly they like you. But I'm afraid in Deliverance Felton you have met a woman that will neither fall at your feet nor ensure you have clean linen and a full belly."

"So what do you suggest?"

"Give her a role in the defence of this castle. Something which gives her a sense of purpose and keeps her out of our way."

Luke's lips tightened and he glanced down to the courtyard where Deliverance was engaged in heated conversation with Sergeant Hale, which to judge from the gesticulating, involved the length of the staves his men were employed in cutting.

"Oh, dear Lord, now what's she up to?" Luke shuddered. The last three days she had driven him to distraction. Ned was right, he had to come up with a constructive solution to the dilemma.

He turned back to the table and picked up his hat. He glanced at the paper on which Ned had been writing, recognising, between the scratching out and ink blots, something that appeared to resemble verse. "What are you doing?" Luke snatched up the paper before Ned had a chance to retrieve it. A flush of

embarrassment coloured Ned's cheeks as Luke read aloud. "*Oh Penitence, so fair of face…*"

He scanned the rest of the appalling doggerel before tossing the paper back at Ned with a shake of his head.

"May I remind you, we are not here to fall in love with Sir John

Felton's pretty daughter," he said.

"We are here for one reason only and that is to ensure that Sir John Felton's..." he sought the right word. He would hardly call Deliverance plain or ugly. She had an unconventional face that in the right moment, caught off guard, he would almost call beautiful. "That Sir John's more interesting daughter is able to defend her home. If you are anxious for female company, there are a couple of pretty and accommodating young women in the dairy."

Ned shook his head. "You don't waste time, Collyer!"

Luke smiled and winked. He retrieved his hat and spinning it in his hand, left Ned to his hopeless infatuation and bad poetry.

Deliverance looked up into the beefy face of the enormous, barrel-chested Sergeant Hale, who served Luke both as Sergeant and preacher. She had heard his fine baritone leading his men in singing psalms as they worked.

The man shifted uncomfortably. "I 'ave me orders."

"But these staves are too short and insubstantial," Deliverance repeated. "They will hardly hold back an attacking force."

"They will if they are placed at the correct angle," Luke Collyer's voice came from behind her. Deliverance turned to face her nemesis, noting the grim line of his mouth.

"Mistress Felton, could you spare me a moment of your valuable time?" "I was just telling your sergeant—"

"I heard." Luke's eyes flashed with anger. "Carry on, Hale, as ordered by me. Mistress Felton, if you would be so kind?"

He took Deliverance's elbow and propelled her up the stairs into the Great Hall. She shook her arm free, and braced herself for the tirade she expected. If she was honest with herself, it was probably deserved. She was behaving like a petulant child deprived of a toy.

Luke Collyer sat down at the head of the table in her father's great oak carver and gestured for her to take a seat.

He ran a hand over his eyes. "Mistress Felton. I acknowledge that this is your demesne and indeed, I am in awe of your knowledge of matters military but we can only have one commander and, whether you like it or not, that person is me." He straightened in the chair and leaned forward, forcing her to look him in the eye.

"But—"

"Hear me out." He held up a hand and she fell silent. "I have a proposal. We need to be ready for that happy day when Sir Richard Farrington takes it upon himself to return to his quest of subduing the rebels of this county."

"Perhaps he has decided to leave us alone?" Deliverance suggested. "We've certainly seen nothing of him or his men since you scared them away."

Luke shook his head. "No. He has just retired to Ludlow to lick his wounds. I have every reason to believe that he will be back as soon as he receives the arms he is waiting on."

"How do you know that?"

Luke smiled and Deliverance glowered. He had an infuriating smile that implied great inner knowledge to which she would never be privy.

"I have my sources," he said. "What arms is he waiting on?"

He shook his head. "That I don't know. However, when Sir Richard, with his well-armed and better- trained men turn up again at your gate, we could find ourselves incarcerated here for quite some time. How many people do you think we will need to feed and quarter?"

Deliverance did a quick calculation. "Upwards of at least one hundred."

"I do not have the time to see to the provisioning of a siege that could last one, two or even three months," he said.

Deliverance's heart skipped a beat. "Three months? But surely someone will come to our aid before then?"

"I don't wish to alarm you, Mistress Felton, but we need to be realistic. Gloucester is already under pressure and could well be besieged itself within the next month or so. There will be no help from Wales and the nearest parliamentary force of any size would be at Warwick. You are sitting in the middle of a very unfriendly neighbourhood."

"Oh." Deliverance's stomach lurched as she realised he was quite right. To all intents and purposes they were completely and utterly alone.

"What I need is someone competent to see to the provisioning of the castle. We have water in the castle well." He paused and frowned. "By the way, I suggest we mount a twenty-four hour guard on the well."

"Even though we're not under siege?" "If we lose the water, then we are lost." "And you want me to do this task?"

"I would like you to be my adjutant and see to the logistics of the siege. Apart from food, we will need quarters, arrangements for the sick and wounded, sanitation and also the security of our powder."

"Doesn't Ned...Lieutenant Barrett do all that?"

"It will free Ned to do other tasks. Believe it or not, we are on the same side and what I need is for you and I to work together, not at odds." The corners of his eyes crinkled and a smile lifted the corners of his

mouth. Rather a nice mouth, Deliverance thought. She had seen the maids stop in their work as he passed by and greeted them. While their blatant simpering annoyed her, she was beginning to see the attraction.

"Does this arrangement suit you?" he said.

Deliverance thought for a moment. The last few days had been extremely stressful as she had waged what she knew to be a losing battle to maintain her authority. Even her men, loyal to the death to the Feltons, had begun to waver and defer to the charismatic and—

she had to admit, competent—Captain Collyer. Much as it chafed her to give up on the command of the castle, what he proposed made sense.

She sniffed. "Very well, Captain Collyer."

"Good. So, shall we call it a truce, Mistress Felton?"

She nodded and he held out his hand. She looked up into the grey eyes and took the proffered hand. Strong, warm fingers closed around hers and she caught her breath as a shiver ran down her spine.

"Truce," she said, hurriedly extricating her hand, and covertly wiping her fingers on her skirts as she rose to her feet. "I shall set a guard on the well."

Chapter Three

The disused castle chapel stood apart from the residential buildings, hard against the east wall of the Castle, the only wall that did not concern Luke. It faced the river and had been built with a considerable fall to the riverbank. No attacker in their right mind would try to attack from that direction. Attack from overhead was another matter and if the chapel were to take a direct hit from a cannon ball then the resulting explosion would cause less damage.

Luke found Deliverance in the chapel counting barrels of gunpowder. She looked up as he entered and scratched a number on the paper she had set out on an upturned, empty barrel in the middle of the room.

"I've given orders for the lead to be stripped from the outbuildings and melted down for musket balls," she said in the sort of tone he imagined an ordinary woman would discuss making pastries, but Deliverance Felton was no ordinary woman.

"Err...good," he said, feeling redundant to the conversation. "I have mounted the cannon on the Bastion tower and the Hawk Tower."

"Excellent. The proximity of those two towers to the village worried me. It seemed the most obvious place for a full scale assault," Deliverance said. Her lips twitched. "Farrington tried that on the third day." "You saw him off?"

"It began to rain and his troops seemed to just give up," Deliverance said. Luke had to bite his lip to stop from smiling.

"There is another matter you can assist me with," he said. "While Sir Richard is still licking his wounds in Ludlow, I would like to make the acquaintance of your neighbour at Byton. I hope perhaps we can be of some mutual assistance."

"I doubt it," Deliverance said. "You've not met Sir Alwyn Curtis. He and Father have not spoken to each other for years, not since the argument over the Brough's Wood."

Luke held up his hand. "I've no interest in Brough's Wood. Surely such petty disputes can be put to one side when we are both facing a greater enemy?"

Deliverance laughed. "Unfortunately, I don't share your optimism on that point. Sir Alwyn is very good at holding a grudge."

Luke shook his head. "It's worth a try. I would appreciate it if you would accompany me."

"Me?" Deliverance frowned. "I'm not sure if I will add much to your cause."

"If nothing else with a woman in the room, he is more likely to listen to what I have to say," Luke said.

"Maybe." Deliverance sounded doubtful. "I'm not sure my presence will be a hindrance or a help." "We can but try. I will have your horse saddled and if you could be ready to ride in half an hour. Does that suit you?"

Deliverance nodded and he turned, leaving her staring after him. As he stepped out into the sunshine, he smiled. It amused him to catch her off guard. He had learned long ago that you caught more flies with honey and he had to admit he quite enjoyed this game of wills he and Mistress Felton were engaged in.

Luke's heart sank at the first sight of Byton Castle. It stood in a pleasant park and garden, the ditches ringing the castle no more than soft, lawn covered indentations planted with shrubs. Apart from a hastily erected, rickety palisade fence that would not have prevented an elderly cow from tumbling it, the present owner appeared to have done little to strengthen the defence works.

'Colonel' Curtis kept them waiting in a parlour for a good twenty minutes. When he appeared, dressed in a stiff, new buff leather coat with a shining gorget at his throat, it was all Luke could do to keep a straight face, until he reminded himself that this idiotic figure held the lives of this small garrison in his pudgy hand.

Curtis acknowledged Deliverance with a haughty inclination of his head. Deliverance curtsied and introduced Luke. Curtis gave Luke a cursory inspection, and from the twitch of his extravagant moustache, he did not approve of what he saw.

Curtis indicated a chair for Deliverance but no such courtesy was extended to Luke who remained standing. Curtis sat himself in a large, oak chair well padded with cushions and crossed his legs as a handsome, red-haired maid entered carrying a tray with a jug of ale. As she offered the visitors a cup, Luke studied the girl, liked what he saw and winked at her. She grinned back. Luke's gaze followed the provocative sway of her hips as she left the room. When he returned his attention to the matter in hand, he had to face Deliverance's furrowed brow and compressed lips. He bestowed a smile on her and gave his attention to the Colonel who had angled his chair toward Deliverance, excluding Luke from the conversation.

"Mistress Felton, your father is in Gloucester, I hear?" Felton said, as if they were discussing a pleasant social engagement.

"He is," Deliverance replied.

"It is only to be expected of your father to leave his estate and two helpless females alone and unprotected," Curtis said, his lip curling in a derisory sneer.

It occurred to Luke that Curtis did not know Felton's daughters very well. He would not have described either of them as 'helpless females'.

Deliverance's shoulders stiffened. "He has sent Captain Collyer and men to strengthen the garrison at Kinton Lacey. We are hardly alone and unprotected." She shot a quick glance at Luke and he thought he detected the shadow of a smile in the twitch of her lips.

Curtis harrumphed. "I heard you had a bit of trouble from that upstart, Farrington?"

"He decided to lay siege to us but fortunately Captain Collyer saw him off and we've seen nothing more of him," Deliverance said.

Curtis flashed a glance at Luke and then turned back to her. "Well, I can understand why you have come looking for my assistance, young lady."

"On the contrary," Deliverance said. "We are here to offer you our assistance."

"You? Offer *me* assistance?" Curtis stared Deliverance. He rose to his feet, colour rising to his florid
cheeks.

"And Captain Collyer." Deliverance gestured at Luke.

Luke moved beside her, forcing himself into Curtis' line of sight. He drew himself up to his full height, topping the irritating little man by a good head. "Sir, I am charged by Sir John Felton to see to the defence of Kinton Lacey Castle and I have come today to see what aid we can be to you, in your support of Parliament's cause. Our security can only be aided by ensuring that Byton is well-prepared for siege."

Curtis dismissed him with a wave of his hand.

"I do not take advice from mere captains," he said imperiously.

Luke took a breath, trying to contain his irritation with this infuriating, pompous little man. "You may not take it, but I shall give it anyway, *sir*. You need to strengthen your defences on your eastern side. The ditches should be re-dug to a depth of at least six feet and a solid palisade erected, not that wicket you have put up. The wall on the south side is also in need of strengthening, and your gate will not hold a charge. Furthermore you should ensure you have water and supplies to survive a siege of at least two months."

Curtis had turned an alarming shade of purple during his recitation. Now he exploded. "How dare you presume to tell me your business, Captain Collyer. Mistress Felton, I will not stand here to be insulted by this... this... tinker's boy!"

"Tinker's boy?" Luke stared at the preposterous man. "I am touching thirty years of age and as for my birthright—" He snapped his mouth shut before he betrayed himself.

Curtis ignored him, rounding on Deliverance. "I have no wish to be lectured to by any lackey of your father's. Take your captain back to Kinton Lacey and leave me to the protection of my own home. Your father showed no such generosity of spirit towards me over the matter of Brough's Wood and I told him then, and I'll tell you now, I will not have any more dealings with Feltons, of whatever gender. Good day to you both."

Luke took a step backwards towards the door. He gave an ungracious bow and as he straightened, he said, keeping his tone low and moderate, an effort in the circumstances, "I apologise if I have offended you, Colonel Curtis. We have only your interests, and those of the souls within these walls, at heart. We will not trouble you again."

"Out," Curtis screamed.

It was not until they had put a few hundred yards between themselves and Byton that Luke looked at Deliverance for the first time. Her face was ashen and her mouth set in a grim line.

She glanced at him. "Stupid, stupid man! I did warn you."

"Unfortunately, this war is full of men just like him," Luke said.

Deliverance glanced at him. "But you were right. Even I could see that castle cannot be defended."

"If Farrington has any sense, he will move on it first," Luke said, thinking aloud.

They rode in silence for a few minutes before Deliverance spoke.

"Why are you only a captain? You clearly have sufficient age and experience to hold a much higher rank."

Luke looked at her in surprise at the question. "I thank you for your confidence in my abilities, Mistress Felton but to answer your question I have an unfortunate habit of annoying my senior officers."

"What do you do to annoy your senior officers?"

Luke fell silent. He did not feel inclined to admit his failings to Deliverance Felton. As well as an unfortunate habit of speaking his mind when he should keep a still tongue in his head, wine, women and a taste for cards would not sit well with her puritan upbringing. That is, if she had such an upbringing. Despite her name, she certainly didn't behave like any puritan he knew. "I think they call it a lack of proper respect," he said.

Deliverance looked straight ahead and he thought he could detect the hint of a smile playing around her lips. "Lack of respect? Really? You surprise me, Captain."

Luke returned her smile. He sensed that she had begun to trust him and that thought gave him more confidence about facing the days ahead. He glanced at her. Away from the castle and her responsibilities she seemed more relaxed and it surprised him to find that the formidable Mistress Felton did have a sense of humour. He liked it when she smiled. It transformed her face. The hard line of her mouth softened and the perpetual crease between her brows smoothed and the large, luminous grey eyes sparkled. A man could drown in those eyes, he thought. He would set himself the challenge of forcing her to smile more often. He liked a challenge.

Chapter Four

W hat are you doing?" Penitence asked.

Deliverance readjusted her position on the north wall, squinting at the distant woods.

"We're being watched," she said. "There's a man on a horse just inside the tree line." She pointed at the woods. "See the large oak?"

Penitence leaned forward on the ramparts, looking in the direction Deliverance indicated. "Oh yes, I see him," she said. "One of Farrington's men?"

"Most likely," Deliverance replied. "Hadn't you better tell Captain Collyer?" "I suppose so."

"Speaking of Captain Collyer, where is he?" Penitence asked.

Deliverance waved a hand in the direction of the west wall. "Oh, he's over there, supervising the men on the earthworks. I suppose I should go and find him."

The two women walked the length of the curtain wall, emerging from the Hawk Tower. As Deliverance looked along the battlements, she realised that quite an audience had gathered. In fact every maid in the castle seemed to be leaning over the stonework, laughing and jesting with the men below.

Penitence leaned over the ramparts. "Oh," she said. "Oh my! I really do think he should put some clothes on."

"What on earth do you mean?" Deliverance joined her. "Oh...I see."

Last time she had seen him, Luke Collyer had been fully clothed, albeit with his jacket unbuttoned and his shirt unlaced at the neck. Now he swung a mattock like one of his men, naked to the waist. His back glowed with the healthy tan of a man used to working outdoors...without a shirt.

Her eyes widened. She had never thought of men as being particularly attractive creatures. There had been no opportunity in her life to spend her time thinking about men much at all. While young, handsome men had queued at the gate for Penitence's favours, the only offers Deliverance had received were from three old, bald and foolish men of her father's acquaintance. Mercifully her father had not sought to force her into accepting any of the offers.

Now, as she watched the smooth muscles across Luke Collyer's back moving rhythmically to the swing of the mattock, she revised her opinion of men in general. She shifted her gaze to Ned Barrett, working a shovel not far away and similarly unclothed. Ned's tan ended at his neck and his body was pale and freckly. Further along the line of straining men, Sergeant Hale, wielded a mallet, his great hairy, bear-like chest heaving under the effort of each stroke of the mallet.

She turned back to Luke Collyer. Compared to Hale, he seemed almost slender and graceful. Almost—she bit her lip ashamed even of the thought—beautiful.

Giggling from the assembled audience of maids reminded her that she and Penitence were not Luke Collyer's only audience. Jennifer Jones, a buxom lass of dubious reputation who worked in the dairy, called out to him. "Captain Collyer, if you pull a muscle, come and see me and I'll rub it for you."

To Deliverance's mortification, Luke stopped his work and leaned on the handle of the mattock, grinning up at the dairymaid. "Ah, the beautiful Mistress Jones." Using the handle of the mattock as if it were a walking stick, he swept her a courtly blow to which Jennifer Jones responded with a curtsey

Curses, thought Deliverance, he even knows her name!

"Now you mention it," Luke continued, "I've an ache that will need a gentle hand."

The girls broke into gales of laughter at the ribald exchange between the dairymaid and the soldier. Even Penitence giggled.

Deliverance rounded on her sister. "Penitence." She clapped her hands, addressing her errant staff. "All right, enough of your gawping. Get back to your work."

The girls shot her disappointed glares and giggling into their hands went back to their duties. Luke

looked up at Deliverance, his head cocked on one side. As she glared down at him, he put two fingers to his forehead in a mock salute and picked up the mattock. As he swung it, the broad muscles of his chest, peppered with dark hairs, slid beneath his skin. Deliverance turned on her heel and fled.

When she heard Ned Barrett and Luke Collyer's voices and the sound of the men's boots on the flagstones behind the screen, Deliverance stopped pacing the floor of the Great Hall.

"Captain Collyer," she called.

He pushed aside the curtain and raised an enquiring eyebrow at her. "Mistress Felton?"

"I would appreciate a moment of your time," she said.

He crossed the floor towards her, carrying his jacket slung over one shoulder. At least he had put his shirt back on, but it clung damply to the sculpted muscles of his chest and shoulders, the tight whorls of hair on his chest, still damp with the effort of his exertion. She forced herself to look up at his face. A smudge of dirt marred his right cheek and his dark brown hair was thick with dust.

She resisted the temptation to wipe the smudge of dirt away.

"Captain Collyer. That was a disgraceful display this afternoon. I would thank you not to upset my servants in future."

"I assure you if I have upset anyone, you have my profuse apologies."

He bowed in penitence, one hand on his chest but as he rose his lips twitched and she knew he was mocking her.

An uncomfortable heat rose to her cheeks.

"Captain Collyer," she began, noticing that even to her ears her voice sounded shrill. "I need hardly remind you, our situation is desperate. We do not have time for frivolity..."

Her diatribe trailed off as she found herself transfixed by his grey eyes.

She saw no trace of humour in their icy depths. He looked down at her, his face grave.

"Mistress Felton, it is precisely because of our situation that the occasional frivolity and jesting is called for. Now, if that is all you wish to say to me, I should go and clean myself up." His voice held a clipped tone that she'd not heard before and she knew she had pushed him too far.

As he turned and started to walk back towards the screen where Ned waited, she said, "No. No...There is something else I wanted to tell you. There was a man on a horse watching us this afternoon. What do you think we should do?"

He turned back to look at her. "Where was this man?"

"In the tree line. I only saw him because the sunlight glinted on something metal. Could it have been one of Farrington's men?"

"Of course it was." Luke's mouth tightened and he turned to Ned. "Send Hale to me, I want to know why our patrol didn't see him."

"What are you going to do?" Deliverance asked.

He scratched his chin and looked up at the dusty beams of the hall. "I think the time has come. I need to see for myself exactly what Sir Richard Farrington is planning."

"I thought you said he was in Ludlow," Deliverance said.

"He is," Luke replied. "But it's what he's doing in Ludlow that interests me." "Shall I send our scout again?" Ned asked.

Luke shook his head. "No. I will go myself."

"Don't be a fool," Deliverance scoffed. "You can't just walk into Ludlow. You would be instantly suspected."

Luke looked back at her, his brows creased.

"Not if I had a woman with me." He raised an eyebrow, a slow, conspiratorial smile spreading over his face. The grey eyes that only a moment ago had cut her down with the force of cold steel, now rested on her with the warmth of soft smoke. "A woman who had a fancy for a little adventure?"

"Do you mean me? Don't be such a fool. Do you really think that I, the daughter of Sir John Felton, rebel, can just walk in through the gates of Ludlow when it suits me?"

"You could if you were suitably disguised. Are you particularly well known in Ludlow?"

Deliverance bit her lip, trying to suppress the sudden surge of excitement within her. What would her father say when he found out? Would he commend her for her courage and audacity?

"Not so well known that I couldn't pass as a goodwife on her way to Ludlow market."

"And when is market day?" Luke asked.

"Collyer, this is folly!" Ned interposed.

"Tomorrow," Deliverance said.

"Excellent," Luke said. "Tomorrow it is."

"Are you both mad?" Ned looked from one to the other. "Do you honestly think that you will get away with this?"

Luke held Deliverance's gaze with his as he said, "Yes, I do, Ned."

"Then let me go," Ned said. "You're needed here."

Luke gave his second-in-command a withering glance. "What am

I doing that's so valuable here? Digging ditches?"

Ned looked at Deliverance. "Of all the people in the castle, the two of you are the ones we can least spare. Please see sense. Mistress Felton, see sense."

Luke's gaze returned to Deliverance. His grey eyes sparkled with irresistible and infectious mischief. "Well? Mistress Felton, it's entirely up to you."

What he proposed was rash, bordering on dangerous, but looking into the smoky depths of his eyes she would have followed him into hell.

The gates of Ludlow stood open, but heavily guarded as the market day traffic flowed into the old town. Seated pillion behind Luke on the oldest cob they could find in the stable, Deliverance's stomach gave a nervous lurch. Even the telling off she had endured from Penitence could not quell the heady anticipation of danger. Every nerve in her body seemed to have a life of its own. The lure of adventure had always called her and now she had the opportunity to shine. She would make her father proud of her, the worthy protector of Kinton Lacey.

She gripped the handle of her basket of eggs harder with one hand while the other, twisted in Luke's belt. He cast a reproachful look over his shoulder. "Relax your grip. I can hardly breathe." he said.

They had rehearsed their story on the journey. She would be Goodwife Chambers of Kersey bringing eggs to sell at the market. In a russet gown borrowed from her maid, Meg, and a starched white cap on her head, topped with a flat crowned brown felt hat that concealed her face, she looked very much a goodwife.

Luke would be her 'man', Tom Perry. Despite much grumbling from Luke, Penitence had rough-cut his hair like a labourer's, and now it stuck out at odd angles from beneath the filthy, battered hat borrowed, like the greasy jerkin he wore, from one of the stable hands. Riding behind him, at such close quarters, Deliverance's nose wrinkled at the smell of man and horse that exuded from his borrowed garments.

The guards on the gate gave them no more than a cursory inspection and asked their business. Deliverance responded in a faultless local accent that would have appalled her father.

Once inside the gate, they found a stable for the cob, and set out on foot for the market square at the gates of the castle. They stood looking up at the magnificent walls and the well-guarded gate. "You're not thinking of trying to get in there?" Deliverance whispered.

Luke didn't respond but his gaze roamed the castle walls.

"How much you sellin' them eggs for?"

A woman's voice at her elbow startled Deliverance, almost causing her to drop the basket. A stout matron waited expectantly.

"How many do you want?"

"A dozen. Are they fresh?" The woman narrowed her eyes suspiciously.

"Fresh today, lady," Luke replied.

"A shilling then, for a dozen," the woman said.

"Fine," Deliverance agreed,

The woman looked surprised. She had evidently expected to haggle. Deliverance concluded the transaction while Luke waited behind her. When the woman had gone away, evidently pleased with her bargain, Deliverance turned back to Luke.

"Stay here and sell your eggs," he said.

Deliverance looked up at his determined, grimy and unshaven face, and a shiver of fear ran down her spine. She wanted to say,

"Don't leave me here by myself" but that sounded childish. She had volunteered for this adventure and she would see it through with the true courage of a Felton.

"Be careful," she said.

"If you sell all your eggs before I'm back, meet me in the porch of that church." Luke indicated the spire of St. Laurence. "And if I'm not there before the clock strikes twelve, leave without me."

"Will an hour be long enough?" Deliverance looked around the crowded market square, noting the large number of soldiers in blue uniform coats.

"It should be plenty of time." He gave her a reassuring smile. "Stay out of trouble, Mistress Felton." She watched him walk away, her gaze following him until he was lost in the bustling crowd.

Word had evidently got around that her eggs were cheap and Deliverance sold them all within half an hour. She wandered around the market square pretending to be interested in the produce, all the while watching for anything that might be of interest to Luke. She had been to Ludlow market many times in the peaceful years but now the familiar bustle of farmers and townsfolk had been padded out with armed troops who all looked better equipped than the rabble Farrington had set down in front of her gate.

She looked up at the clock. The hour of twelve approached so she set off at a brisk pace to the church of St. Laurence, the beautiful medieval building, with a square tower that rose high above the roofs of the town. The presence of more soldiers surrounding the porch of the church and bristling with weapons and smart new uniforms, slowed her step. The church had evidently been appropriated for military purposes.

"Now then, goodwife, move along," one of the soldiers said as she hesitated at the gate to the churchyard.

"I came here to pray," Deliverance responded. "How dare ye turn a house of God into a ... what are you doing with it?"

"Gunpowder store," the man said.

"Oh, that's shameful," Deliverance said, guiltily recalling the chapel at Kinton Lacey, presently lined with barrels of powder. "And what need 'ave ye for such a large store? From what I 'ear tell in the market, there's only a handful of rebels in this county."

"Aye, and it's Sir Richard's intention to blast 'em to hell," the man replied. "He's ordered a siege gun to deal with the bastards."

"A siege gun? And what's so special about a siege gun?"

"Ah lady, 'tis the length of two men with a mouth that a grown man can put his head in. God have mercy on the rebels, is all I can say."

Deliverance's guts clenched. God have mercy on them indeed. "And when is this 'ere gun to arrive?" Deliverance asked.

The men looked at each other. "Why it came yesterday, lady. Ye'll find it outside the town walls on the water meadow."

"Really?"

"Aye. Not seen it myself but they say 'tis too big to bring into the town."

Deliverance glanced down the street and a wave of relief washed over her at the sight of a familiar greasy hat that marked Luke's progress through the crowd.

"Well, 'tis a sad day when a church becomes a harbinger of death," Deliverance returned to the street and waited for Luke to join her.

"Where have you been?" she asked.

He shrugged. "Here and there. Farrington's brought in a whole regiment of reinforcements, well- armed and well-trained. It will be no raggle-taggle troops, afraid of the rain, that we will face."

"Well I have intelligence too," Deliverance said, her heart racing at the thought of what lay ahead of them. "There's a siege cannon in the water meadow."

Luke's eyebrows rose to meet his hairline. "A siege gun. How did you find that out?"

"Sometimes men will talk more easily to a woman," she said with a smile.

Luke's mouth tightened. "If you're right, that one piece of information is far more worrying than anything I've managed to glean. You've done well."

Deliverance flushed. She heard praise so rarely that when it came it was a nugget to be treasured.

He looked up at the town walls. "Anywhere we can get a sight of the gun?"

Deliverance nodded and led him across the town, through the narrow streets lined with half- timbered buildings. A gaggle of townsfolk lined the town wall, indicating the presence of the siege gun had excited some interest in the local populace.

They pushed their way through the crowd, ignoring the grumbles. Deliverance drew breath as she caught sight of the object of the attention. Below them on the far side of the river Teme, another crowd had gathered around to watch blue-coated soldiers drill with the massive gun and several smaller pieces. Luke whistled and Deliverance cast a sideways glance at him.

"That is a serious siege gun," Luke said in a low voice. "A forty eight pounder cannon, unless I am greatly mistaken."

"No, you're not, friend." They turned to see a young man, one of the townsfolk, Deliverance presumed. "A whole cannon they call it. Over ten feet long, she is. They call her the 'Thunderer'."

"I didn't know guns had names?" Deliverance cast a questioning glance at Luke.

"Only the special ones," their informant told them. "God help those poxy rebels when they meets her, is all I can say."

"Indeed," Luke replied. "God help them."

The onlookers were ushered back by an officer, and the artillerymen set the fuse alight. Fire spurted from the mouth of the mighty weapon with an accompanying roar that rocked the walls on which Deliverance and Luke stood.

With her ears still ringing, she looked at Luke. He stared at the gun, his mouth set in a grim line. "Time to go," he mouthed and taking Deliverance by the arm he guided her back into the town.

They turned down the High Street towards the stable where they had left the cob.

They were only a matter of yards from the lane that led to the stables when a body of soldiers wheeled around the corner. Luke and Deliverance stepped back into the shelter of a doorway to allow the troops to pass them. At their rear, a young officer in well-polished breast and back plate and gorget, glanced in their direction.

"Go on," she begged him silently. "Just walk on, ignore us." Too late, she pulled the hat brim low down across her face.

The young man stopped, his mouth dropping open in surprise. She had been seen and recognised.

"Deliverance?"

She looked up and forced herself to smile into the puzzled face of Jack Farrington.

Chapter Five

"Deliverance? What are you doing in Ludlow?" A mixture of pleasure and puzzlement, mingled with anger crossed Jack's face. Jack had never been good at hiding his feelings.

Deliverance cast her eyes around the street and lighted on the apothecary. For the first time in her life she lied. "I had to fetch some medicine from the 'pothecary." When he looked unconvinced she compounded the lie, using the one weapon in her armoury she knew would find its mark with Jack Farrington. "Penitence is unwell."

She scored a hit. The expression on his face changed to one of the deepest concern. "Is she all right?"

"The recent trouble at the castle affected her deeply and she has contracted a chill to her chest," Deliverance continued. "I had to take the risk of coming to Ludlow." Jack's gaze strayed to Luke. "Who's this? I don't recognise him?"

"Oh that's only poor Tom Perry, Jake Peverill's nephew from Gloucester." She leaned conspiratorially towards Jack. "Was dropped on his head when he was a babe." She tapped her skull. "Quite mazed, but he's good with horses, so Father sent him north."

Jack looked at Luke again, who affected a glazed stare into the middle distance. He frowned. "He looks a strapping fellow. Strange of your father to send him away from Gloucester."

"Quite useless with weapons," Deliverance said. She glanced anxiously around the street. "Are you going to let me go, Jack? I really must get this medicament back to Penitence."

For a moment Jack looked confused. Loyalty to his father dictated he should detain her, possibly indefinitely. Loyalty to Penitence told him to release her.

"Go," he said, adding in a tone that he no doubt intended to sound fierce, "but don't let me catch you here again, Deliverance."

"Now, Jack, don't be so hasty."

Jack visibly flinched as a hand gripped his shoulder and Deliverance's heart lurched. The dark shadow of Charles Farrington shadow fell across them.

Deliverance glanced around. Except for Luke, who moved in closer behind her, and the Farrington brothers, they were alone in the narrow street.

"Kind of you to pay us a visit, Mistress Felton." Charles sneered and gave her a mock bow. "And what brings you to Ludlow on this fine day?"

Deliverance opened her mouth and her words stumbled out, the lie sounding even more unconvincing now. "Penitence is unwell. I came to see the apothecary."

Charles looked down at the basket. "You come away empty handed I see. Did the apothecary not have what you were seeking?"

"I...no..." Deliverance faltered.

Behind her she heard Luke's sharp intake of breath.

Charles did not appear to hear. "Dear Penitence may just have to wait for her medicaments. I absolutely insist, Mistress Felton, that you join us in the Castle as our guest."

"No, thank you, Charles. I really should be getting back." Deliverance's hand tightened on her basket.

Charles pushed past his brother, grasping her right forearm in his hand. As Deliverance tried to shake him free, his grip tightened.

"Deliverance, you are not such a fool as to think this is an invitation? You, my girl, can now consider yourself a prisoner."

She summoned every bit of her courage and glared up at him. "You have no right to detain me. Unhand me this instant."

"I have every right," Charles said, bringing his face down so close to hers that she felt his spittle on her face. "The moment you shut your castle gates on us, you forfeited your liberty, Mistress Felton. I am sure that once your father knows you are a prisoner in Ludlow Castle, he will have no difficulty in turning over Kinton Lacey to the King. Jack," he nodded his head in Luke's direction, "bring that man she has with her." "Don't be silly, Charles. Tom's quite harmless," Deliverance said. "Take me but let him go."

Charles jerked his head in Luke's direction. "Secure him, Jack. I'm not the gull you might think I am, Deliverance." As he spoke he pulled a pistol from his belt with his free hand and levelled it at Luke. "One look at this man is enough. He's no simpleton. This has to be one of your garrison, and you can only be here for one reason. Spying."

"I told you, I needed medicine for Penitence." The lie became less convincing by the moment. "I'm not here to spy."

Jack drew his pistol and approached Luke. He lifted the rough leather jerkin Luke wore exposing the brace of pistols tucked into Luke's belt.

"No good with weapons, is he, Deliverance?" Jack cast her a hurt glance. "What's your name, man?"

Luke's gaze flicked across to Deliverance and then back to Jack. He affected a tight-lipped smile and shrugged.

"Collyer," Luke replied. "Your servant, sir."

Charles stiffened, releasing Deliverance's arm and facing up to Luke. "What a pair of fools you are. Who is left at Kinton Lacey?" He glanced at Deliverance, his lips curving in a sneer. "That soft sister of yours and a few old men? Father will be pleased when he finds I have not only Deliverance Felton but the scurvy knave—"

"Who whipped your useless men all the way back to Ludlow," Luke cut in with a half-smile lifting the corner of his mouth.

Deliverance, forgotten, swung her basket at Charles Farrington's knees, dropping him to the ground. In that moment Luke launched himself at Jack, knocking the hand that held the pistol. The weapon discharged, shattering the window of the nearest shop.

Luke seized Deliverance by the right arm, and they turned towards the gate. Beneath her bodice her heart hammered and her lungs felt as if they would burst. Her shoes slipped on the cobble-stones but he dragged her on, his fingers biting into her arm.

Behind them she heard Charles shout, and the sound of other men's voices and heavy boots on the stones as Farrington gathered his men in pursuit of the fugitives.

The crack of pistols reverberated off the walls of the houses lining the narrow street. Innocent bystanders pressed themselves into doorways, too shocked to obey Farrington's command. "Stop them!"

A fiery jolt ran through her left arm and she gave a yelp, stumbling in her headlong rush but before she fell, Luke had his arm around her waist, lifting her into the air.

"Fortune favours us. Up here, my lady."

As the world spun giddily around her, he threw her across the bow of a saddle leaping up behind her. A man shouted, "Hey! That's my horse..." and the world went black.

Luke put his heels to the horse and careened down the High Street towards the gates. The soldiers on duty, alarmed by the cries of their comrades, had started to close the massive gates. However even the bravest was not prepared to stand his ground before a madman on a galloping horse, and leaped aside as Luke, riding as though the fiends of hell were after him, passed out of Ludlow onto the open road that led back to Kinton Lacey.

With one arm securing Deliverance, he forced the horse onwards, not daring to slow until he was certain that his pursuers had fallen behind. Only when he could find a secure place to rest the lathered beast did he stop. The horse, a fat, bay gelding that had probably never been called on to perform such a wild duty in its life, dropped its head, its flanks heaving.

Deliverance slumped against him, quite limp, her eyes closed and her face ashen. Her hat and respectable cap had been lost in the flight and her dark brown tresses tumbled loose over his arm. Impulsively he tightened his arms around her slight figure. It had been his mad suggestion to go to Ludlow. What perverse fate had put the Farrington brothers in their path? Now Deliverance had been hurt and he was to blame. He shuddered to think what Sir John Felton would say when he heard about his daughter's injury.

"Deliverance?" he whispered. "Where are you hurt?"

Receiving no response, he flung himself off the horse, and lifted her down on to the soft grass of the clearing. Her cloak fell away. The sleeve of her left arm was dark and wet with blood. He swore under his breath. If Deliverance Felton died as a result of his reckless action not only did he risk Sir John hanging him on the spot but he would never forgive himself.

Fumbling for a pulse in her neck he held his breath. "Thank the Lord," he said aloud as the slow, steady beat pulsed beneath his fingers.

He steeled himself and with shaking fingers he undid her cuff and without ceremony tore the sleeve to the shoulder, revealing the wound left by Charles Farrington's pistol ball.

Mercifully, on close inspection, it appeared to have only grazed her arm and the bleeding had all but stopped. He set about manufacturing a bandage torn from the hem of her petticoat.

A stream flowed through the clearing and he tore some more

cloth, wet it, and bathed her face, silently exhorting her to wake up. It seemed like an age before he was rewarded by the fluttering of her eyelids and a little colour flowed back into her ashen cheeks.

"Welcome back," he said gruffly.

"Ow!" Her brow puckered when she tried to move her arm. "What have you done to me?" "A pistol ball nicked it. You'll live," he said.

She frowned. "A pistol ball?" She struggled to sit up and looked around her. "Oh, I remember. The Farringtons...have they followed us? Are we safe? Where are we?"

"To answer your first question, we got away, although undoubtedly they will be searching for us and will have the road to Kinton Lacey well patrolled. As to the second, I don't know where we are. I just put heels to the horse and fled. You'll have to show me another way to get back to the castle without running into the Farringtons."

She squinted at the horse. "That's not our cob!"

"No, I borrowed a better looking horse that just happened to present itself at an opportune moment."

Deliverance ran a shaking hand through her tangled hair. Her shoulders heaved, and she let her hand fall before turning to look at him. Her mouth drooped at the corners and tears filled her eyes, clouding the sky blue to a dreary grey.

"There's something I should have told you." Tears glinted on her eyelashes. "Jack and Penitence were betrothed before the war."

Luke rose to his feet. With his hands on his hips he glared down at her. "Why didn't you tell me this from the first? It changes everything."

Her mouth trembled. "How? I just saw it as unfair that two people who loved each other had to be torn apart by this cursed war."

He shook his head. "It betrays a weak link, Deliverance."

"But Pen is utterly loyal, Luke. She would never betray us." She looked up at him, the tears rolling down her cheeks and regret for his harsh tone plucked at his conscience. "Will it be all right, Luke?"

He knew what she meant. She had remembered the terrible gun

and the ruthless efficiency of Farrington's well-trained troops. Luke resisted a sudden, inexplicable urge to draw her in his arms, kiss away the tears and tell her, yes of course it would all be all right.

He would be lying.

When he didn't respond, she lowered her head, tears dropping on to her skirts. She wiped her face with her left arm. "Poor Kinton Lacey," she said in a voice muffled by her sleeve. "It was never built to withstand a weapon like that."

Luke had no comfort to give her. Kinton Lacey had been built to withstand bows and arrows or at the worse, slingshots, not a siege gun the size of the Thunderer.

He knelt down beside her. "Deliverance," he said, using her given name for the first time. "Deliverance," he repeated softly and laid a hand on her dark head. "What do you want to do?"

She shook her head. "I don't know. I just can't give it up, Luke."

He raised his right hand, and touched her hair. She made no protest, leaning her head against his chest. He stroked the dark, tangled locks and she sighed, closing her eyes. This time he surrendered to his impulse and folded her in his arms. She had shown incredible bravery and kneeling on the ground with this strange, defiant little woman in his arms, he made a silent vow to do whatever it took to protect her, save her castle, and make it right for her.

Sir John Felton's daughter. What was he doing? He disengaged her and rose to his feet.

"We have to keep moving, Mistress Felton," he said. "Farrington's men will be looking for us. On your feet."

He took her by her uninjured arm and hauled her to her feet. She sagged at the knees and he caught her before she fell.

In a softer tone he said, "I need to get you home. You've lost a deal of blood. Now, can you stand if I let you go?"

She nodded and stood, swaying on her feet as he swung himself into the saddle.

"You will need to ride before me," he said. "I can't have you fainting and falling off."

"I don't faint," she protested, with a touch of old defiance, a smile catching at the corners of her mouth.

"You have already have done so at least once today. Put your foot in the stirrup and I'll lift you up." He swung her into his arms. "Comfortable?"

"No."

As he readjusted her position he reflected that the short rest had done wonders in restoring her normal prickly disposition. She perched in his arms like a steel rod. He sighed.

"Relax, Deliverance, otherwise we are both going to be in for a very uncomfortable time of it."

She cast him a reproachful glance and taking a deep breath as if this were the most distasteful thing she could think of, she lay back against him. Luke looked down at the dark head, resting against his shoulder. She fitted within the shelter of his arms as if she belonged there. He tightened his grip around her, and gently kicked the horse on.

Deliverance closed her eyes and let the gentle rhythm of the horse's gait soothe her. Her arm burned but the pain was endurable. The close proximity of Luke Collyer was more disconcerting. In the borrowed jerkin he smelled of man and horse, but not in an unpleasant way. She also liked the way his arms encircled her. The hard cast of his muscles flexed against her back, as he guided the horse.

"Tell me more about Penitence and Jack Farrington." Luke said, the tone that of the soldier not the man who had held her in his arms and stroked her hair.

Aroused from her reverie, Deliverance forced her drowsy mind back into action. "Sir Richard made Jack break the betrothal once father declared his allegiance to Parliament. Take the right turn at the next cross roads."

Luke fell silent.

"What are you thinking?" she asked.

"I was thinking Jack Farrington seemed a decent enough man." "He is. They adored each other. It is so unfair."

"It is the nature of civil war, Deliverance. And now? Does Penitence still hold a candle for him?" Deliverance didn't answer for a long time. She hadn't really stopped to consider how Penitence may be feeling. She had just assumed her sister accepted her fate. "Penitence is a dutiful daughter," she said.

"What sort of answer is that?"

"She accepted Father's decision on the matter."

Luke laughed, a low rumble in the chest against which her head rested. "Knowing your father, I can well imagine she had little choice but to accept her fate."

A few long minutes passed in silence before Deliverance ventured, "I assume you are not married, Captain Collyer?"

"Me? Do I look like a married man?"

"No heartbroken girl awaiting your return from the war?"

"Oh, plenty of heartbroken girls," Luke said, "but not one in particular."

His arms tightened around her. She closed her eyes and let herself relax against him. Despite the smell of the borrowed jerkin, she liked the feel of those strong arms and the steady beat of his heart. For the first time in her life, she wondered if this was what it was like to have someone else to rely on or whether the giddiness was simply the effect of loss of blood.

"Deliverance?"

Deliverance's eyes had closed and she slumped against him, a dead weight against his right arm. Luke put his heels to the horse and urged into a gentle canter. He had to get her to help.

Deliverance stirred at the change of pace, her eyelashes fluttering for a moment but the rhythm of the horse's gait, seemed to soothe her and with a sigh, she drew closer to him, murmuring to herself.

Sleep, or unconsciousness, softened her face and took away the hard edges that the responsibility of her position gave her. He wondered for a moment how she would look in a satin gown and pearls, her hair done up in the fine ringlets the women of his father's household had favoured.

With a snort of laughter, he dismissed the picture. Fine ringlets and pearls may become Penitence but they would not suit Deliverance. Deliverance Felton had something more than physical beauty, she had intelligence and character.

That thought sobered him and he looked down at the dark, burnished head resting against his chest. For the first time in his life, he had met a woman whom he could consider his equal in so many ways. She may frustrate him beyond measure, but he couldn't imagine Kinton Lacey without its mistress—and he had almost got her killed.

They had skirted through the back lanes, narrowly avoiding a patrol of Farrington's men. It had made the return journey considerably longer than it should have been and the lengthening shadows crept across the fields before the outline of the castle appeared above the trees.

For a fleeting moment Luke could imagine that no war lurked like some menacing beast in the dark. No forty-eight pounder siege gun, and four times the number of troops waited at Ludlow to bring the castle to its knees. Instead Kinton Lacey drowsed, golden in the setting sun, the pretty wallflowers that grew from the crevices of its mighty walls, a strange contrast to the new earthworks and the churned fields marking the recent altercations.

"Deliverance," he said. "We're home."

"Hmmm?" She stirred and opened her eyes and looked up at the familiar walls rising above her. She stiffened and the old, familiar Deliverance flashed back into her eyes as she pushed away from him. "Let me down, I can walk," she said. "They cannot see that I'm hurt."

Far from letting her go, Luke tightened his hold and chuckled. "If I let you down you will fall flat on your face, my lady,"

They had already been spotted by the sentries, and the tall figure of Melchior, accompanied by Penitence and Ned, was visible beneath the shadow of the gatehouse.

Penitence reached them first. "Liv! You're hurt."

"She'll be all right," Luke said. "It's just a graze but she has lost quite a deal of blood. You, man." He hailed one of the Kinton Lacey garrison. "Truscott, take your mistress."

The big man with a pleasant, round face hurried across to the horse and reached up to take the woman.

"Put me down, Truscott," Deliverance protested. "I can walk."

"Now then, Mistress Deliverance," Truscott said. "We won't have any of that nonsense." "What happened?" Penitence glared at Luke as he dismounted.

"We encountered your friend, Jack Farrington," Luke said.

Penitence gasped, her hand flying to her throat. "Jack? Jack, did this to her?"

"No, that was his brother."

"He was trying to shoot Captain Collyer. Pity he missed," Deliverance interposed over Truscott's sturdy shoulder.

"I told you it was a foolish plan," Penitence stood in front of Luke, her cheeks flushed with anger. "Now look what you've done? Truscott, carry her up to her bedchamber. Meg," she turned to one of the maids who stood at the foot of the stairs, "fetch water and bandages."

Luke, still holding the reins of the horse, stood in the middle of the courtyard watching as the little party, with Deliverance still protesting she could walk, disappeared into the residence.

"Well done," Ned said in an ironic tone. "I hope your precious excursion was worth putting Sir John's daughter's life on the line?"

Luke turned to look at his friend. "She'll live."

"That's not the point. Sir John Felton will not thank you for getting his daughter shot."

"Then Sir John Felton should not have left her in command of the defence of his home. I need a drink."

He handed over the horse to one of his men, and climbed the stairs into the house, where he slumped into a chair in the Great Hall and sent for Melchior Blakelocke, Sergeant Hale and a jug of Sir John's best wine.

"Well?" Ned demanded when they were all assembled. "What did you find out?"

"Not only do they have at least four hundred well trained and equipped troops, they have a forty eight pounder, a demi-cannon and two culverins."

"God help us." Ned glanced out of the window at the illusory solidity of the castle walls. "Oh dear," Melchior Blakelocke said with a shake of his head. "That is not good news, sir." "No," Luke said with a grimace. "Not good at all."

"How long have we got?"

Luke studied the grain on the wooden table for a long moment, tracing it with a finger. "If I was Farrington I would take out Byton first and when that is secure, move on us. We have probably less than two weeks, if that."

"With Mistress Felton indisposed..." Blakelocke began.

Luke pushed back his chair and stood up. "We should be able to get a great deal done. Gentlemen, let's take a walk."

Chapter Six

D eliverance lay looking up at the bed hangings. The sun streamed in through the windows, catching the dust motes that danced in the golden light of the late morning, as she replayed the headlong events of the previous day. Her arm hurt enough to remind her of her own mortality, and how close she had come to losing her life.

Penitence must have given her some poppy juice to ensure she slept through the night and her eyelids began to droop once more. Through her torpor, she heard a sharp rap on the door and the sound of Meg's shoes on the floorboards as she crossed to the door, followed by a whispered exhortation from her maid.

At the sound of a man's voice, her eyes sprang open. A shadow fell across her and she squinted up into Luke Collyer's face.

"Good. You're awake."

She squeaked with alarm and scrabbled at her bedclothes with her good hand, drawing the sheet up to her chin while he leaned one hand against the bed post, and looked down at her with a smile, tugging at the corners of his mouth, the corners of his smoky-grey eyes creased with amusement.

"This is most improper," Deliverance said.

"Meg is here to insure your honor is not impugned." He indicated the maid sitting on a chair by the table, her back rigid with disapproval. "How's your arm?"

"It hurts...a little." Her voice sounded high and tight even to her ears as hazy memories of their ride back from Ludlow began to seep back into her consciousness.

Luke straightened and crossed his arms, and as he did so, an uncomfortable recollection of being held in those arms sent a warm glow rushing through her body. She closed her eyes and took a deep breath. Loss of blood must have made her silly as well as light-headed. What had she been thinking to allow herself to be held by a man in such a fashion? On the other hand it had not been unpleasant. For the first time in her life someone had stepped in to take her cares and worries away and keep her safe. "Pistol balls do have that effect," he was saying. "You'll be fine in a few days."

Luke's brisk tone punctured the warm memory of their shared intimacy and the throbbing in her arm gave a lie to his words.

She narrowed her eyes. "Have you ever been wounded?" Luke raised an eyebrow. "I'm a soldier, what do you think?"

"I didn't notice any scars..." Deliverance said without thinking, remembering the sight of his well-muscled body as he wielded a mattock in the trenches. As he grinned, the warmth flooded into her cheeks.

"Ah, so you were not just keeping watch on the castle wall? Shame on you, Mistress Felton!" He wagged a reproving finger at her.

"My attention was fixed on the man in the trees, not you. You had more than enough female admirers on the wall."

His lips parted as if he were about to say something but he must have thought better of it. He straightened, the soldier once more.

"I came to tell you that Farrington has moved. He marched out of Ludlow this morning." "Is he coming here?"

He shook his head. "As I predicted he is heading for Byton first.

It will only take him a day or two to wipe out that minnow, and then he'll turn his full attention to us."

All humour had gone from Luke's face. The smoky-grey in his eyes had turned once more to burnished steel.

Deliverance sat up, the protective sheet falling away unregarded. "Are we ready?"

"We'll never be ready," Luke said. "But we are as prepared as we can be."

Deliverance pushed back the sheet and swung her legs over the side of the bed. "I should get up. There are things to do."

As she rose to her feet, the room swayed and the world began to roar in her head.

A strangled cry came from Meg as she jumped to her feet. "Now, that's enough, Captain Collyer. Mistress needs to rest. She lost a deal of blood yesterday."

Luke was faster. His strong hand steadied Deliverance, easing her back on the bed and pulling the covers over her. Embarrassed by her weakness she looked away as he sat himself on the side of the bed.

"You must rest, Mistress Felton. Thanks to your hard work, we are already well prepared. The last remaining defences are my responsibility," he said.

"You should not be sitting on my bed," Deliverance protested, clutching the neckline of her voluminous nightdress.

The corners of his eyes creased as he smiled. "I assure you, you are in no danger while you are encased in that ridiculous night gown."

"Captain Collyer, what are you doing in here?" Penitence demanded from the doorway.

Luke stood up, giving Penitence the benefit of a deep, courtly bow. "Just ensuring Mistress Felton has responded well to your tender care," he said.

Penitence stood back and gestured at the door. "Out! I am sure you have work to do, Captain Collyer."

Luke strode to the door where he paused and inclined his head, taking in all three women as he said, "*Adieu*."

They waited until the sound of his strong, purposeful stride had died away.

"Pen, you're very hard on him," Deliverance commented as her sister sat down on the bed beside her, taking the place where Luke had sat just a few moments ago.

Penitence raised an eyebrow. "He nearly got you captured and killed. He is trouble, Liv, and it was quite improper that he visit you in your bed."

Deliverance lay back on the bolsters and looked up at the carving of nymphs sporting above her, unable to meet her sister's eyes. "Yes, of course, you are right. But I think I might have misjudged him. I must concede he is quite good at what he does," she mused.

And, she had to admit to herself, their excursion to Ludlow had been the most exciting thing that had ever happened to her, with or without a sore arm to show for it.

Penitence raised an eyebrow. "Since when have you become such a petitioner for the talents of Captain Collyer? Is there something I should know about?"

Deliverance shoved a dim memory of a man stroking her hair to the back of her mind. "Of course not. He was a perfect gentleman. I just meant that now I have got to know him a little better, I have slightly more respect for his talents...his military talents."

Penitence narrowed her eyes and studied her sister for a moment before she said, "Ned says Farrington could be at our gate within the week. Is it true about the guns?"

Deliverance nodded. "Yes. I need to send a message to Father. He must know what we will be facing."

"I think Captain Collyer has already done so." Penitence hesitated. "I didn't want to worry you, but Ned has had word that Gloucester is now besieged." She added with a downcast mouth. "We need Father here."

Deliverance stared at her sister. Luke hadn't imparted that piece of news. It changed everything. Her one hope had been that they would hold out long enough for Sir John to reach them.

"If Gloucester is besieged then we cannot expect Father to come running at our beck and call, Pen." As Penitence bit her lip, a habit when she was worried, Deliverance added, "We are well prepared and I'm sure he will come as soon as he is able." She patted her sister's hand and hoped she sounded reassuring.

Privately her heart sank. If Gloucester were truly besieged, they could not count on any help from that quarter.

Penitence lowered her head. "Luke said you encountered Jack and Charles yesterday." Deliverance nodded.

Penitence bit her lip again and looked out of the window to the soft summer day beyond. "Did Jack ask about me?"

"It was hardly the occasion for social discourse," Deliverance said, her tone softening when she saw the naked yearning on her sister's face. "Yes, he did ask after you and I think he misses you as much as you do him."

"Do you suppose Jack will be with his father and brother when they come here?"

Deliverance didn't reply. She didn't need to. Of course he would and it would be agony for Penitence knowing Jack was outside the castle walls. She recalled something of a conversation with Luke Collyer from the previous day when loss of blood and shock had loosened her tongue.

"Do you really still love him, Pen?" she asked.

Her sister looked up, her blue eyes misted with tears. "With all my heart." "Pen, if you want to leave and go to Father in Gloucester or Aunt Jane..."

Her sister shook her head. "I won't leave you, Liv, and maybe Jack can bring some sense to the situation if he knows I am within the castle walls." She sighed heavily and her blue eyes misted with tears that she dashed away with the back of her hand. "Pay me no heed, I am just being foolish." Deliverance studied her sister. "Pen, how do you know if you're in love?" Penitence looked at her sister, all tears forgotten.

"Oh, Liv, how can I explain it? It's the most delicious pain you can ever know. Your heart beats and the breath stops in your throat and you just want to be near the person—" Penitence stopped, frowning. "Why do you ask?" Her eyes widened. "You're not in love with Captain Collyer, are you?"

Deliverance's mouth fell open. "Captain Collyer! That insufferable...arrogant...good gracious, Pen, how could you even think that?"

Penitence rose to her feet and looked down at her sister. "There are far more worthy men to fall in love with than penniless soldiers of fortune." She placed a hand on her sister's brow. "I think you might be a little feverish. You are not to stir from that bed today. Meg will bring up some broth for your lunch and you are to rest."

Deliverance sank back against the bolsters as her sister and her maid closed the door behind them.

In love with Luke Collyer? What a preposterous suggestion, she thought and closed her eyes.

There must be another explanation for her racing heart and shortness of breath when she had seen him looking down at her. Not to mention the alarming heat flashes when she thought of his arms around her.

Loss of blood—that was it.

It occurred to Luke, as he went about his business the following day that he should have considered the efficacy of a pistol ball in Deliverance's arm earlier in their relationship. For the first time since he had arrived at Kinton Lacey, he enjoyed undisputed command over the entire garrison.

He had paid her another visit after breakfast, and found her up and dressed but still looking pale and wan, and apparently content to pass the day in the parlour, looking for the entire world like a demure goodwife and not at all like the bossy, determined little person who made his life difficult.

And yet part of him missed their sparring. He had, he admitted to himself, become accustomed to her presence as a comrade and as an equal. He missed seeing her slight form everywhere he looked, supervising ditches, ordering provisions to be stored, countermanding his orders, confusing the men...

He left Ned supervising a small herd of cattle purchased for the provisioning of the castle and strode across the courtyard. Looking up at the residence he saw Deliverance sitting at the window of the upper parlour, her chin resting on the hand of her uninjured arm. In that unguarded moment she looked so sad that he stopped in his tracks.

She saw him and straightened, the moment of candour gone, but the recollection of her drawn, pensive face lingered. He waved at her and decided they should both take a short break from the responsibilities that weighed upon them so heavily.

Luke washed the dust of the day off and made himself as presentable as he could. He found Deliverance in the parlour, still sitting by the window where he had seen her, looking down over the courtyard, her arm in a neat blue silk sling. Penitence sat in a chair beside her, the ever-present embroidery in her hand. She looked up as Luke entered and seeing him she frowned. Luke swept both women an all encompassing bow as Deliverance turned around and looked at him.

"Where did you get the cattle?" Deliverance asked without preamble.

"Purchased quite legally from a farmer over by Stanton," Luke replied. "I have some news. Charles Farrington has just sat himself down in front of Byton with three hundred men."

The women looked at each other and Penitence's hand went to the chain at her throat "Three hundred?" Penitence stared at him. "How do you know that?"

Luke's lips compressed. "The game of war, Mistress Felton. He watches us and I watch him." Her eyes widened. "And Byton? Are you going to help?"

He frowned. "What help can I be now they are under siege? When I offered Byton help, it was refused."

"Can't you attack Farrington from behind?" Penitence asked. "I have fifty men. He has three hundred."

"But you did it before!" Penitence said.

"I had the element of surprise and Farrington's force was untrained and ill-equipped. It is quite a different army that is encamped before Byton. Two of my patrols have already been involved in skirmishes with Farrington's men. I'm sorry, Mistress Felton, but Byton is on its own. I've sent word to Gloucester but as you know that is also under siege. We can do no more and my men are all needed here."

Deliverance sank into the chair across from her sister. "Luke...Captain Collyer is right, Pen. There is nothing we can do for Byton." She looked up at him. "How long do you think we have?"

"Only a matter of days."

She sighed and looked away.

Penitence looked him up and down. "You look unusually tidy. Do you have an assignation planned, Captain Collyer?"

He looked down at his best coat of fine wool, dyed a deep ruby, alleviated by a spotless linen collar edged with a good quality lace that he had chosen. Just for a few minutes it felt good to have left his military persona in the bedchamber, even if he still wore a sword and had a small pistol tucked into his belt.

An unaccustomed heat burned his cheeks and he cleared his throat.

Looking at Deliverance, he said, "I was wondering if...that is... if you're up to it, Mistress Felton, you would care to take a walk?"

Penitence gasped and, he amended his invitation. "I mean both of you, of course."

Penitence glanced at Deliverance. "I have chores to see to," she said, "but I think a stroll would do you good, Liv."

Deliverance looked from her sister to Luke. "Me?"

Thankful any confusion had been avoided by Penitence's tact, Luke continued with more confidence, "When Farrington takes Byton, he will move on to us and then our chance for a walk in the fresh air beside the Teme will be lost."

"A walk?" Deliverance repeated.

"That is an excellent idea," Penitence said. "A little fresh air will put some colour back in your cheeks, Liv."

Deliverance looked out at the fine summer evening and nodded. "Very well. Thank you, Captain

Collyer. I really don't need this," she said, removing the sling.

He bowed low to her and offered her his arm. For a moment she hesitated, glancing at Penitence who just smiled.

As they walked out of the residence into the mellow afternoon sun, a shout went up. The entire garrison had gathered in the courtyard and were clapping and cheering. Deliverance cast a questioning glance at Luke. He smiled and shook his head, gently disengaging her arm and standing back, leaving her alone at the top of the stairs.

Sergeant Hale disengaged himself from the crowd and climbed the stairs to her, one hand behind his back.

As he stood before her he drew the hand out, and thrust a bunch of meadow flowers, already wilting, at her. She took them in her good hand and looked up at the huge barrel-chested man.

"Thank you, but I don't know what I have done to deserve this."

Hale whipped his hat off his head and stood turning it in his huge hands. "Lady, 'twas a brave thing you did and we," he indicated the entire garrison, "want you to know that you has our loyalty, to a man."

Deliverance scanned the disreputable ranks of unshaven men, still covered in dirt from their day's work on the defences.

She cleared her throat and looked down at the nosegay, the scent of the meadow sweetening the air around her. A lump rose in her throat and she swallowed it down. Tears were not appropriate at this moment.

With an effort she looked up and spoke, keeping her voice strong and clear. "Thank you, all of you. What I learned on our reconnaissance to Ludlow is that we will be faced with great adversity over the coming weeks, and there will be times when we will need all the strength God gave us. It heartens me to know that we have such loyal men beside us."

"Amen!" Sgt Hale declared. "Let us join together in prayer for the safe delivery of this castle from the hands of the foul fiends."

When the seemingly interminable prayer had ended, Luke stepped forward. "Enough. Back to work all of you."

The men dispersed and Deliverance looked down at the wilted flowers in her hand. "I didn't expect this," she said in a small, quiet voice.

"That is why it is important," Luke said. "Those men will die for you now."

She looked back at the empty courtyard and sighed. "They shouldn't have to. They should be home with their own families, bringing in the harvest." "That is the tragedy of war."

Luke took the flowers from her hand and handed them to one of the maids who had come out of the residence with a bucket of water.

"Put these in Mistress Felton's chamber, girl." He crooked his elbow. "Now, Mistress Felton, about that walk."

As they strolled out of the castle, Luke glanced at his companion. He had ample opportunity to study her face on the long, fraught ride back from Ludlow. In the dark of the largely sleepless night that followed their safe return he had reached the conclusion that while she paled in the shadow of her classically-beautiful younger sister, there was strength of character in her strong jaw and determination and intelligence in her bright eyes and the curve of her mouth.

For some reason, he had never had cause to consider before, he found those characteristics infinitely more attractive than Penitence's oval face, blue eyes and golden curls.

"You seem remarkably well-armed for a pleasant stroll by the river," Deliverance remarked.

Luke rested his hand lightly on the hilt of his sword. "It would be pleasant not to take such precautions, but with Farrington practically on our doorstep, I would prefer not to take unnecessary risks."

He allowed her to lead the way and they took the gentle path that meandered down the side of the hill towards the river.

Luke looked up at the east wall of the castle towering above them, searching out the one weakness in the wall, the sally port, the secret entrance to the castle. Deliverance followed his gaze.

"What are you looking at?"

"I was trying to see where the sally port is. It's completely concealed from this angle."

"Well it wouldn't be a very good sally port if it was quite so obvious," Deliverance smiled. "You see that large outcrop of rock," she pointed. "It is behind there."

"So how do you get down that cliff? It's almost sheer."

Her generous mouth curved in a conspiratorial smile. "Oh there's quite a safe path if you know where to look but I don't think you need to worry about it, I can't see a force attacking up it."

"Maybe not, but I should set a guard on it. It is still a vulnerable place in the wall of the castle."

They reached the river, where a weir had been constructed to turn the castle mill, and struck out to the north along a narrow wooded path.

"Where are you from, Captain Collyer?" Deliverance asked.

"Warwickshire," Luke replied in the clipped tone he reserved for occasions where he didn't wish to encourage any further conversation.

He should have known better. Undeterred Deliverance continued, "And what of your family?"

"What about them?"

"Do they fight with you for parliament's cause?"

Luke hesitated before replying, his silence giving the answer.

Deliverance stopped and looked at him, her eyes wide. "They don't! Your family is divided?"

He swallowed. "My family was divided long before the war, Mistress Felton. My father and my brother fight for the King."

She narrowed her eyes and studied him. "So, is Collyer even your real name?"

Luke looked up at the trees above him. "You ask a lot of questions. My family is not your concern."

Her cheeks coloured and she looked down at the ground. "Sorry. My mother always used to say my curiosity would get the better of me."

Luke quickened his stride. No one, except Ned, knew his antecedents and, in his opinion, that was already one person too many but he owed her his trust and he knew whatever confidence he shared with her would go no further.

"I was christened Lucius," he said.

That was half the truth. He had been christened Lucius William Absalom Harcourt. His father, Viscount Harcourt, had been a close confidante of the King and when the irretrievable rift between himself and his family had occurred, he had deemed it prudent to adopt a new identity. He didn't need or want his father's name to play a part in this war.

She stopped and stared at him, a smile curving her lips. When she smiled her eyes seemed to light up. He wished she smiled more often.

"Lucius?"

"Lucius."

She shook her head. "Oh, no. That doesn't suit you at all. Lucius demands a much grander surname than Collyer. You are not a Lucius."

How right, he thought. Lucius Harcourt was another person all together.

They had reached a curve in the river where willows and elms reached down to a still, deep pool. The fisherman in Luke told him that some magnificent specimens would lurk in its dark recesses. In a more peaceful time there would be nothing he would like better than to drowse away an afternoon at such a spot with a rod and a good companion.

Beside him Deliverance stopped, wrapping her arms around herself. Glancing down, he saw something glisten on her eyelash. A tear?

"Drat these cursed midges!" Deliverance unsuccessfully tried to dash the tears from her eyes while pretending to swat midges. She probably hoped he didn't notice.

His mother's propensity to tears at the slightest provocation had inured him to a woman's tears but in Deliverance, tears seemed so out of character.

"Deliverance?" He laid a hand on her shoulder.

She swallowed. "My brother died here. He came swimming on a warm, summer day like today and...and...he drowned."

Luke stared at her. He had not expected such a confidence. He looked across the still, deep pool, seeing the beautiful place through her eyes as a dark and foreboding place of grief and tragedy.

"I'm sorry," he said. "How old was he?"

"Thirteen. He...he was my twin. My mother was grief-stricken. She never recovered and died the next winter. Father was away so much with parliament and county duties. It all fell to me..." She trailed off, fresh tears catching at the corners of her eyes.

He slid his hand from her shoulder around the back of her neck, drawing her in to him. She rested her head against his chest and they stood together looking out over the still water, as a brightly coloured kingfisher dived into the water coming up with a wriggling fish in its bill.

Deliverance stiffened, extricating herself from his arm. Once again, the woman she wanted the world to know. She turned to stride along the path ahead of him, her head bowed.

Luke stood for a moment watching her. At fourteen, Deliverance Felton had found herself mother to her younger sister and mistress of this rambling castle. No, he thought, life had not dealt fairly with her.

He caught up with her and they walked side by side in silence to a place where the tree line broke and a green expanse of grass and wild flowers ran down to the river bank. Deliverance sat down and drew her knees up, wrapping her arms around them. Luke sprawled beside her, plucking at the long grass stems and chewing their ends, a childhood habit.

Deliverance leaned her head on her knees and looked at him.

"I suppose you must think that I cannot bear to go anywhere near the pool," she said.

He looked up at her; a frown puckered her forehead. "I love going there. I go when I need to think." She stopped and looked away. "You'll laugh..."

"I won't," Luke promised.

"If I have a problem I go there to talk to James."

"He was your brother and your twin. It's natural that you still feel the connection with him."

She tore at the grass around her shoe, a slight colour staining her pale cheeks. "It calms me. I can always see the solution to my problems when I've sat with James." She looked up, scanning his face. "I've never told anyone about that before, not even Pen."

66

"I am honoured," he said. "Accept my assurance that your confidence will go no further."

"Thank you for understanding."

The heat rose to Luke's face and he coughed to cover his embarrassment. Any other woman and he probably would have laughed and ribbed her about her fancies but not Deliverance. She had told him something about herself that she had not even told her closest confidante. He appreciated the value of the trust she had placed in him. It was to be treasured.

Deliverance stretched and lay down in the grass beside him. "It all seems so peaceful. This was a good idea, thank you, Luke...Captain Collyer."

He smiled. "Luke is fine. May I claim a similar familiarity?"

She nodded. "That seems fair."

"Deliverance Felton. Deliverance..." He tried her name on his tongue and looked down at her, smiling. "What were your parents thinking when they named you and your sister?"

Deliverance smiled. "My mother's choice, I think. She came from a very strict puritan family. My brother ended up with the perfectly acceptable name of James. My family calls me Liv. I...I wouldn't mind if you did as well."

"Liv?" Luke tried the shortened name out. He twirled the feathery grass stem in his fingers and reached out and batted her on the nose with it. "No, I like Deliverance. The right to contract a person's name has to be earned, I think."

Deliverance swatted the grass away. "Stop that!"

He rolled on to his back beside her with his ankles crossed. Above them, small, fluffy white clouds scudded across a sky the colour of Deliverance's eyes, like lambs playing in a field.

"So, what will become of the castle and estate when your father dies?" Luke asked

"It's not entailed. I believe it will come to me...I hope it will come to me. I've tried to show father that I'm worthy." She paused. "Sorry--that sounded grasping."

"And your sister?"

"She has a respectable dowry."

"I'm surprised she's not had every eligible man in the county after her," Luke observed.

"She has, but only one she cared for," Deliverance said. "Jack Farrington."

Luke sighed, contemplating that particular doomed relationship. "What about you, Deliverance?"

"Me? What man would have me?"

Luke looked up at the outline of the castle rising above the tree line, the soft grey stone of its walls, picturesque against the green. Any man who wanted a castle and substantial estates would have her, he thought cynically.

"I think," Deliverance continued, oblivious to his train of thought. "I think I may have been too preoccupied to notice if any man seriously paid me court."

"How old are you?" Luke asked.

She stiffened. "Twenty-five." She looked down at him. "I consider that an extremely personal question. How old are you, Captain Collyer?"

He smiled. "Twenty-nine and I've been a soldier since I was eighteen."

"If I'd been a man I would have been a soldier..." Deliverance began but didn't continue.

"If you'd been a man you would have set yourself to be the best rider, the best swordsman, the best at everything wouldn't you?"

She flushed scarlet to the roots of her hair. "I'm good at all those things." She pulled a face. "What I'm not good at is domestic duties."

"You are good at swords?" Luke asked.

"Not good...but passable," Deliverance said.

Luke rose to his feet. "Show me."

Deliverance looked up at him. "What do you mean?"

"Show me how you wield a sword?"

Deliverance spread her hands. "I've no sword with me."

"Wait here."

Luke walked into the glade, returning with two long stout sticks of even length and weight that he had cut.

"This is foolish," Deliverance said as he threw one to her. She caught it deftly in the hand of her uninjured arm.

"On your guard, madam," he said with a laugh. "You're serious?"

He assumed the *en garde* position. "Very. I've never fenced with a woman before."

"You have something of an advantage over me," Deliverance observed as she brought her stick up to rest against his. "To start with you are considerably taller than me, you have a longer reach and, sir, you are not wearing petticoats."

Luke moved to flick the hideous cap off her head and found himself parried. They circled gaining each other's measure and then with a lightning fast move, Deliverance lunged, the stick skimming his right sleeve.

"Very good," Luke said in genuine admiration, parrying her next lunge.

He could have used his height and reach advantage but chose not to. Deliverance's own size and weight made her fast but the skirts were obviously a serious impediment, so they indulged in a bit of back and forth until the ghastly cap she wore fell from Deliverance's head and the shining dark hair tumbled around her face. She put up her weapon and pushed the hair back from her face. The exercise had brought colour to her cheeks and her eyes danced with laughter. Luke wondered how much opportunity she had in her life to laugh.

She rubbed her sore arm. "Enough, Captain Collyer. I am just out of my sick bed, remember."

Her breast rose and fell from the exertion and, with her collar askew, for the first time he noticed that the plain gown hid a shapely figure. His eyes held hers, and he saw an answering longing in their blue depths.

He let the stick fall and took a step towards her as she did likewise. She stood within arm's reach of him, her gaze locked on his eyes. Her lips parted and her eyelids fluttered and as one they leaned in towards each other.

A low growl of thunder rolled across the peaceful landscape, causing the birds to take flight. They flew upwards carolling alarm as Luke and Deliverance jumped apart.

"Cannon?" Deliverance whispered, her eyes still locked on Luke's wide and fearful.

Luke nodded. "Byton. It has begun. We must get back to the castle, Deliverance."

Deliverance paused only to scoop up the linen cap and they both strode swiftly back towards the castle and their responsibilities.

Chapter Seven

With Byton now under siege, Luke redoubled his efforts on Kinton Lacey's defences. Every able bodied person, man, woman or child bent their back to the ditches and fortifications. Even the weather turned against them with cold, sleeting rain turning the clay to mud and the task to one of Herculean proportions.

As the men laboured in the ditches, up to their knees in cold, muddy water, everyone's spirits began to sag. Patrols of Farrington's men harried the troops Luke sent out to gather provisions and he had lost three good men in the ensuing skirmishes. He could ill afford to lose any more.

Luke hunched down under his sodden cloak while the rain dripped off the brim of his hat. He looked down from the curtain wall at the toiling labourers below him. It had been Deliverance's idea to line the ditch with the antiquated weapons from the great hall. The old halberds and pikes were of little use in siege warfare but still quite serviceable and would make a nasty deterrent to anyone foolish enough to try to storm the weakest wall. The gate caused him no concern. Despite the stone bridge, replacing an earlier drawbridge, the double fortified gatehouse had two solid, working portcullis and it would take an enormous force to take the gatehouse.

"Is there anything more we can do?" Ned asked.

Luke shook his head. "Of course there is more we can do, but with the time we have left, we have done as much as we can. If Farrington wants this castle, he will have to work for it,"

Without the siege gun Farrington would have to starve them out. Deliverance's careful provisioning of the garrison ensured they could hold out for months. The only thing that could, and probably would, break them would be the Thunderer and at the thought of that enormous weapon, he shuddered.

He turned and looked down into the courtyard where Deliverance's slight, bedraggled figure stood in the centre of the mired yard, directing barrels of salted meat towards the cellars. He stood watching her for a few minutes, smiling when he saw her hair hanging unregarded in sodden rats' tails down the back of her

cloak. A lesser woman would have disappeared indoors at the first drop of rain, but not Deliverance. Until the job had been completed, she would be out there all day.

He sighed and gathered himself together. Ever since that moment on the water meadow when he had nearly kissed her, being in her presence caused him acute embarrassment and he found himself going out of his way to avoid her. However, this time it couldn't be avoided and, dearly as he might have liked to escape through the Gatehouse, he had a matter he needed to discuss with her.

As if aware she was being watched, she turned and looked up at him. He gestured for her to join him and she left her post, taking the slippery, unguarded steps to the walk at the top of the curtain wall with an ease born of familiarity.

As she reached him, she pushed the matted hair back from her face. "I'm very busy, Luke. Is this important?"

"Yes. I wanted to tell you I intend to raze that line of cottages." He indicated four cottages a mere three hundred yards from the castle gate.

Her jaw fell open. "You can't do that," she protested. "People live there."

"When Farrington comes those cottages make perfect cover for him and whoever lives there now, most certainly won't be there for long."

She looked up at him, her blue eyes fierce with anger. "Luke, where will the people go?"

"They can be rebuilt when this is over, but for now, Deliverance, they are coming down." He turned back to the wall and gave a sign to Sergeant Hale to proceed with the demolition. The sound of axes crashing into wood pierced the still air. A child began to cry. Luke set his jaw. He could not afford sentimentality.

"I have already told the villagers that they have three choices. They can stay where they are and face Farrington, they can come inside the castle walls or they can take themselves off to a safer place."

Deliverance looked at him. "What sort of choices are those?"

"The only ones they have," he said. "And the same applies to those within these walls, yourself and Penitence included." He hunched his shoulders, straightening as he looked down into her angry face. "In fact, it would be preferable if you both left the castle."

Deliverance turned to him, her hands on her hip, her chin lifted in defiance. He knew that look and his heart sank.

"And where do you think we would go?"

He shrugged. "Surely you have some kindly relative in a quieter part of the country who would take you in? Frankly, Deliverance, I would prefer it if I didn't have you and your sister to worry about."

Rain ran down her face, failing to cool the anger that coloured her cheeks and the fire that burned in her eyes.

"You are...insufferable," Deliverance said. "We are not going anywhere and you know it!"

"Suit yourself." He shrugged. "But don't come bleating to me, two weeks after the gates shut, that you've had enough and want to get out."

He heard the hiss of indrawn breath and her mouth opened to let forth a response but it didn't come. She clamped her mouth shut and turned on her heel. He turned back to the wall to watch the destruction of the cottages.

"That was a bit harsh," Ned spoke at last, having maintained a judicial silence during the confrontation with Deliverance.

Luke leaned on the wall and let out his breath. He hadn't been aware how braced he had been for that conversation with Deliverance. He had fought many battles but none had drained his energy so much as a conversation with Deliverance Felton.

"I'm serious," he said. "They have no idea what they are in for. I don't want to be responsible for them."

"I rather suspect it is the lady who feels responsible for you, rather than vice versa," Ned said.

"What do you mean?" Luke stiffened, guilt clutching at his sleeve. He wanted Deliverance away from this hellhole, because that is what this castle would become. He wanted to know she was safe and if he had to drive away with cruelty he would. It was the only way he could protect her, keep her safe from the horrors he knew were coming.

Ned shrugged and swept a hand across the castle and lands beyond the wall. "Her father left her with task of defending her home and she feels that responsibility as well as the lives of everyone in it, you included."

Luke gave an unconvincing snort. Ned could be uncomfortably perceptive and despite his harsh words, he knew in his heart Deliverance could never walk away from Kinton Lacey. If she died in its defence, she would consider it her duty and honor to do so.

"Do you have any word on Byton?" he asked, changing the subject. He turned to look in the general direction of their brother garrison. There had been no noise from the guns for at least twenty-four hours and the silence was ominous.

His scouts had confirmed that Charles Farrington had command of the siege. Sir Richard hadn't wasted his big gun on such a small prize but he had a couple of the smaller siege cannons in place and these had proved quite effective on the inadequate preparations of the castle.

Ned shook his head. "They've held out nearly two weeks but it can't go on much longer."

Luke gave his friend a sideways glance. "They've beaten the odds I would have given them."

The rain lifted by evening and a perversely serene twilight descended on the castle. Luke only left his position on the curtain wall to catch a snatched meal before returning to keep watch.

The smouldering embers of the cottages he had razed that afternoon provided a strange comforting glow as darkness fell.

Every nerve in his body was on edge, the soldier's instinct telling him to expect trouble. It came late in the afternoon when he heard the sound of several explosions coming from the direction of Byton.

The soldier standing beside him, Truscott, one of the Kinton Lacey men, glanced at him. "Byton?"

Luke nodded. "Farrington is slighting the castle."

Truscott frowned. "Slighting, sir? What's that?"

"He is destroying it to make sure it cannot be defended again."

Truscott's eyes widened. "And that's what he'll do if he takes Kinton Lacey?"

Luke nodded. "It's what I'd do."

He heard a rustle of skirts and Deliverance joined him, greeting Truscott like an old friend. The man grinned, saluted and moved away, leaving Luke and Deliverance alone together. Deliverance leaned on the bulwark, looking out at the glowing remnants of the cottages.

"I'm sorry about the cottages," Luke said at last.

She shook her head. "You were right. They can be rebuilt. My people have gone to relatives. You were right, the ground needed to be cleared."

'My people'. Luke recalled Ned's words. He had been right. Deliverance took the responsibility for everyone in Kinton Lacey on her slender shoulders.

She took a deep breath of air that smelled of smoke. "The guns at Byton have gone quiet. Do you think...do you think it is over?"

He looked at her. "I will send a couple of scouts out in the morning, but I am sure it has fallen."

"There's no chance—" She stopped as he shook his head. "When do you suppose they will march on us?"

"Tomorrow. I've no doubt the guns are already on the move."

She shivered and he resisted a sudden urge to put his arm around her and draw her in towards him.

Too many eyes, and she wouldn't thank him.

"I haven't asked how your arm is faring," he said, changing the subject. "Healed well, thank you. I will have a nice scar to show my daughters."

He smiled. "Now there is a terrifying thought. A whole clan of small Deliverances." She smiled in response. "Thank you."

Grateful for a change of subject, he continued. "Have you any desire for children?"

"I have yet to meet anyone I would care to have children with," she replied, "but I am grateful that I at least have that choice. So many women don't."

"Aye, my mother was married off at fifteen. She and my father hated each other on sight. It made for a happy childhood," Luke said, unable to disguise the bitterness in his voice.

"My parents were a love match," Deliverance said. "My father was broken by her death. I think that was why he spent so much time in London with parliamentary duties. He couldn't bear to be home."

Luke nodded. "My father was rarely at home either and when he was–" He broke off, pushing the memories of his father's temper and their furious confrontations, to the back of his mind.

"I am fortunate that Father let me have so much independence," Deliverance said. "I would like to think it was because he cared, but I think it is probably because he didn't care. He even let James' tutor stay on to teach Penitence and me for several years after James' death."

"Oh, don't misjudge him, Deliverance. Your father cares very much about you and Penitence." "How do you know that?"

Luke broke a loose piece of stone off the wall and threw it down, listening for the faint splash as it hit the water that had pooled in the bottom of the ditch. "We had a very frank discussion before he sent me here."

Deliverance laughed. As she opened her mouth to respond, a shout went up from the sentry stationed on the far side of the village and a shot rang out. A lone horseman, a bundle over the pommel of his saddle, rode into plain view of the castle. He upended the bundle on to the ground, raised his hand in an impudent salute to the watchers on the wall and galloped away, the shots from the out posted sentries ringing around him.

For a moment Luke and Deliverance stood frozen staring at the bundle on the ground that moaned and moved.

"It's a person," Deliverance cried.

Luke moved first, shouting an order for the gate to be opened even as he took the stairs two by two. Deliverance followed close behind him.

Ned, who had been on watch in the gatehouse, was ahead of him as they ran across the bridge and he reached the crumpled body first. He fell to his knees beside the figure, as the others joined him, panting from their exertion.

Ned went down on his knees, pulling the swaddling from around the moaning figure.

"It's a woman," Ned said and even in the gathering gloom, Luke could see that the bundle that had been treated with such disdain was a girl wrapped in a rough cloak.

Ned lifted her up and as the cloak fell away, the girl's long red hair tumbling across Ned's knees. "Lay still, lass," Ned said. "You're safe."

Luke caught his breath, recognising the pretty face.

"It's the maid from Byton," he said and hearing the word, the girl's eyes opened and fixed on Luke.

"Get her inside," Deliverance ordered.

As Ned hefted the girl into his arms, Deliverance glanced at Luke and he saw that she too had recognised the girl.

"What have they done to her?" Deliverance said in a low voice, adding. "What have they done to Byton?"

Ned carried the girl in and laid her on one of the oak settles in the upper parlour. The men retired to the doorway while the women swung into action, peeling back the cloak. Penitence gasped and looked up at her sister, distress written in her beautiful blue eyes.

Deliverance's lips tightened as she saw the girl's clothing was torn and stained and livid bruises had begun to colour her face and arms. If these were the bruises on show to the public what other injuries did this poor girl carry?

She glanced across at Ned and Luke.

"I think it best you leave us," she said. "Wait in the library and I will report to you later." Luke shook his head. "I need to question the girl."

Deliverance opened her mouth to argue but Meg entered the room, carrying a bowl of water. The maid held the bowl and dipping a cloth into the water; Penitence began to gently sponge the girl's battered and bruised face while Deliverance knelt down beside the girl and picked up her hand.

"Can you hear me?"

The girl's eyes flickered open and she gave a great, shuddering sigh, tears beginning to pour silently down her cheek.

"Hush," Penitence said. "You're at Kinton Lacey. You're safe now."

In two strides Luke had joined her. He leaned over Deliverance's shoulder. "Can you talk?" he asked. She nodded and recognition animated her face. "I remember you. You tried to warn 'em and the Colonel he wouldn't listen. I thought you had a nice face." Fresh tears started in her eyes.

"Your name?" Luke sounded cool and in command, compelling a response from the unhappy girl. Her lip trembled. "Lovedie. Lovedie Brown. I am...was...maid at Byton Castle."

Luke, hearing the past tense, glanced at Deliverance. "Has Byton fallen?" he asked.

"He said...he said...to tell you... You would be next." A note of hysteria rose in the girl's voice and she tried to sit up.

Deliverance placed firm hands on her shoulders pushing her back down again. "Sir Richard Farrington?" Deliverance asked in a tight voice.

The girl shook her head. "Not him. The other one."

"Charles?"

The girl nodded.

"And the garrison?" Luke asked.

Lovedie pushed aside Deliverance's constraining hand and sat up. She looked around the anxious faces. She took a shuddering breath and spoke clearly. "We held out for as long as we could and then the Colonel, he said, we had to surrender. We'd no more food and the powder were all gone. He spoke with Farrington and came back and said he'd negotiated honourable terms. The garrison marched out unarmed to surrender." Her lip trembled. "They took the Colonel, said they were taking him to Ludlow Castle and then, then...they tied the others together in pairs..."

Her face contorted and her audience held their collective breath, dreading what was to come. "They slit their throats. Every man. They threw the bodies into the ditch."

Dropping the cloth she held, Penitence's hands flew to her mouth and she gave a stifled cry.

"Charles Farrington," Deliverance said in a low voice. A man who would kick a puppy to death would have no end to his cruelty.

"A man who does not respect the rules of war," Luke responded. "And the castle?"

Her chin quivered. "They blew it up. My brother..." she sobbed burying her head in her hands.

Luke squatted down and took the girl's hands in his own. This was war and he knew the atrocities women could suffer at the hands of a triumphant enemy. "And you, lass? Did they...? Did he...?"

She looked at him and shook her head as she gleaned his meaning. "No...Not that." She touched her face. "Farrington, he hit me a few times, just to teach me some manners, he said. Then he flung me over the saddle of one of his men with the message I've just given to you."

"So we're next?" Luke sounded grim.

"That's what he said," the girl replied.

"Enough," Deliverance snapped. "Pen, take Lovedie to our room and Meg, organise a pallet to be made up for her."

Penitence put her arm around the girl and led her from the room. Meg followed, carrying the basin.

Luke crossed to stand by the window, looking out over the darkened castle, his shoulders tense and his back ramrod-straight. Ned sat down at the table and began tapping his fingers on the table.

Deliverance addressed Luke's rigid back. "What are you going to do?"

"The first thing I am going to do," he said slowly. "Is verify the girl's story for myself."

"Don't be a fool, Luke." Ned rose to his feet. "Byton is an hour's ride away and Farrington could be anywhere between us and Byton."

"Farrington will be back in Ludlow," Luke said.

"How do you know?" Deliverance asked.

Luke turned to face the room and shrugged. "I'm guessing that Farrington's returned to Ludlow to report to his father, celebrate his success and gather reinforcements before he marches on us. Ned, send out a scout to report if he's left a guard on the castle. If he's just marched away we will go and see for ourselves at first light."

Ned rose to his feet and left the room. "It could be a trap," Deliverance said.

A thousand thoughts crossed her mind. If he were to be captured on this escapade, what would become of the castle? Of her? She could not imagine how she could sustain a siege without Luke Collyer. He had taught her to depend on him and that thought caused a rush of anger. Before Luke she had managed quite well. She had never been dependent on anyone else in her life and the thought frightened her more than the threat of Farrington.

"Don't argue with me, Deliverance," Luke said. "I'm not in the mood."

"No, you're feeling guilty," Deliverance said. "You're thinking that you should have gone to Byton's aid."

She could see from the anguished twist of his mouth that she was correct.

"You wouldn't have achieved anything," she said. "You said yourself Farrington's men outnumbered anything we have to throw at him and you were right. We had no choice but to stay here. Stay safe."

He scowled. "Safe? Deliverance we have less than a hundred men to hold this castle."

"Yes, but we have something Byton didn't have and that is ample supplies and a clean water supply and we're well prepared. We can hold out until help comes. If you're riding out into a trap we are losing the only other thing we need...you."

To her surprise he laughed. "I thought you would be pleased to see the back of me?"

She sniffed. "You are quite good at what you do and I've grown rather accustomed to having you around."

He crossed over to where she stood and placed a hand on her shoulder. Beneath its warmth and weight, the gesture gave her a curious comfort.

"You've read all the books, Deliverance. There is no science to shutting the door and letting Farrington knock away to his heart's content. I doubt your father will let Kinton Lacey go unrelieved for any length of time. Good night." He pulled his hand away and turned for the door, walking with a slow heavy step as if he, not she, carried the world on his back.

Deliverance touched the place where his hand had rested. She had to stop him, whatever it took.

As he reached the door she blurted out, "Luke, you've heard Lovedie's story. What are you going to accomplish by riding out to Byton?"

He stopped at the door and turned to look at her. "Peace of mind," he said.

Chapter Eight

The scout Ned sent out reported back that Byton castle appeared to be deserted. The man admitted that he hadn't gone right up to the ruins, and Luke decided to see for himself.

They set out before first light and encountered no enemy on the road from Kinton Lacey. The acrid smell of smoke reached them even before the former stronghold of Byton loomed out of the dawn mist, grey and ominous. He remembered how he had last seen it, golden and soft in the summer sun, a family home not a fortress. Now the broken, jagged teeth of the walls reached to the sky from a mire of trampled gardens and destruction.

He drew rein, his nose twitching. Over the stench of burning from the slighted castle, even from two hundred yards distant, he could smell death. He dismounted and led his horse across the battle-field to the ditch that lay before the castle, steeling himself to look down.

He counted twenty eight bodies lying in the inadequate defensive ditch below the castle walls. Just as Lovedie had said, the men of Byton's garrison had been tied in pairs and their throats savagely cut. Farrington hadn't even spared the powder for a merciful bullet.

Luke's own men dismounted and stood beside him looking down at the carnage, the horror on their faces undisguised. The man beside him turned away, retching and two went down on their knees, their hands clasped in prayer. Luke reflected, with some gratitude, that at least they had not heard Farrington's message.

'Kinton Lacey will be next'

Even as they stood there, the sound of women's voices and weeping came from the broken building and a group of four women appeared in the gateway. They walked towards him, past the shattered remnants of the gate hanging drunkenly from its hinges, their hands outstretched beseeching the newcomers to retrieve their menfolk for decent burial.

Without the necessity of him giving the order, Luke's men set to the gruesome work retrieving the bodies and giving the dead some dignity in their last resting place.

Luke left the men to their grisly task. With his pistol primed and at the ready, he entered the ruined stronghold. Farrington had set charges and brought down the towers and much of the curtain wall. Byton would pose no more threat to the royalist cause again. He thought of Kinton Lacey and the fate that awaited it—that awaited the garrison—if they should fail to hold it.

An attempt had been made to torch what was left of the place but the fire had not taken hold completely. In the remains of the hall, he stepped over the charred and still smoking timbers, and climbed the stone stairs to the upper level of the only tower that had survived the destruction.

A rattle of stone above him, alerted every nerve in his body and he softened his step, his hand tightening on the stock of his pistol.

The stairs opened out into a square room that had apparently been used as quarters for the garrison. Straw mattresses had been piled in a corner with neatly stacked blankets. He scanned the room, and in the soft morning light caught the faintest flicker of movement from behind a buttress.

He braced and cocked his pistol, levelling it in readiness. "Come out," he said.

"Please don't fire." The voice sounded young and frightened.

A slight figure stepped out from the narrow space formed by the buttress and the wall, holding shaking hands above his head. He fell to his knees and looked up at Luke. The boy could not have been more than about thirteen, a scrawny youngster, his dirty face streaked with the tracks of tears.

Luke lowered his pistol. "It's all right, lad. I'm not one of Farrington's men. We're from the garrison at Kinton Lacey."

The boy gave a choked sob and slid down against the wall. He wrapped his arms around his legs, lowered his head on to his knees, and began to rock back and forth.

Luke crouched down next to him. "I don't need to ask you any questions, lad. I've eyes in my head.

Can you tell me your name?"

The boy sniffed and said in a muffled voice, "Toby, sir. Toby Brown." He raised his head and looked into Luke's eyes. "They're all dead, aren't they? I heard them screaming." His face crumpled. "I hid meself. I should've been out there with them."

Luke laid a hand on the boy's shoulder. "And you would be dead too. Nothing you could have done would have changed anything, Toby. You're alive. That's what matters."

The boy continued to rock back and forth, locks of red hair covering his face.

Luke squatted down. "You wouldn't be related to a Lovedie Brown would you?"

The boy stopped his rocking and looked up. "She's my sister. What's happened to her? I thought her safe in Ludlow with our aunt."

Luke regarded him for a moment. "Why would you think that?"

"She escaped from here not long afore the final assault." Lovedie had not made it to safety. Farrington had caught her.

"Is she dead?" The boy looked up at him, his face stricken.

Luke held up a placatory hand. "Don't worry. She's safe at Kinton Lacey." How she had got there and the grim message she carried was for Lovedie's telling, not him.

The boy closed his eyes. "I prayed for her so hard." He raised his face to the ceiling. "Thank you, Lord."

He held out his hand, raising the boy.

Toby swallowed and ran a hand through his hair. He took a deep breath. "Where are they? I've got to see for meself," he said.

Luke knew he meant his murdered friends and he didn't argue. He followed the boy down the stairs and out of the stinking ruin. The bodies of the slain had been laid out and it made grim viewing. Luke told the corporal about the blankets in the tower room and the man nodded, gesturing for two of the men to go and fetch them.

The boy looked down the line of slain men. The women knelt beside the bodies of their menfolk, the keening of their grief almost too much to bear. Luke placed a hand on the boy's shoulder and Toby turned to look up at him.

"Can I go to Lovedie?" he asked.

"Of course, but first tell us who the dead are so we can give them proper burial."

Toby nodded and they walked the line of the dead, giving the grisly corpses the humanity of their names. These men who twenty four hour earlier had walked, talked, and laughed with the boy. Luke had little time for monsters like Charles Farrington. He would see him dead before this affair was over.

They could not do much more than lay the bodies back in the bottom of the ditch and cover them with earth. Sergeant Hale said prayers over the dead, and with the morning sun high, the men mounted their horses and turned back for Kinton Lacey.

An uneasy feeling prickled at Luke. It had all been too easy. It gnawed at him that Charles Farrington had apparently just walked away from Byton. The dramatic flourish of dumping Lovedie with her message only made him more suspicious. He wondered if this was what trout felt after it had been tickled and had taken the bait.

Dearly as Luke would have loved to have put his heels to his horse and ridden hell for leather back to the safety of Kinton Lacey, a soldier's natural caution held him back. Small party though they were, he sent a scout out in front and proceeded at a leisurely walk. An hour's ride would take a little longer but he had to ensure they all arrived back in one piece. He could not afford to lose a single man.

He rode with every nerve on edge. Behind him, his men rode in single file down the narrow country lanes, each man lost in his own thoughts. The horror of what they had dealt with that day reflected in their grim faces and their silence.

To reach Kinton Lacey they had to cross a bridge over the River Teme. They were quarter of a mile from the bridge when the forward scout came galloping down the lane toward them. He drew rein, his face white.

"Soldiers," he said. "Cutting off the bridge."

Luke took a deep breath and uttered a silent prayer of thanks that he had not given in to emotion. Farrington had guessed, rightly, that Luke would respond to the situation at Byton and had laid the amb ush for his return, certain in the knowledge that the parliamentary troops would be caught off guard.

"How many?"

"A hundred maybe more."

They stood no chance against those odds. "Were you seen?"

The man hesitated. "I don't know."

Of course he had been, Farrington would have his own scouts out and they would have seen them all coming.

"Fight the bastards," one of the men growled.

"Not today," Luke said. "Split up. Half of you go around to the north and half to the south. Get across that river and we will meet back at Kinton Lacey."

Even as he spoke, a musket ball whistled overhead and he heard the pounding of galloping horses. Farrington must have realised his ambush had been sprung and was coming after them.

Without need for further discussion, Luke's men turned their horses in the narrow lane and they galloped for the nearest crossroad where they split up. Luke, Hale, with the boy Toby riding pillion behind him and three others went north with a squadron of horsemen in the Farrington livery of blue coats hard on their heels.

One of the men with him was local, and he turned them across country down towards the river but even as they reached the bank, he could see more blue-coated soldiers on the far bank.

"There's a ford about quarter a mile further on," the young man said as they paused with blue soldiers closing in on them from behind.

Luke nodded and they followed the river bank, the men on the far bank keeping pace with them. The occasional pistol shot slowed them but failed to hit any marks. A heavily wooded copse on the far bank slowed their pursuers and the parliament men put their heels to their horses in the knowledge that if they could get across the river before the soldiers on the far bank reached the crossing, they stood a chance of making it to Kinton Lacey, two miles further on.

Luke crouched low over the horse's head and prayed.

Deliverance had been up and down to the tower watching for the men since mid-morning. As the evening drew on, annoyance turned to concern. Her fears had been justified. Luke had walked into a trap and was probably captured...or dead. At the last thought, her heart tightened.

Penitence, calm as always, looked up from her needlework as Deliverance paced the floor of the parlour.

"He will be fine, Liv," she said.

"I have a bad feeling," Deliverance blurted out. "I told him not to go. If anything's happened to him, it will be his own fault." She clasped her hands together. "I tried to get Ned Barrett to go out after them but he says his orders are to stay within the castle. He won't defy Collyer's orders." Deliverance did another round of the parlour. "Collyer's so stubborn, arrogant and...and..."

"A man?" Penitence suggested.

Melchior entered the room without knocking. "Some of Captain Collyer's men are back," he said. Deliverance's heart lifted for a moment before sinking back as she realised what Melchior had said.

Some of his men...not Captain Collyer.

Melchior signalled to a man waiting outside the door to enter. He all but stumbled into the room, his face drawn and grey, his eyes red-rimmed and haunted. Deliverance took one look at him and knew that something had occurred at Byton--something terrible. Her first thought was of Luke and that terrible nagging fear that had haunted her all day crystallised. She took a deep breath. She had to maintain control. If she fell in a weeping heap on the floor, that would serve no purpose.

"What happened?" Deliverance refrained from grasping the man by his dirty collar and shaking him. "Farrington was waiting for us at the bridge over the Teme. We got away but we had to split up."

"Captain Collyer?"

"He's with the others. They're not back yet?" The man shot a glance at Melchior who shook his head.

Deliverance glanced through the window at the darkening sky. If Luke was in trouble surely he would wait until the cover of darkness to make his way home?

The man sensed her concern. "He'll be fine, ma'am. I've served with him this year past and he can look after himself."

The man's assurance provided no comfort. If he was still alive, Luke was out there when he should have been safe within the castle walls.

A shout went up from the courtyard. Deliverance hurried across to the window and saw a small group of horsemen riding into the castle confines. The heads on their beasts sagged with exhaustion as they drew rein.

As people ran out with torches, Deliverance counted the horsemen in. Ten men had gone out, five had returned in the first party. She counted...three horses... there should have been five.

She gathered up her skirts and ran down to the courtyard as the last two horsemen entered. Sergeant Hale with someone riding pillion on the horse with him and the unmistakable outline of Luke Collyer, hatless behind him. The gates slammed shut behind him.

Deliverance took a steadying breath. All the patrol was now accounted for. Her fears had been unfounded. Now she could afford to be angry.

She gathered her skirts and descended down into the courtyard but as she approached him and saw Luke's grim face, her caustic greeting stopped in her throat.

She looked from Luke's face to the other men and saw the story confirmed in their eyes. She could smell it on their clothes, the stench of smoke and something else, a sickly sweet smell of decay. Lovedie's story had been true, all of it. Charles Farrington had murdered the garrison at Byton before slighting the castle.

Luke dismounted, leaning against the animal's neck as if too weary to move any further. A red-headed boy slid off Sergeant Hale's horse and stood looking around at the gathering crowd. Deliverance heard a shriek and turned to see Lovedie pushing her way through the crowd.

"Toby! Oh Toby, ye're safe!" Deliverance glanced at Luke.

"Her brother," he said, his tone heavy. He looked spent, dark circles under his eyes that had not been there the previous day.

The Brown siblings threw their arms around each other, both crying with relief. Lovedie looked up at Luke. "Oh, Captain Collyer, how can I ever thank you?"

Luke stiffened and he shook his head. "It was the boy's own wits that saved him, not I." Lovedie seized his hands. "We owe you our lives, sir. We'll not forget your kindness."

Luke extricated his hands and shook his head.

"Nothing any good Christian wouldn't do." He looked around the assembled garrison. "Farrington is on the move and he will be with us come the morning. It's time to shut the gates. Those who want to go, leave now."

No one moved.

"We're here to the end, sir," Truscott said and the Kinton Lacey men nodded in agreement. "Lovedie?" Luke looked at the girl. "You and the boy've just been through a siege, there's no call to go through another."

Lovedie straightened, tightening her arm around her brother. The siblings exchanged glances.

"We're not leavin'," she said. "I told you, we owe you our lives and if that's what the good Lord wants of us, then we'll stay and see it out."

Toby looked up at Luke with undisguised worship in his eyes. "I'm your man now, Captain Collyer. I can fire a musket as good as any."

Luke clapped the boy on the shoulder as Hale held up his arms and boomed, "On your knees and let us pray to God Almighty for the souls of the slaughtered at Byton and for our safe delivery from the enemy. And let us beseech God to smite our enemy and give us victory."

As one every man, woman and child sank to their knees in the muddy courtyard to echo Sergeant Hale's fervent prayers.

As Luke rose, brushing the mud from his breeches, Deliverance put her hand on his sleeve. "Luke?"

He looked down at her, his face grim. "We don't have time for pleasantries, Deliverance. We need to get as many of the villagers as want to come in here along with as much livestock as we can fit. Ned..."

He strode off leaving her standing in the middle of the courtyard. Halfway to the gate, he stopped and turned, looking at her with a smile on his face.

"Well, my lady? Are you just going to stand there? I can't do this by myself."

Chapter Nine

They heard Farrington's advance long before he arrived. The steady cadence of his drums and the tramp of feet drifted toward Kinton Lacey with the soft summer breeze, long before the first soldiers came into sight.

Deliverance watched from the castle wall, anxiously scanning the road for the patrol Luke had led out at first light. The five horsemen came galloping up the road toward the castle. A shout went up from the Gatehouse and the horse's hoofs clattered on the cobbles as they entered the castle. Hitching up her skirts, Deliverance and ran down into the courtyard to meet them. As she placed her hand on the bridle of Luke's horse and looked up into his grim face, she knew the news would not be good.

He unbuckled the heavy steel 'pot' helmet he wore and pulled it off, shaking out his sweat dampened hair.

"Well?" she demanded.

A wry, humourless smile twisted his lips. "We're honoured. Sir Richard himself is riding at the head of the column." Luke paused. "I calculate he has three hundred men with him as well as all the guns we saw at Ludlow."

At the memory of the impressive arsenal they had seen demonstrated on the water meadow at Ludlow, Deliverance's courage wavered. She looked away and took a deep breath to steady her nerve, as Luke swung off his horse.

"Is everyone inside?" he asked.

She nodded and Luke turned to Sergeant Hale. "Shut the gates, Hale."

"Sir!" Hale turned on his heel, already bellowing the orders.

It took three men to shut the heavy gates, stoutly reinforced with new cut oak. With its chains clattering, the newly repaired portcullis juddered to the ground behind the gates with a resounding thump.

Kinton Lacey had become once more the fortress it had been designed to be.

Deliverance looked up at the walls and saw the garrison already deploying to their rehearsed positions, the sun glinting from the metal on their muskets and helmets. Buckets of water had been placed at strategic positions on the walls and around the courtyard, ready to deal with the inevitable fires. They were as ready as they would ever be.

A hand rested on her shoulder and Luke said, "Nothing more to be done, Mistress Felton."

"When will he be here?"

"Within the hour."

Deliverance nodded and gave Luke a brave smile. "Then I will be waiting for him."

Preparing for the imminent arrival of a besieging force held some odd similarities with the expected arrival of an exalted guest. One dressed for the occasion. Luke considered his rather limited wardrobe, and decided on grim, military efficiency.

Toby had burnished the steel breastplate, helmet and gorget, and the leather of his baldric shone like glass. He donned the stiff leather buff coat and allowed Toby, who had, unasked, assumed the role of his manservant to buckle on his armour.

"You terrify me," Ned said with a smile as Luke turned to leave the room.

Eschewing the heavy pot helmet for his hat, Luke clapped his friend on the shoulder and the two men clattered down the grand stairs of the residence to wait for Deliverance.

She came running down the stairs, dashing past them in her haste to reach the battlements.

Luke caught her arm as she passed and ran his eye down at her slight figure, clad in a man's breeches and leather jerkin. In her right hand she carried a handsome Wheelock musket, nearly as long as she was high. He seized the weapon and thrust it at Ned.

She squirmed in his grip. "Unhand me, Captain Collyer," she fumed.

Luke shook his head. "You cannot wear that ensemble."

Deliverance shook off his arm and glared up at him. "I've worn it before." "What do you mean you've worn it before?"

"Last time Farrington was here. I took my place with my men on the wall." She looked at Blakelocke.

"Melchior will tell you, I am a very good shot."

Luke glanced at Melchior's impassive face. "I have no doubt you are, Mistress Felton, but I am not letting you out of this house dressed like that."

Her eyes narrowed. "I am not staying in here like some helpless milksop while you negotiate with Farrington."

"I am not suggesting you do that," Luke took a deep breath and schooled himself to patience. "What I am saying is that I do not need you on the wall. I do not need to risk you being killed. You are too valuable."

"Oh." The defiance went out of Deliverance's eyes. "What do you mean?"

"I will hate myself for saying this, but the men seem to adore you." He paused and the corners of his mouth quirked into a smile. "Obviously they don't know you well enough."

Anger flared again in Deliverance's eyes again and he held up a placatory hand. "You have earned their respect and their admiration precisely because you are a woman who has shown incredible bravery. That is what is needed. They want to protect you and you need to show them you are worthy of their protection."

Penitence, who had followed her sister down the stairs, laid a hand on her sister's arm.

"Peace, sister. I understand, Captain Collyer. You need Deliverance to be a woman worthy of their affection," she said.

Luke gave Penitence a relieved smile. "Precisely." He addressed Deliverance. "Think of good Queen Bess...What did she say? *'Although I have the body of a weak and feeble woman, I have the heart and soul of a King of England'.* Those men at Tilbury would have died for her on the spot. I need you to be Queen Bess."

"But this is my castle and I will defend it as I see fit."

Penitence shook her head. "In this case, Liv, I think Captain Collyer has a point." She looked at Luke and smiled. "Leave her to me. We will be right back." She took her sister by the arm and propelled her back up the stairs.

It seemed to take forever before Penitence reappeared at the top of the stairs with a smile on her serene face.

She looked down at the men. "Ready?"

With the full attention of all three men, Penitence pulled her sister forward out of the shadows into the light. Luke clamped his jaw tight to stop his mouth falling open.

Deliverance stood with one hand resting on the banister. Her sister had clothed her in a gown of deep, rich burgundy velvet. She wore no collar, cuffs or jewellery and her hair, lightly pinned back from her face, fell in dark, glossy tresses around her shoulders. The colour of the gown was perfect on her, accentuating the ivory of her skin and the rich brown of her hair. The simple hairstyle framed and softened her face and Luke thought she looked both beautiful and ethereal. A woman worthy of his sword and his honor.

He shook his head in admiration.

"I knew it. I look ridiculous." Deliverance ruined the effect by nearly tripping on the skirt as she attempted to take the stairs at her usual pace.

Luke stepped forward and swept a deep, courtly bow. "Mistress Felton, the admirable Mistress

Felton. You look wonderful."

He took her hand and kissed her long, slender fingers. His own work-hardened and calloused fingers tightened on the fragile bones. Deliverance contrived to wrench her hand free.

She looked defiantly from one man to the other, her gaze coming to rest on Luke. "Well, now you have me looking like something out of an Arthurian legend, what do you want me to do?"

Luke smiled. "We will show Sir Richard Farrington, just what he is up against," he said. "Would you do me the honor of taking my arm, Mistress Felton?"

Beneath the heavy lacing of her bodice Deliverance's heart beat a rapid tattoo. She glanced back at Luke who gave her an encouraging smile as Sergeant Hale held out his hand to assist her to step up on to the box he had placed for her. Farrington needed to see her and as she barely topped the curtain wall, some additional height was needed.

It seemed like the eye of every man in the garrison was fixed on her and she began to see what Luke had meant. As she had stepped out into the courtyard on Luke's arm, a mighty cheer had gone up. They needed an idol, a figurehead. It may have been a tableau, a pantomime, but she could feel the responsibility of these men's lives weighing on her shoulders.

Perched on the box, she drew herself up, standing ramrod straight. A gentle breeze flapped the standard above her, lifting her hair. No one watching from below could fail to see her and it would only take a reasonable marksman to pick her off, but she had no fear. Luke Collyer had been right, she needed to make a statement to Farrington and she would not do it hiding behind the walls.

Her heart skipped a beat as she saw what lay beyond her walls. Rank upon rank of blue-coated soldiers drawn up in battle order and Sir Richard himself, immediately identifiable by his own banner and the chestnut horse he rode, formed the centre of a small circle of senior officers. The sight of him almost came as a relief. She had hoped that he would not leave such an important mission to his brute of a son.

Sir Richard Farrington would find Kinton Lacey a different foe to the one he had faced in his half- hearted siege of only a month ago. The village buildings previously crowding up to the castle walls had been razed, leaving a couple of hundred yards of bare ground, between the nearest cover and the ditch that surrounded the castle. The ditch itself had been excavated to a depth of ten feet and bristled with staves and the antique weaponry.

Farrington and his officers seemed to be in conversation probably debating how best to deal with this troublesome woman. As she watched, Farrington turned his dancing chestnut towards the castle, his gaze scanning the walls until it rested on her. Across the distance Deliverance stared back at him.

"Is Jack there?" Penitence, on the curtain wall below her sister, tugged at the red skirt.

"Of course he is," Deliverance said with a dash of impatience. "And several of our good neighbours. I can see William Linnet and Samuel Parr."

"It must be somewhat awkward for them," Luke, leaning on the curtain wall beside Deliverance, looking out at the scene, observed. "I am sure they have been guests at your father's board in happier times." "William Linnet and my father were boys together," Deliverance said. "But that, as you would know,

is the perverse nature of Civil War." She shot him a sideways glance, remembering his revelation about his own family.

Sir Richard disengaged from the party and rode to the edge of the village within plain sight of the castle, and well within a musket's range.

"Smith could take him," Sergeant Hale whispered to Luke. Out of the corner of her eye Deliverance saw him nod to his best sharp shooter who began priming his weapon.

"No," Luke said. "This is a carefully arranged dance and that would be quite the wrong move. Let him say his piece."

"Mistress Felton," Farrington hailed her across the distance between them. "I call on you now to lay down your arms and surrender up the castle to me. You have my word that neither you nor any of your garrison will be harmed."

"Is that not the same promise made to the garrison at Byton?" Deliverance replied, her voice ringing out clear and strong in the silence.

"Byton made the grievous error of resisting," Farrington replied.

"I am not resisting, merely defending my home," Deliverance responded. "You have my answer, Sir Richard."

"So be it, Mistress Felton." He doffed his hat to her and turned back to his fellows.

Luke held out his hand and helped Deliverance off the box. She looked up at him, her eyes wide and bright. He tightened his fingers on hers and smiled.

"That was well done, Mistress Felton." "Is that it? What happens now?"

She took a step, and almost tripped on the infernal skirts again.

Penitence was a few fingers taller than her and the skirts of the red gown were far too long.

"No. Farrington will send you a formal letter requesting your surrender," Luke said. "And what do I do in the meantime?"

"You sit quietly and wait," Luke suggested.

Penitence smiled. "We have some sheets to turn into bandages, Deliverance dear. Join me in the parlour."

As Penitence ripped the castle's oldest and most darned linen, Deliverance watched from the window as the garrison went about its last minute preparations.

Ned and Luke stood in the centre of the courtyard, their heads together, in deep conversation. They both looked up at the sudden blast of a trumpet from beyond the walls. Luke, displaying no sense of urgency, took the steps to the curtain wall.

"This is agonising," Deliverance complained. "I need to know what's happening."

Penitence joined her at the window. As they watched, Luke returned to his position in the courtyard, his eyes on the gate. The portcullis raised and a lone figure wearing Sir Richard Farrington's uniform jacket of blue with silver trim, ducked underneath it and walked forward. The men greeted each other with a formal bow and Luke stood to one side gesturing for Farrington's man to enter the residence.

Penitence gave a sharp indrawn breath and her hands flew to her mouth. "Oh, no. It's Jack." Deliverance caught her sister's arm giving her a reassuring squeeze.

"Who did you expect? He sent the least objectionable person, thinking we will capitulate to Jack's charms. Try not to think about him as Jack, but as the enemy who wants to destroy our home and murder our garrison as he did Byton's."

Her sister's lower lip trembled. "Oh, not Jack...he would never..."

"If you can't control yourself you can wait here." At the sight of her sister's stricken face, she continued in a softer tone. "Otherwise I would like to have you by my side."

Melchior appeared at the door. "Sir Richard Farrington's envoy is awaiting you in the Great Hall." Deliverance reached for her sister's hand. "Coming, Pen?"

Penitence took a deep breath. "I am Sir John Felton's daughter, too. I just wish I was as strong as you, Liv."

If only she could see how my stomach is churning, Deliverance thought, pausing at the screen to straighten her skirts.

She swept into the Great Hall, the skirts of the red gown making a satisfactory swish through the rushes on the floor. She had the satisfaction of seeing Jack's eyes widen with surprise as he bent into a low bow. As he straightened, his eyes flicked to Penitence and Deliverance saw the naked misery in his face. What a pair, she thought.

"Good afternoon, Jack," Deliverance said, deliberately using his forename.

"Del...Mistress Felton," Jack said. "It pains me that we must once again meet in these circumstances."

She glanced at the officers of her own garrison, who stood behind Jack. Both Luke and Ned wore expressions of military inscrutability. She was the lady of the castle and she had never felt so completely alone.

"I bring a letter from my father." Jack handed over the stiff parchment, bearing the Farrington seal in a pool of red wax that had been applied with such haste, or anger, that it sputtered across the paper, like drops of blood.

Deliverance broke the seal and read the missive aloud.

"*My dear Mistress Felton, I assure you of the great respect I hold for you and your sister and our long relations with your family make me careful to prevent, if I can, any further inconvenience to you. However my orders are to restore your castle to the good graces of His Majesty the King and you may do well to reconsider your position. Prince Rupert has taken Bristol and is even now before Gloucester, so that you cannot expect any relief from that quarter. If you persist in your obstinacy I cannot promise to pay you the respect due to your position, nor indeed any quarter to those who are with you.*"

She looked up at Jack. "Is your father threatening me with the fate that befell Byton?" she asked, her voice glacial.

Jack shifted uncomfortably, unable to meet her eyes. "Mistress Felton. I had no hand in the fall of Byton. I was with my father in Ludlow."

"Let me remind you, Jack. The garrison surrendered on honourable terms only to find the word of your brother meant nothing. Twenty-eight men murdered in cold blood." She indicated Luke. "Captain Collyer can attest to the atrocity. Your brother should be called to account with his neck for such brutality. I speak the truth, do I not, Captain Collyer?"

"You do, ma'am. The garrison had surrendered on terms. The men were tied together and their throats cut, their bodies flung in the ditch."

The colour drained from Jack's face and he swallowed. "I...I...didn't..." he stuttered.

Deliverance decided to put him out of his misery. Tormenting Jack Farrington brought her no pleasure. She believed him innocent of the atrocities committed at Byton.

"Bring me paper," she said. Melchior stepped forward setting paper, pen and ink on the table.

Deliverance sat and wrote her reply. In the silence, the scratch of her pen seemed to echo around the ancient beams of the hall. When she had finished she looked up and read out what she had written.

"Sir Richard Farrington. Sir, you have my assurance that I am a faithful subject of the King who at his coronation, promised to maintain the laws and liberties of the kingdom. I cannot believe that this same King would give an order to take anything away from his loyal subjects, much less my home. If you are set upon this path then I have no choice but to rightfully defend what is mine."

She looked around the circle of faces, doubt gnawing at her heart. Was she doing the right thing? As if reading her mind, Luke inclined his head, his mouth quirking at the corners into an encouraging smile. As she poured the red wax on to the sheet of paper, she thought of the blood that would be spilled in the next few weeks. She hoped the men would not see how her hand shook as the seal of the Felton's pressed carefully into the wax.

She rose to her feet and handed the paper to Jack who bowed as he took at it. "That is your final answer?" he enquired as he straightened.

She nodded.

He looked down at the paper in his hand. "You have my word, as a friend, Deliverance, that I will do whatever is in my power to see no harm comes to you." His eyes drifted to where Penitence stood behind her. "Or any of your family."

"Thank you, Jack, but I am not convinced your word holds much sway with your father or brother, but I am glad to know someone in the Farrington camp will speak for our case."

As Jack bowed to Deliverance, Penitence stepped forward and Jack turned to her.

"Mistress Felton," he said in a strangled voice and, bowing low took her hand and kissed it. He straightened, gave Penitence one last, lingering look, turned on his heel and with Melchior and Ned as his escort, left the room.

Penitence gave a choking sob and fled, leaving Deliverance alone with Luke. They stood unmoving, looking at each other.

"Will she be all right?" Luke asked.

Deliverance didn't think he referred only to Penitence's current distress. He meant could she be trusted?

She nodded. "My sister is a Felton. She knows what is expected of her."

Luke regarded her for a moment, his head on one side. "The heart is a curious master, Deliverance. It does not always listen to common sense."

"And what do you know of love, Captain Collyer?"

"More than you I warrant, Mistress Felton," he replied.

She snorted. "What you think of as love, most people would call lust."

His eyebrow twitched but he gave no other sign that her barb had gone home, until he spoke.

"You are harsh, Mistress Felton." His voice dripped with ice. "If you want to learn about what it means to love, ask your sister. One day there will be a man who will teach you the difference. Now if you'll excuse me, there is work to be done."

He strode past her, so close she could smell the now so familiar tang of soap and leather.

Deliverance watched him go. She wanted to run after him and tell him she regretted her impetuous words but he wouldn't thank her for demeaning herself. She sank back into the chair and rested her chin in her cupped hands.

Before Luke Collyer had come into her life, no man had affected her the way he did. When he walked into a room, she wanted him beside her. When he looked at her, her guts clenched, and when he smiled at her, she just wanted him to fold her in his arms.

She closed her eyes and prayed. *'Oh, dear lord, make these feelings go away. I want to go back to how I felt before. I don't need this distraction.'* Her eyes, brimming with unshed tears, opened. *'But don't let him be killed, I would die...'*

She laid her head on the table. Love...lust...whatever it was she suffered from, it afflicted her badly and now she had to endure possibly weeks of incarceration with a man who clearly saw her as nothing more than a nuisance.

The clock in the great hall had struck twelve midnight, but Luke still prowled the castle, checking and double checking that everything was in order, making certain the sentries were awake and that no possible chink existed in the castle's defences.

Since Deliverance's message had been sent to Farrington the besiegers had redoubled their preparations. Those within the castle could do nothing except watch as earth bastions were thrown up, wicker palisades erected and the great gun manoeuvred into position beyond the reach of the small cannon mounted in the castle's towers.

By chance, Luke glanced up at the Hawk Tower and caught a fleeting movement as the cloud parted from the moon. He frowned. He had not, to his knowledge set a sentry on that tower.

Drawing his sword he took the stairs lightly, emerging on to the platform of the tower undetected by its sole occupant. Deliverance, dressed in her normal drab gown, stood leaning against the wall looking out at the flickering campfires below her.

He sheathed his sword and at the hiss of the weapon, she jumped, looking around. "Luke! You gave me a fright. I thought you abed."

"The same could be said of you, lady."

He joined her at the wall, leaning on the old, grey stone ramparts. A cold wind rose from the river, lifting Deliverance's hair and whipping it against her face. She pushed the strands back, trying unsuccessfully to tuck them behind her ear, while not shifting her gaze from the enemy encampment.

"How many men do they have out there?"

"Ned and I estimate that they have about four hundred foot and at least fifty horses."

"And that awful gun!" Her fingers twisted the chain of a gold locket she wore around her neck. She looked up at him, her brow furrowed in anguish. "Luke, have I done the right thing?"

Luke considered the question and probably mistaking his silence for reproach she continued. "I have prayed and hoped that God would give me some indication that I have chosen the right course."

"If," Luke spoke slowly, thinking through every word, "it had been me, I would have made exactly the same decision."

"But there are innocent souls within this castle. What if the same fate befalls them as did the defenders at Byton?"

"Sir Richard Farrington has more sense than to allow that to happen again. Or at least I hope he does. What his son did runs contrary to every rule of war. Your father is not like that fool at Byton and the repercussions should any harm befall either you or your sister would not be worth the effort. Byton was meant merely as a warning, to scare us into early submission."

Even as he spoke, he hoped he was telling the truth. This was war, there could be no certainty.

"I never thought it could be this hard," Deliverance's voice shook as if she struggled to control her emotions. "When Farrington came the first time, it seemed easy. I'd read the books, I knew what to do but Byton changed it all. Now I don't feel very brave."

Without conscious thought, he reached out and pushed one of the dark, wayward strands back behind her ear, allowing his hand to fall to her shoulder.

She looked up at him, her eyes wide and dark in her shadowed face.

"You are the bravest woman, I have ever met," he said. "I am afraid you are going to need every ounce of that courage in the next few weeks."

"Weeks?" Her voice shook.

He shrugged. "Maybe months. If relief can't reach us from Gloucester."

She turned her face away, the shoulder beneath his hand tensing with suppressed emotion. She had accused him of mistaking lust for love, but she had been wrong. He knew the difference.

Lust was Betty Jones in the dairy, an object of physical desire he had steadfastly resisted since his arrival. Love was reserved for someone deserving and there had been other girls with whom he had known love but the spark that had lit when he met Deliverance Felton went beyond all previous experience. The unknown emotions terrified him far more than Farrington.

He gently squeezed the slender bone beneath his hand, resisting the urge to run his hand around the back of her neck and pull her against him. Desire stirred, quickening his breath. It would be so easy to hold her tight, kiss the dark hair and tell her it would be all right.

He moved closer to her, smelling the soft, sweet smell of lavender that wafted from her clothes as she turned beneath his hand to look at him. Her lips parted and her large eyes glittered in the pale light of the waxing moon.

"Luke," she whispered.

The breath caught in his throat and he dropped his hand, taking a step back. *Dear God, she felt the same way!*

A vision of impending disaster flashed into his mind. Within the close confines of the castle with over a hundred people watching their every move, they needed to maintain the distance. Whatever might be developing between them, they could not afford to step over that invisible line that separated Sir John Felton's daughter from her captain of the guard.

"It's late," he said, a noticeable crack in his voice. "Go and get some rest while you can, Deliverance. I fear tomorrow may be a difficult day."

She straightened, her chin coming up in that small gesture of defiance he had come to know so well. "You're right. Nothing is served by standing here in the cold worrying. Good night, Captain Collyer."

Without a backward glance she turned for the stairs, leaving him alone. The cold wind whipped the Felton standard above his head. He glanced up at it, and then out at the twinkling lights of the watch fires.

No, he didn't need the distraction of entertaining feelings for Deliverance Felton. He leaned against the wall to give time for his ardour to cool, and smiled at the irony of his situation. Of all the women he had ever met, why this small, determined virago should have wakened a hitherto unknown emotion in him, he had no idea.

God really did move in mysterious ways.

Chapter Ten

A massive explosion followed by a jolting crash of stone, rocked the residence. Deliverance sat bolt upright in bed, her heart hammering as the drum within the castle grounds beat 'Stand To'.

Beside her Penitence sat up and Meg, who like Lovedie, slept on a pallet in the bed chamber, began to scream. "We'll be murdered in our beds."

"Don't be a fool, Meg." Deliverance swung her feet out of bed. "That is just the Thunderer roaring her disapproval and I am afraid this is how it is going to be. Find my clothes."

Resisting the temptation to don her breeches, Deliverance fretted while Meg dressed her. She looked around for the musket and remembered Luke had confiscated it on the first day.

"That man," she muttered as she raced down the stairs and out into the courtyard.

In the grey light of the early morning she could see that the garrison already lined the east wall at the action position. Behind them, Luke stood in conversation with Ned Barrett and Sergeant Hale. As another explosion rocked the castle, she saw him instinctively duck, one hand going to the hat on his head. As the massive cannon ball crashed into the Hawk Tower, spraying the courtyard with bits of stone, he straightened.

Deliverance raced across the courtyard.

"Don't just stand there," she screamed. "Do something!"

He looked at her. "What, exactly, do you think I should be doing? Calm yourself, Mistress Felton. They are just softening us up but please go inside and ready yourself for casualties. I expect a full scale assault shortly."

Deliverance snorted with exasperation, and turned for the curtain wall. Even as she reached the stairs, from beyond the walls came the crackle of musket fire and bellowed orders reached her. Above her Sergeant Hale shouted the order to fire and the Kinton Lacey muskets flared, the smoke bathing the soldiers in a ghostly light.

She started up the stairs, only to be dragged back by Luke's hand on her arm. "Where do you think you're going?"

"I need to see what is happening."

"I don't want you getting shot. We have everything under control, Deliverance Felton. Go back to the house."

She shook his hand free, and bolted up the stairs to her familiar vantage point. Even as she peered over the wall, a musket ball hit the stonework just inches from her. She sank down with her back against the wall.

A shadow loomed up behind her. "I told you to leave the battlements, Deliverance. Do I have to carry you down myself?"

She glared at Luke. "You cannot tell me what to do and I would appreciate the return of my musket. I am as good a shot as any man on this wall. I took my turn on the last occasion."

Luke's eyes narrowed. "Were you standing there the night we relieved the siege?"

A musket ball sang over his head and he ducked, crouching down to bring himself down to her level. Deliverance glanced away. There could be no denying it. "Yes, what of it?" she said with a careless shrug of her shoulder.

Luke's eyes widened for a moment. "You are responsible for this?"

He whipped his hat from his head and put his finger through a hole in the crown.

Deliverance swallowed. "How was I to know who you were?" Luke stared at her "You could have killed me!"

"I did point out her error, sir." Melchior had come up behind Luke during the exchange, making her mortification complete. *Et tu*, Melchior, she thought.

To her surprise Luke began to laugh.

"God save me." He stood up and replaced the hat on his head. He threw his hands in the air. "I give up. Stay if you must, Mistress Felton. If you can knock the hat from my head at that distance then you are as

good a shot as any man here but we don't have time to go looking for your weapon. Just stay down and out of the way."

He turned away from her and glanced over the battlements. He turned to Melchior. "Blakelocke, bring fire to bear on that party of men. They are carrying petards."

"What's a petard?" Deliverance asked, cautiously rising to her feet again.

"If you'd read your books, you would know it is a metal object shaped a bit like a hat, that is full of powder. Our friends would like to nail it to the gate. They will then light the fuse and duck as the gate is blown in. Here they come in force." He raised his voice so it could be heard along the length of the wall. "Fire at will!"

The attacking force carried long, sturdy ladders that spanned the ditch with its vicious stakes. The sheer press of men overwhelmed the musket fire of the defenders and Deliverance heard the cries of her men go up as two of the ladders swung up against the walls. They were quickly pushed away, accompanied by the screams of those foolish enough to already have put their feet on the rungs.

Deliverance sank down on her haunches again. This was nothing like the pathetic attempt Farrington had made only a few short weeks ago. That had been a tame affair where Farrington had simply sat his troops down just out of range. A few musket shots had been exchanged but no one had been hurt and nothing had been damaged...except Luke's hat.

She put her hands over her head as the Thunderer roared again, the ball flying high and crashing down through the roof of the residence. A few of Farrington's men had gained the curtain wall, swinging their legs across the ramparts as the Kinton Lacey men, their weapons to slow too load, swung their muskets like clubs.

She looked around for Luke. He had his sword drawn, engaged with a soldier wearing Farrington's blue and she realised with a jolt that Luke Collyer was all that stood between her and the melee on the curtain wall.

He had been right. Far from being a help, her presence presented a very real danger to him and to every one of the defenders. She swallowed and looked around for a way to remove herself but her only exit was blocked by Luke. She had no choice but to stay put, frozen with fear and weaponless. She crouched down low, while the battle raged across the wall.

If she just had a sword or a pistol...but even as those thoughts crossed her mind, she became aware that the Kinton Lacey garrison seemed to have prevailed. The men in the blue coats were going back down the ladders, their screams filling the air as the garrison pushed the ladders away from the wall.

Hardly daring to breathe, she rose slowly to her feet, her legs trembling beneath her, and peered over the wall. Below her wounded men were clambering from the ditch, helping their injured comrades. Several blue-clad bodies lay motionless, others impaled on the ancient pikes still twitched. The heavy cloying smell of blood mingled with gunpowder hung in the air. Her breakfast rose in her throat, and she crouched down against the wall fighting back the nausea.

Along the length of the wall, the defenders peered over the stonework. No one fired at the retreating soldiers and a ragged cheer went up from the wall as Farrington's men regained the shelter of their own defences. She twisted to look down at the gate. The man carrying the petard, along with his escort, lay among the fallen lacking only a few yards to the bridge.

"Are you all right?"

Deliverance turned to see Luke Collyer, leaning with his back to the wall, panting with the exertion, his sword still held in his hand. He had lost his hat and his dark hair clung damply to his forehead.

She nodded and he looked away.

"See to the casualties," he shouted to Hale.

"Aye, sir."

Deliverance straightened. "Take any of the injured to the Great Hall and my sister and I will see to them."

This at least was something useful she could contribute to the day. "Ma'am." Hale saluted her.

Luke bent, his hands on his knees, as he regained his breath. He looked across at Deliverance. "Well?" He arched his eyebrow at her. "Still want to be a soldier, Mistress Felton?"

"If you hadn't taken my musket..." she began and then gave him a wry smile."The reality of war is very different from the books," she conceded. "Now I will go and see to the wounded."

She found the residence in uproar. The household staff were gathered at the foot of the stairs, several of the maids were crying, others white-faced with shock and fear. Penitence's eyes were also red from crying and on seeing Deliverance, she seized her sister's arm, pointing up the stairs.

"Liv, it came through the roof. The upper parlour is destroyed." She began to shake and Deliverance put an arm around her sister's shoulders. "This is just the start, Pen," she said. "If I'd been in the parlour..."

"Ssh," Deliverance whispered, stroking her sister's hair. "We must be brave for everyone. Hale is bringing the wounded into the great hall. Let's go and make ready and you" she pointed at the weeping maids at the foot of the stairs, "stop that mewling and go and clean up the mess."

"Is anyone hurt?"

The women turned to see Luke standing at the door, hatless and breathing hard. Deliverance released her sister and faced him.

"No. The upper parlour took the brunt of it, but mercifully no one was in the room."

"There is a massive hole in the ceiling. The ball came through the attics and the room above the parlour as well," Penitence said, her tears forgotten.

Luke nodded. "I'll go and have a look. I need to be sure that it hasn't affected the structure too badly, otherwise we will all be sleeping in the stables."

Penitence shook her head. "It just seems to be a very large hole. My ancestors built solid stone floors."

As he mounted the stairs, he turned. "I have four wounded men who need tending. Nothing too serious. Can I leave them in your tender care, ladies?"

"Was anyone killed?" Deliverance asked, not wanting to know the answer as she thought of the men of Kinton Lacey and Luke's men whom she had come to know so well over the previous weeks.

He shook his head. "No, we were lucky."

Penitence nodded. "Have them brought into the Hall. I will see that we have everything in order."

Luke thanked her and started up the stairs. Halfway up, Deliverance caught up with him. She laid a hand on his arm to detain him.

"I owe you an apology, Captain Collyer," she said in a low voice, her eyes darting to the hall below, fearful someone might overhear her. "You were right, it was no place for me."

He looked down at the hand on his arm and she hastily removed it.

"I have no doubt, Deliverance, that had you been armed, you would have held your own, but it is in my own interest that you are not hurt." He ran a hand through his hair. "God knows I've already got you shot once, your father would have me hanged from the nearest tree if anything worse happened to you. Let me be quite clear about this because I will brook no more opposition from you. I am in command of this garrison and while I hold that position my word is law." She opened her mouth but before she could protest, he held up a warning finger. "You have your role in this matter and I have mine. As long as we are fed and our hurts tended then that is one thing I do not have to concern myself with. Do we understand each other?"

Deliverance nodded.

His stance relaxed. "There I have said my piece. Now the fighting is done, my men...and yours...would be greatly cheered by a few words from you."

"Would they?"

"They are waiting outside."

Deliverance nodded and leaving him standing on the stairs walked outside. Below her in the castle courtyard those men not keeping watch on the wall, had gathered to clean their weapons and count the cost of the attack.

Sergeant Hale saw her and straightened. "Silence for the mistress," he bellowed. As one they turned grimy, strained faces towards her.

She cleared her throat.

"Thank you," she said in a clear, strong voice. "Thank you from the bottom of my heart for the work you have done this morning." She looked back at the house. "This is just the start but if we hold true to the belief in the rightness of our cause, we will prevail. Sergeant Hale, I think we should give thanks—"

"Aye, for our Deliverance" A voice called from the ranks, provoking general laughter. "To our Deliverance!" Another voice called and the men cheered.

"Our Deliverance," echoed a low voice behind her.

Deliverance turned and smiled at Luke Collyer.

Chapter Eleven

After the first abortive attack, Farrington retired his troops to a safe distance and resumed digging in. Like giant moles, great mounds of earth began to appear just out of musket range. Luke fired a few cannonade shots at the new trenches which provoked some return of fire from Farrington's smaller guns. The Thunderer brooded in her own trench behind a sturdy wicket palisade.

The fourth day of the siege dawned as a glorious late summer day, where the world beyond the affairs of Kinton Lacey Castle, glowed with sunshine. When Luke did not appear for the midday meal, Deliverance wrapped bread and cheese in a cloth. She packed the meal together with a small flask of wine, a beaker and a couple of apples, into a basket, and went in search of him.

The soldiers pointed to the Hawk Tower where Luke had placed one of his small cannons. She sighed. He would choose the tallest tower with the steepest and narrowest stairs. Gathering her skirts in one hand, and balancing the awkward basket in the other, she made the arduous climb, emerging into bright sunshine on the rooftop.

She blinked for a moment, not so much at the sudden glare of sunshine but at the sight of Luke, stripped to the waist, his body glistening with perspiration from the exertion of cleaning the gun.

He hadn't heard her approach and it allowed her a moment to stop and admire the hard, muscled planes of his chest, peppered with dark hair. Her heart beat a little faster and her breath came in shallow gasps. She tightened her fingers on the basket as she wondered what it would be like to touch him, slide her hands across the taut, golden skin...

She swallowed and stepped back into the doorway, where she stopped to catch her breath and wonder at these wayward thoughts. He had made their relative positions perfectly clear the last time... that night when she had almost kissed him. Dear Lord, she was turning into some sort of hoyden. This would never do.

I am Deliverance Felton. He is a common soldier. We have four hundred angry men sitting outside our door. This is not the time or the place.

Repeating this to herself, she retraced her steps part of the way down the stairs. She took a deep breath and humming a familiar soldier's song, she re-emerged. This time he had heard her and was engaged in the act of hurriedly resuming his shirt as she stepped through the doorway. He didn't bother tying the neck or wrist laces, or tucking it in.

"Deliverance. What brings you up here?"

"I've brought some food. You didn't come down for dinner." She set down the basket on the firing step beside the rampart and sat down. "Isn't that a task for your gunners?"

He looked at the gun. "I like to do it myself occasionally. Guns are sensitive beasts and liable to misfire or worse. I don't need to injure my own men."

He plunged his hands into a bucket of water and wiped them on a cloth. Deliverance spread the cloth and laid out the simple repast.

"You're not eating?" he asked.

She shook her head. "I ate with the others."

His eyes crinkled at the corners as he took a bite of the slab of bread. "Sorry, I forgot the time. Thank you for thinking of me," he mumbled with his mouth full of bread.

She shrugged and leaned back on her elbows looking up at the sky. "On a day like today, it's almost possible to believe this is all a dream."

"Except that four hundred men on the other side of the wall are hardly quiet," Luke observed. "True." Deliverance listened to the sound of men shouting, spades in dirt and the general hum of humanity both within and beyond the castle walls. Someone in the royalist camp was singing. He had a fine baritone and the words carried up to the top of the tower.

'When cannons are roaring,
And bullets are flying,
He that would honour win, Must not fear dying...' Deliverance shivered.

"That's an old song," Luke said. "I heard it sung in Germany." He started to sing, in a good tenor.

'Sentinels on the walls,
Arm, arm a-crying. Petards against the ports, Wild fire a-flying...'

He trailed off and took a bite from one of the apples.

"You have a good voice," Deliverance said. She cocked her head and looked at him. "Luke, if your family supports the King, what is your reason for fighting for Parliament's cause?"

"I probably did it just to annoy my father," he said.

Deliverance studied him, seeing the fleeting expression of regret that flashed into his eyes. "No," she said. "You did it because you believed in a cause."

He didn't answer for a moment, munching thoughtfully on the apple. "Not much escapes your eagle eye does it, Mistress Felton? I returned to England in early '42 to a country ruled over by a King who would not listen to the voice of the people. A silly, stubborn little man. I could not in all conscience give him my sword."

"Why did you leave England in the first place?"

He leaned over and tapped her on the nose. "Too many questions,

Deliverance. My personal business is none of yours." When she continued to fix him with her gaze, he sighed. "If you must know, my father banished me."

"Why?"

His mouth twitched. "It began as a stupid argument with my brother over a woman, nothing more." Deliverance's stomach lurched. *A woman, of course.* It had to be a woman. She looked up at him and her heart started to race again.

"Is there still...a woman?" she asked in a small tight voice.

He shook his head and smiled. "No."

Her heart beat a little faster. *Please kiss me.*

As if he had heard her silent plea, he set his apple down and reaching up, he stroked her cheek, his touch searing her skin like a brand.

"I don't think any woman I have ever met is your equal," he said, his tone soft and uncertain and quite unlike the Luke Collyer she thought she knew.

With shaking fingers she responded, brushing his face, feeling the rough stubble of his cheek, his skin warm to her touch. Her fingers moved to his lips and in a swift movement he caught her wrist. For a moment she thought he would cast it down but he held her fingers against his mouth, gently kissing the tip of each in turn.

He released her hand and Deliverance slid her hand behind his neck, meshing his thick, dark hair as she drew his face down towards hers. Their lips met with a sudden bruising intensity, caused by her eagerness and inexperience. He pulled back a little, his eyes widening before he took her in his arms and pressed his lips to hers, gentle but firm, and infinitely more experienced.

Deliverance went limp, her lips parting beneath his. A burning longing ignited deep in her being for this man to hold her like this forever. Her breasts began to tingle as if they strained against her bodice, willing him to touch them.

His long, hard, body pressed against her and the realisation that he desired to possess her both terrified and exhilarated her. Despite her genteel upbringing, she was not entirely ignorant of what could follow. There had been a particularly embarrassing incident when she had walked in to the stable and tripped over one of the stable boys and a girl from the dairy. She had thought it quite amusing--her father had other ideas.

Was this what that girl had felt for the stable boy? Was this what it felt like to want a man so badly that all caution and sense blew to the wind?

Here they were on the top of a tall tower with hundreds of people within yards of them and yet it was as if they were the only two people in the whole world. They could be discovered any minute and that heady thought made this unplanned tryst even more exciting.

"Captain Collyer? Are you there?" A voice came from deep within the stairwell.

Luke jumped to his feet, with the speed and grace of a cat, hastily tucking his shirt into his breeches. Deliverance sat up, read-justed her clothing and began making a show of packing away the remnants of Luke's lunch, as she fought to return her breathing to normal.

The soldier who came out on to the tower didn't seem to notice anything amiss.

"I've given the gun a good clean, Smith," Luke said and Deliver-ance cast him a quick glance, hearing the check in his voice. He coughed. "Thank you for the food, Mistress Felton. Now if you'll excuse us, I need to discuss the disposition of the gun with Smith, here."

Deliverance rose to her feet, hoping the flush in her cheeks did not betray her. She waited till the rest of the gun crew had come huffing up the stairs and clutching her basket to her chest, she stepped into the cool, dark of the stairwell.

She leaned against the wall while her eyes adjusted to the gloom and wondered if her breathing would ever return to normal. With trembling fingers she touched her lips that burned and tingled from the intensity of their desire for each other.

Glancing back at the tower she could see Luke, the soldier, deep in conversation with his gunners.

Luke the soldier...Luke...the lover?

Her knees threatened to buckle under the weight of the emotions that flowed through her, and she put her hand out to the wall to steady herself. She had never thought much about love, let alone the physical expression of love between a man and a woman. Beyond what she had seen in the stable, her notions of what it entailed were vague at the very best and the thought of this man teaching her, made her head spin.

She reached the ground and stepped out into the bustling courtyard, instinctively ducking as a musket ball spun unheeded past her shoulder. The danger of her position, the threat to the castle...all of these matters receded into insignificance.

Is this love? she thought. Or am I just indulging in some foolish fantasy brought on by the situation I find myself in?

She had no answer to her own question and, taking a steadying breath, she crossed back to the residence, determined to find something to keep herself busy that afternoon—until the next time she and Luke were alone together.

As Luke gained the dark recess of the stairwell, he took a deep breath. He had no idea how he had managed to conduct a lucid conversation with the gunners when his body and mind was absorbed with Deliverance Felton. The betraying ache in his groin had not subsided, and he sat down on one of the narrow window ledges that lined the stairwell. Even on such a bright day, the light barely penetrated the narrow embrasure.

He groaned aloud and leaned his head on his hands. What had he been thinking? Deliverance Felton? If it was just about sex, why couldn't he just slake his lust with any of the other women still within the castle confines?

He took a deep breath and looked up. He didn't want any of the other women. He wanted Deliverance. He remembered the taste of her mouth, her impatience and her response to his touch and smiled, shaking his head in disbelief at his own foolishness. A virgin. Oh dear Lord, of course she had to be a virgin. Her inexperienced touch and her eagerness had betrayed her innocence. He touched his lip where her teeth had accidentally cut him and shook his head.

Why not Deliverance Felton? He thought. He had never contemplated a permanent liaison with any woman, why should Deliverance be any different? And yet she was different, she was his equal in everything—his soul mate?

He rose to his feet, straightening his jacket and tying the strings on his shirt collar. He was her equal in status. Even if she only thought of him as a soldier of fortune, he would have to confide in her at some point. Her father could not possibly disapprove if he knew that Luke was Lord Harcourt's son.

As he took the stairs down the tower he considered the mechanics of conducting a relationship in such a crowded castle. They would have to be careful. He would have to be careful. The garrison must not know that they had formed an attachment but it could be done. It would be done. They could both be dead tomorrow. Why not? Today was for the living.

"You're mad," he said aloud and stepped out of the tower stairwell into the bustling courtyard.

Chapter Twelve

"H ave you and Captain Collyer argued again?" Penitence enquired.

Deliverance nearly dropped the bowl she was holding, feeling the colour rise to her cheeks. "Why would you say that?"

"You seem to be avoiding each other. I can't help but notice when he comes into a room, you leave and I haven't seen you talking to each other for days now."

Deliverance made pretence of carefully measuring out the beans for the days ration. What Penitence had not seen were the careless meetings in dark corridors, when Luke would seize her by the waist, pressing her back into the wall as he kissed her. Neither had Penitence noticed the way their feet touched at the dining table or their hands brushed as they passed each other. The thrill of these illicit encounters made her forget, just for those few fleeting moments, the danger to the castle.

"No," she said. "We haven't argued. We just have our own tasks. He's busy and I'm busy."

"That's a relief," Penitence said. "You were getting on so well."

Deliverance opened her mouth. Her heart burst with the frustration of keeping the relationship clandestine. She yearned to confide in her sister, as Penitence had confided every nuance of her growing relationship with Jack. At the time Deliverance had found the lovelorn longings of her sister quite nauseating. Now she understood.

The women flinched as a loud explosion followed by a juddering bang in another part of the castle rocked the foundations of the residence..

"Lovedie." Deliverance summoned the maid. "Take over. I'll go and see the damage." She found Luke in the centre of the courtyard looking at the west wall.

"I'm not sure the wall is going to stand much more of this," he said as she drew level with him. "They've found the sweet spot and they'll just keep hammering at it until it gives way. They just have to bring Hawk Tower down and we will be in trouble."

Deliverance looked up at him. "Is there nothing we can do?"

"I'll have to think about it, but nothing occurs to me at the moment." He looked down at her, his grey eyes smouldering. The breath left her body and a warm surge of desire rushed through her. They were discussing possible annihilation and all she could think about was the touch of his hands.

"Perhaps if you could spare some time, Mistress Felton, we should inspect our powder supplies," he said in a husky tone only matched by the glint in the depth of his smoky eyes.

"I think I can spare some time, Captain Collyer," she responded, hoping no one overhearing them would detect the answering quiver in her voice.

Luke unlocked the door of the chapel and stood aside to let her in. The building smelled of must and gunpowder. The barrels stood neatly stacked against the walls. After the hustle of the world outside and the cramped conditions of the residence, the cool quiet chapel came as a relief. You could, Deliverance thought, almost believe it was still a holy place, not the most dangerous place in the whole castle.

"I think the last time this was used, was for my parents wedding," she said aloud. "My mother will be turning in her grave to see it so desecrated."

Luke shrugged. "Needs must. Now shall we start at this end?"

He began counting the barrels. Deliverance blinked. Had she misunderstood him? Did he really intend to check on the powder supplies?

She fought back disappointment. "Will it be enough?"

Luke shrugged. "If the siege ends tomorrow, then yes it will be enough. If the siege lasts until Christmas then we will have surrendered long before then." He gave a hollow laugh. "Although we will probably have run out of food first and be reduced to eating rats and cats."

Deliverance looked up at him. The light from the windows, once filled with coloured glass but now, mostly broken and boarded over, cast the lines of strain on his face into sharp relief. Hesitantly she reached up and touched his face, seeing for the first time, the dark shadows under his eyes. He leaned against her hand, his own hand rising to grasp her fingers, placing them against his lips.

In the gloom, his face caught the light from a sliver of the painted glass window, showering it with coloured flecks as he drew her toward him, his other hand slipping around her waist.

"I thought this might be one place we could be alone and undisturbed for a little." His voice held an unfamiliar husky tone.

She laughed, suddenly nervous. This moment had occupied her thoughts for days and all she could say was, "A strange place for a lover's tryst, Captain Collyer."

"I'm sure there may have been stranger but none I can think of." He tilted her face up to look at him. "You have a smudge of dirt on your cheek, Deliverance. No, don't rub it off, it looks rather endearing."

"This pretence is killing me," she murmured leaning her head against his chest as he gathered her into his arms.

Even beneath the thickness of his wool jacket, his heart beat steadily against her cheek, and she wound her arms around his neck, pulling his face down so their foreheads and their noses touched. She closed her eyes, feeling Luke's lips on hers. His arms tightened around her and they sank to the dusty floor, locked together.

Deliverance shut her eyes, surrendering to her other senses. The cold, hard flagstones beneath her, the warm smell of man, the rasp of his stubbled cheek against her, the sweet salty taste of his mouth on her lips and the sound of their own desire, mingled in the strange silence of a room filled with gunpowder.

She meshed her fingers in his hair, gasping as his hand cupped her breast. Even through her bodice, her nipples responded, aching for his touch. She began tugging at the laces of her bodice, loosening them enough to allow his questing fingers to find the sensitive nubs. She thought she would scream as a shudder of longing ran through her body. She wanted him to touch her there...and there...

She arched her back, her hips grinding into his. "Luke," she cried out, remembering at the last minute to lower her voice.

Luke paused and his body stiffened. Deliverance moaned with frustration. He laid a finger against her mouth and she opened her eyes.

His concentration seemed to have moved from her. He poised above her, like a dog that had picked up another, more interesting scent.

"Ssh," he said. "Can you hear something?"

'Only the beating of my heart', she longed to say. He released her, rolling off her to lie on his stomach on the floor beside her, his head turned to look at her and his ear pressed to the stonework.

"Listen."

Reluctantly she rolled over and copied his actions. Her eyes widened as she heard the unmistakable sound of metal striking rock.

"What...?" she began.

"They're mining," he interrupted. "The bastards are mining."

Deliverance sat up, hastily retying her bodice laces and trying to restore some order to her hair as Luke continued to listen to the sound rising through the rock that lay beneath the castle's own foundations. "What do you mean?" she asked.

In one movement he was on his feet, brushing the dust from his clothes. He put out a hand and pulled her to her feet, rearranging her collar and brushing dead leaves from her hair. His hands rested on her shoulders and he looked into her eyes.

"It means they are digging a tunnel beneath the chapel, Deliverance. They must know the powder is being stored here. What they will do is lay explosives in the tunnel and set them off. That will in turn cause a

massive explosion within the castle. We will be lucky to survive. I need to alert the others."

Deliverance thrust her tangled hair behind her ears, lingering long enough to allow her heartbeat to return to normal, before following him out into the courtyard where he had already gathered Ned and Sergeant Hale. They all returned to the chapel and stood in the middle of the floor looking down at the flagstones.

Ned shook his head. "I don't understand how we've not detected them?" He paused, frowning with concentration. "How on earth did you hear them?"

Luke hesitated for a fraction of a moment before replying, "I bent to retrieve that... he pointed to an empty barrel that had conveniently rolled off the pile. How could they have got so far without our knowledge?"

Deliverance cleared her throat. "I think I know." The three men looked up at her.

"There is a crypt under the altar and an old tunnel runs from it down to the riverbank,"

Luke's eyes flashed. "And you never thought to mention it?" Deliverance bridled. "The tunnel caved in years ago."

Where does the tunnel come out, Mistress Felton?" "On the path to the sally port," Deliverance said. "Farrington would know about this tunnel?"

She nodded and he gave her a reproachful glance. They had discussed the security of that path and she had assured him it posed no risk. She had forgotten the long lost tunnel under the chapel.

Stupid, stupid.

She thought about her answer before saying slowly, "Farringtons have been coming to Kinton Lacey for years. Sir Richard himself as a boy, and then his sons. Jack was a friend of my brother's. They spent hours playing in the hidden corners of the castle." She swallowed.

Luke looked around the group.

"Then we can assume they've managed to clear the tunnel. We've not been keeping a vigilant watch on that wall so it would have been easy to slip in under cover of darkness. They're probably camping in the

tunnel and working in the day when we're too busy to notice the noise. Mistress Felton, show me the entrance to this crypt."

A large stone altar still stood in the sanctuary of the chapel. Deliverance led the way behind it and pointed to a flagstone with a heavy ring sunk into it. With a nod from Luke, Hale lifted the stone aside and they stared down into a dark hole.

"We can't use a light, not with all this powder," Luke fumed. "I'll just have to trust to the other senses."

Narrow stone steps led down into the crypt and Luke took these with a degree of caution, his head disappearing from view. It seemed an age before he reappeared, his hair covered in cobwebs.

As he dusted himself off, he looked around the little group. "I found the entrance to the tunnel. There's a rock fall just about ten feet in and my guess is they're just behind it. I could hear them quite clearly. That puts them dead centre of the chapel, about where you're standing, Ned. All they need to do is lay their charges and..." he left the last thought unspoken.

"Are they still down there?" Ned asked.

Luke nodded. "Of course they are not to know that all they have to do is stop now and lay the charges. The fact they are still digging would suggest that they are trying to clear the whole tunnel and by my reckoning they will be through to our side of the tunnel in a couple of hours. Hale, find me six men. We will have a welcoming party for our visitors."

Chapter Thirteen

With the element of surprise on their side, it had not taken much to foil Farrington's plan to blow up the chapel, and at dinner they celebrated their triumph over Farrington's miners with the last of Sir John's French wine.

Luke studied Deliverance's face, as she listened to Ned's account of the victory, soft and gold in the candlelight. He liked the way her nose wrinkled when she found something amusing and he found himself remembering the feel of her pliant body beneath his hands as they had lain together on the dusty floor of the chapel. Another part of his anatomy responded to that memory, and he took a hefty gulp of wine and turned his attention to Ned and his now much repeated account of the day's victory.

"And we took them completely by surprise," Ned continued. "Killed two of them before the others beat a hasty retreat."

"Will they be back?" Penitence asked.

"We've blown the far end of the tunnel. They'll not be back," Luke said. "And the best part is we have another half dozen barrels of powder to add to our stores." He pushed back his chair. "Excuse me, please. I have a report on today's action to write."

Luke sat in Sir John Felton's chair, playing with the feathers of the pen as he looked down at the half-written report. He wondered why he bothered with these daily reports, except as an exercise to prove to Sir John that he took his responsibilities seriously. All of them... except the prohibition about his daughters.

Luke snapped the pen. He had seen Sir John Felton hang a man for stealing a loaf of bread.

He looked up at a knock on the door. Lovedie Brown entered carrying a flask and a cup. She shut the door behind her and walked over to the desk.

"I thought you might be thirsty," she said, setting the cup and flask down on the table in front of him.

"Thank you, Lovedie."

Luke lifted the jug but Lovedie reached out and took the jug from him. "Let me, Captain Collyer."

The wine splashed into the cup, blood-red in the candlelight. Lovedie walked around to his side of the table and set the cup down on the report Luke had been writing. As she did so she leaned forward offering a provocative view of the swell of her breasts. Luke swallowed, and the hair on the back of his neck prickled.

Lovedie moved behind him, resting her hands on his shoulders. She began to knead the taut muscles of his neck and shoulders.

Far from a relaxing experience, Luke's muscles tightened, as her hands slipped inside his shirt. "What are you doing?" He managed to croak as the questing fingers moved down his body.

"I've seen how hard you work, Captain Collyer," she whispered in his ear. "I thought you might like a little fun."

Despite himself, his own body responded to her touch.

"Lovedie..." he began, embarrassed to hear his voice crack with lust. "This isn't going to happen..."

Her full lips parted and her hand slid lower, seeking his groin. "Are you sure? Because that's not what you're telling me." Expert fingers stroked his erection through the cloth of his breeches.

The other hand continued to caress the back of his neck. He knew he should resist, but he had no power to move of his own volition. It was as if he had become a puppet in her hands and what hands...he groaned as she tugged at his belt, unbuckling it, and sliding her hand inside.

She straddled his lap and cradled his face in her hands, her luscious lips parting as she bent toward him.

With a supreme effort, Luke pushed her away and jumped to his feet. She fell to the ground with a thump and sat in the circle of her skirts, looking up at him, anger flashing from her eyes.

"Don't you want me?"

He swallowed, ignoring the ache in his groin. "Yes...no...I...I made a vow," he said "Of chastity until the end of this siege."

Lovedie rose to her feet, smoothing down her skirts. She gave him a scornful look, her lip curling in derision. "You? Chastity? A man like you needs to forget his cares." She paused, tilting her head to one side. "It's Mistress Deliverance, isn't it? I've seen how she looks at you. Why would you want her when I can show you pleasures you've never dreamed of?"

He had no doubt she could, and at that thought, he took a deep breath.

"Lovedie, it is a kind thought, but I've no need of what you have to offer and I would thank you not to speak of Mistress Felton in that way. You owe her your life."

The girl sniffed, tossing the thick, red locks as she stalked toward the door. As she put her hand on the latch and she turned, looking at him from beneath lowered eyelashes, she said. "I'd not meant to offend, but if you change your mind, Captain Collyer..."

"I won't. Thank you, Lovedie."

As the door shut behind her he came out from behind Sir John's chair and looked down at his report. The cup of wine had spilled in the altercation and spread across the paper and the table. He cursed, and walked out of the room, slamming the door behind him.

As he stepped out on to the curtain wall, he turned his face up to the dark night and let the rain cleanse him of the disgust at his own reaction to Lovedie's advances. He could have so easily succumbed to what she had to offer. The base man in him whispered: *Are you mad? A beautiful, experienced woman, throwing herself at you? Why didn't you take what she had to offer? Deliverance would never know.* The lover in him answered, *You knew it wasn't right. You did the right thing.*

He couldn't face Deliverance or anyone for that matter so he climbed the stairs to the top of Hawk Tower and leaned on the battlements looking out across the enemy encampment. He let the rain soak through his jacket and shirt, rapidly cooling what was left of his ardour.

"What in God's name are you doing up here?" Ned's voice came from behind him. Luke turned his head, rats' tails of sodden hair whipping his eyes.

"Escaping," he said.

Ned wisely remained in the shelter of the doorway. "Deliverance been giving you trouble?" Ned asked.

Luke shook his head. "No, not Deliverance." He straightened. "Escaping from myself, Ned."

He crossed to join his friend in the doorway. Ned turned to go down but turned back as Luke sank on to the top step with his head in his hands. He had to talk; guilt was consuming him, distracting him from the task at hand. He needed Ned's counsel, even if he already knew the answer.

"I'm a fool, Ned."

"I've known that for years," Ned responded.

"No, you don't understand," Luke said. "I've broken my own cardinal rule. "What do you mean?"

"I've let myself fall in love."

"What?" Ned sounded incredulous. "You? In love? Not that dairymaid?"

Luke looked up and fixed his friend with a cold glare. "Give me some credit," he snapped.

Slow realisation crossed Ned's face. "You're in love with Deliverance Felton?" He sank down on the step next to his friend. "You are indeed the biggest fool in Christendom, Collyer."

"That's not the worst of it..." In a shaking voice, Luke recounted Lovedie's attempt to seduce him. When he had finished, he closed his eyes and ran his hands down his face. "Now what am I going to do?"

"You weren't considering throwing yourself off the tower?" Ned suggested.

Luke glared at him. "I'm not that desperate." He groaned. "It's Deliverance. I can't even think straight when I'm near her."

"Well, we need you to think straight, Collyer. Maybe throwing yourself off the tower wasn't such a bad notion. Does Deliverance feel the same way about you?"

Luke nodded.

"God help us." Ned threw his hands in the air. "You haven't actually bedded her, have you?"

"No, but not for want of trying. We just can't seem to find the right moment."

Ned stared at him. "Just stop and think, Collyer. Beyond that wall are four hundred men intent on killing us. The two people in this castle on whom one hundred souls are relying for their lives, are behaving like a pair of moonstruck calves. You are going to have to put your woman troubles to one side and start behaving like a soldier. Love is a luxury which you can ill afford now."

Luke looked up at his friend and nodded. "I know that. I've been telling myself that for days now." "And you're going to have to talk to Deliverance and tell her the same thing. She is sensible enough to understand that whatever has happened between the two of you cannot interfere with the conduct of this siege. End it, Collyer."

Luke buried his head in his hands and groaned. "And what do I do about that trollop, Lovedie?"

Ned stroked his jaw. "Nothing. It's her choice. She can stay here and behave herself or she takes her chance out there with our friend Farrington." Ned put a hand on Luke's shoulder. "Come on. You'd better get out of those soaking clothes and get some rest. You're no good to us with lung fever."

Luke nodded and rose to his feet. No battle he had fought had left him feeling so drained.

Chapter Fourteen

Deliverance woke to the now familiar sally from Farrington's guns. The residence shuddered at the impact of the Thunderer's anger and the smaller cannon balls that smashed against the walls, sending reverberations through the whole castle. She lay in bed looking up at the panels of the wooden canopy above her as the curtain rings rattled. She was alone in the bed. Penitence must have already arisen.

She drew back the curtains and called for Meg, but the maid did not reply. Like Penitence she must have also started her morning chores. They had decided to leave her to sleep.

Deliverance swung her feet out of bed and padded over to her chest to find some clothes. As she raised the lid on the ancient coffer, the window crashed in sending glass shards flying across the room. Deliverance dived to the floor beside the chest as a leaden cannon ball, mercifully not one of the huge balls that spewed from the Thunderer, hurtled through the room, hitting the far wall with a mighty crash. The solid stonework stopped it dead and it bounced back, coming to rest in the fireplace.

Deliverance didn't move, shocked into immobility by the violence of the shot. The door burst open and she gathered herself together, peering over the chest to see Luke standing in the doorway, his jacket undone and his shirt unlaced at his throat.

"Deliverance, are you all right?"

"I'm fine. It missed me... by a few inches..." Deliverance struggled to speak. She shut her eyes and wrapped her arms around herself as the realisation of how close she had come to death.

Luke's feet crunched on the broken glass and she smelled the familiar tang of soap and leather as he came to stand over her.

"Deliverance, look at me."

She opened her eyes and he sank to his haunches, his brow knitted as he reached out to touch her face. "You've blood on your face."

Now he had mentioned it, her cheek burned. With a shaking hand she touched the sticky wetness on her cheek, and then looked down at her fingertips with surprise.

She blinked and looked at him. "Is it...is it bad?"

He shook his head and smiled. "Just a cut. Nothing to worry about but there is glass all over the floor. Don't take a step until you have shoes on."

Before she could protest, he lifted her up and dumped her unceremoniously back on the bed. Deliverance wrapped her arms around herself, aware that she only wore her nightdress. She pulled her feet up, wrapping her arms around her knees in an effort to stop the shaking.

Luke bent to pick up the cannon ball. "Leave it," Deliverance said.

He raised an eyebrow at her.

"I want to leave it there to remember..." she began, but couldn't finish '...*how close I came to death*'

Luke picked his way back to the door where he inclined his head and said. "I'll send someone up to board the window as soon as you are dressed."

She had expected him to come to her, take her in his arms, and reassure her of his love...kiss her...

He was just going to leave her?

"Luke...?" she began but he had gone.

Meg came running in through the door, closely followed by Penitence.

"Thank the good Lord, you are safe!" Penitence threw her arms around her sister. They may not have been the arms she longed for but they would do.

After a moment she pushed her sister away with a brusque, "Don't fuss, Pen. Meg, find me some shoes and my clothes, and organise some help to clean this room."

As soon as she was dressed, Deliverance went in search of Luke. She had hoped to find him in the library but the room was deserted. She wandered over to the old oak table, which had been cleared of all but a pen and ink stand and a scattering of papers.

A cup of wine had been spilled across the table, spoiling the papers and she wondered why no attempt had been made to clean it up. She righted the cup and picked up the still sodden papers, recognising Luke's handwriting.

The door opened and Luke walked in. He stood frozen in the doorway, his hand still on the latch.

"Deliverance. What are you doing here?"

She set the paper down and smiled. "Looking for you."

"I'm very busy." He shut the door but didn't advance any further into the room.

Deliverance came out from behind the table and walked over to him. She laid her hand on his chest and leaned forward, intending to kiss him but he took a step back gently disengaging her hand.

"Deliverance." He took a breath. "We can't go on like this. I am here to do a job, not dally with Sir John's daughter."

She blinked in disbelief. "What do you mean?"

"There will be no more dalliance."

Deliverance stared at him as she tried to understand what he had just said.

"You don't want me anymore? Is it something I did?" she said, mortified by the crack in her voice.

He didn't answer for a long moment and his gaze drifted to the table behind her. He shook his head. "It's nothing that you have done, Deliverance. You are an extraordinary woman. But you must know I have an unsavoury reputation--"

"For trysts with buxom girls from the dairy?" Anger flared in Deliverance's chest.

A look of surprise crossed his face. "No...yes...but that's not it. It's you I am concerned for. Deliverance, I am a soldier. I could be dead tomorrow. I don't want to leave anyone grieving for me, so whatever feelings we may have begun to entertain for each other, we must put to one side and work together for the common cause in which we are both engaged. Now, I have matters to attend to." He bowed stiffly. "Good day, Mistress Felton."

Deliverance stood in the middle of the floor staring at the door as it shut behind him. She sank down on her father's chair, buried her head on the table and wept as if her heart would break.

Her heart had broken, into a thousand razor-sharp shards.

"Liv, what's happened? Are you all right?" Deliverance raised her head. Penitence stared at her with a look of horror on her beautiful face.

Deliverance shot to her feet and walked to the window, keeping her back to her sister.

"It's nothing." But her voice sounded thick from weeping and Penitence was no fool. "Just very tired." She cleared her throat, hastily wiping her eyes on her sleeve. "I need a little time alone today."

Penitence crossed to her sister, putting her arms around her shoulders. "You're doing a wonderful job, Liv, but no one will blame you if you sometimes have to seek some solitude."

"That's it exactly, Pen." She leaned her head against her sisters. "Just leave me here for a little while."

"Are you sure?"

Deliverance nodded.

She waited until her sister had left the room, closing the door behind her. From the window she could see Luke deep in conversation with Ned and Melchior over the latest damage to the west wall. At the sight of the familiar silhouette, her heart turned a somersault. She closed her eyes and allowed herself the shameful indulgence of remembering how he had held her, how he had kissed her and then in the chapel how—

She shook her head as if by doing so she could dispel the memories. She had behaved like a hoyden, and he had repaid her by pushing her away.

She had cried her tears over Luke Collyer like a foolish lovelorn maiden. That would never happen again.

Below her the castle bustled with soldiers and the household staff, all going about their business as if everything was normal. Their world had not been turned on its head. Hers was the only broken heart within these walls. She sniffed back the threatening tears. Broken hearts mended.

A cannonball slammed into the Hawk Tower and the castle shuddered and groaned as if it were a living being. She wondered how much longer the walls could withstand the battering. Should she surrender now before her home was completely destroyed?

Surrender now and Luke Collyer would be gone from her life. That would solve one problem. She turned, glancing up at the portrait of her father above the fireplace. No, she couldn't surrender Kinton Lacey, not for such a pathetic reason.

Next time she saw Luke Collyer she would be cool and polite. Their relationship would revert to one of pure professionalism. She would not give him the satisfaction of letting him see how he had hurt her.

She searched her pile of books and sank down on to the chair opening her copy of "The Exercise of Armes" at the marked page. But the words blurred and she sighed. She couldn't blame Luke. He had been right. To indulge in a romantic liaison had been a foolish thing to do in the middle of their current predicament. They both needed clear heads, untrammelled by attachments that could never be sustained once the siege was over.

Chapter Fifteen

✦

As if God sensed the heaviness in Deliverance's heart, the weather turned foul. All that day and through the night driving rain poured relentlessly through the holes in the walls and roofs of the castle buildings and the courtyard turned to a quagmire.

After a sleepless night, during which she had smothered hot, shameful tears in her bolster, Deliverance leaned on the castle wall in the grey, dreary light of another dawn looking out over the enemy encampment. She took some consolation in the equal misery the weather imposed on the besieging force.

Rain had dampened their powder and the cannons had fallen silent.

"Mistress Felton," She turned at the sound of Melchior's voice, hearing a note of urgency in it she had never heard in the usual phlegmatic steward.

"Melchior?"

He stood behind her, his chest rising and falling as if he had just run to find her. Sudden fear gripped her. Melchior Blakelocke never ran.

Her hand instinctively went to her throat. "What is it?"

"It's our food supply, Mistress Felton," Melchior said.

"What about it?"

"I think you need to come and see for yourself,"

With a sinking feeling, Deliverance followed her steward to the cellars, below the residence, where the carefully hoarded food supplies had been stored.

Her mind rushed over the possibilities. Had the rain flooded the cellar? Had rats got into the flour? Melchior stopped at the heavy oak door and turned the key he carried. Deliverance stepped inside, allowing her eyes a moment or two to accustom to the gloomy light that came from several small window embrasures high in the wall.

Even before she could make out the extent of the damage, her nose told her something was amiss. The smell of ale, mixed with other food smells such as flour rose to meet her.

Melchior lit the lantern that sat on the ledge outside the room and holding it high, he stepped around her, illuminating a scene of devastation. Deliverance gasped.

Every flour sack had been cut open, spewing their contents on to the floor where the white powder mixed in a lake of ale from the broached casks. Tubs of apples had been upended and the cheeses hacked apart and thrown to the ground to mingle in a gelatinous mess.

"How...? Who...?" She leaned against the door jamb to gather her breath as the enormity of the destruction and what it meant for everyone within the castle sunk in. "Melchior, what are we going to do?"

Melchior shook his head. "See what can be salvaged and clean up the mess," he suggested, ever practical.

"You better fetch Captain Collyer. He needs to see this," she said sinking on to the bottom step.

It took at least ten minutes before Luke clattered down the stairs. She had gone out of her way to avoid him for the last twenty-four hours but seeing him so close, the familiar skip of her heart, accompanied by an almost physical pain threatened to betray her.

Part of her just wanted to put her face in her hands and cry—and not for the ruined food.

Luke had been awake most of the night, pondering on the most urgent repairs to the castle, and had just managed to find a quiet moment in the library to close his eyes when Blakelocke had burst into the room without knocking. One look at the man's face had told him something had gone seriously wrong.

His first thought had been for Deliverance but no, she sat on the bottom step her chin resting on her hands, her shoulders slumped. She didn't bother to look up or to speak, just waved a hand at the cellar.

Luke's chest tightened as he took in the extent of the devastation. Someone had done a comprehensive job of destroying their food supplies.

He responded by blaspheming volubly and sank down on to the step beside her. "Is it all gone?" he asked at last.

"I don't know what can be salvaged yet." She looked up at him. "Who could have done this?"

"Someone within these walls," Luke said. "Someone who does not have our interests at heart."

She blinked and said slowly, "You mean there is a traitor?"

"Yes," he said, his mouth a grim, tight line. "Do we know when it happened?"

She shook her head. "I always check the door before going to bed. It was locked last night"

"And this morning?"

She looked up at Melchior. "Who found this?"

"I did, ma'am when I came to dole out the day's rations. The door was locked." Melchior shook his head. "I blame myself."

Luke rose to his feet. "Don't be a fool, Blakelocke. This isn't your doing. Someone had access to a key. Who else, besides yourself, holds keys, Mistress Felton?"

If she noticed the deliberate use of her formal name, nothing in her face responded. She stood up and faced him. "There are only two keys. I have one and Melchior the other." She held up her ring. "It doesn't leave this ring."

"Has anyone borrowed the key?"

Deliverance frowned. "I have given it to a few people who had need to access the cellar for food preparation but it has always been returned to me."

"Who?"

Deliverance named the cooks and several of her household staff, adding, "They have all been with our family for years and I would stake my life on their honesty. Surely you don't suspect--"

"War changes people, Mistress Felton." Luke ran a hand through his already dishevelled hair. "We won't be able to keep news of this disaster quiet. See what you can do to mitigate it and also what can be saved. Blakelocke, come with me."

He found his way blocked by Penitence who stood at the top of the stairs, looking down at her sister.

"Oh, this is terrible. What are we going to do, Liv?" Penitence said.

Deliverance looked up at her sister. "Gather the maids. We are going to clean up as best we can and salvage what can be salvaged. The cheeses can be washed and dried, the apples may be bruised but they are still edible. There is still some flour in the bags and ale in the vats."

"But surely not enough to last us more than a few days?" Penitence added unhelpfully.

"We are just going to have to ration ourselves. Save every ounce of flour that can be saved," Luke said as he passed Penitence, thoughts whirling through his mind.

He had convinced himself that an estrangement with Deliverance was for the best but seeing the unguarded misery in her face when she had first looked up at him, tugged at his heart. For all his fine words, nothing could change his feelings for Deliverance Felton.

He stopped at the top of the cellar stairs and took a deep breath, pushing all thoughts of Deliverance to one side. The greater good of the castle and every soul within it had to be considered and he had a traitor to find.

Luke paraded the garrison in the courtyard despite the pouring rain. He stood at the top of the steps and looked down at the gathered throng. Water dripped from the brim of his hat down his collar. If he felt tired and dispirited, weary of the siege, then he could only imagine what the garrison must be feeling. In their present mood the news that their food supply had been compromised could well provoke mutiny.

Behind the ranks of men, the household staff, who had also been summoned, milled in the poor shelter of the buildings surrounding the courtyard, whispering to each other. He wondered if they were speculating on whether he brought them news of capitulation.

As he scanned the faces, his resolve hardened. No matter how wet, miserable and hungry they were, among them was a traitor, a traitor hoping that the destruction of the food supplies would lead to a speedy capitulation.

He glanced over to the corner of the courtyard where the small herd of cattle had been confined. The miserable beasts would not feed a hundred mouths for very long. Before calling the muster he had checked with Melchior Blakelocke, who confirmed that almost all of the flour was gone. Half the cheese had been saved, along with turnips, carrots and dried beans. They had water to drink but at best they could last another two weeks. After that—

He held up a hand commanding instant silence.

"There is a traitor among us," Luke began. A murmur rose from the crowd as each man looked to his fellows. "Last night, someone broke into the cellars and attempted to destroy the castle's food supplies."

A surge of anger rose from the soldiers. To steal a comrade's food was one of the lowest crimes a soldier could commit. Luke scanned their faces, hoping to see a guilty face but all he could see was stunned disbelief.

"Fortunately the perpetrator was not entirely successful and there is food enough for us to survive on for the time being. However our rations will be severely cut."

"How long 'ave we got?" A voice called out.

Luke hesitated. They had a right to know. "Two weeks, maybe three."

A rumble of anger surged among the men and he held up a hand. "If any person here knows who may be responsible, there is no shame in turning them over to me. You all know the price for such treachery."

Hanging...the unspoken word fell on the crowd, subduing it into silence.

"If anyone has any information as to the identity of the perpetrator, they can speak to Sergeant Hale, Lieutenant Barrett or myself."

One of the men, who had been with him at Byton, pointed a finger at Toby Brown.

"What about him? Convenient he's the only one to survive Byton, and then comes here all whey- faced and eager to help."

Toby's mouth fell open, his eyes widened. "Me? Oh, no, I'd never... I'm Captain Collyer's man to the death."

But a tide of sentiment swiftly turned against the boy. The

garrison needed a culprit and whatever the boy's guilt or otherwise, he made a convenient scapegoat.

Two of the soldiers grabbed the boy pushing him forward to the steps.

Luke looked down into Toby's frightened face. He wanted to believe the boy's protestations but he could see logic in the argument put to him by the others. Toby was the outsider and the circumstances of his coming to Kinton Lacey could give rise to suspicion.

"Take him to one of the cells and lock him up," Luke said.

"You don't think...?" Ned whispered in his ear.

"For the boy's own safety if nothing else," Luke replied. "They'd hang him here and now if they had half a chance."

He turned on his heel and strode back into the residence.

In the Great Hall, Luke leaned on the table, looking down at its ancient surface, polished to a gleam by age and many applications of beeswax.

"We should have put a guard on the cellar."

He straightened at the sound of Deliverance's voice and turned to face her.

"It's enough I have a guard on the water supply. I couldn't spare another for a sturdy, locked, oak door." He saw the unhappy look on her face. "Don't blame yourself, Del... Mistress Felton."

"But it was my key."

He shrugged. "It is easy enough to make a copy."

She frowned. "Is it?"

He shook his head and allowed himself a smile at her sometimes endearing naivety. "Deliverance, you are so innocent. All you need is a mould of clay, press the key into it and then fill it with molten iron and you have a copy. There is a blacksmith's forge working here. Anyone could have done it."

"But only if they had the original."

"You said yourself, there are people you have trusted with the key to run errands." She sank into the great chair at the head of the table and rested her chin on her hand. "How long do you think we can we hold out?"

"Much longer than you think. When we run out, we can always eat the horses...and then there are the dogs, the cats and the vermin."

She looked up at him, her mouth opening in horror. "Surely you're jesting...no, I can see you're not."

"This is the reality of our situation. I'm not going to paint a pretty picture for you. The certainty is Farrington will keep banging away at our walls, while we grow physically weaker. In the end he will simply walk in."

Her expression was one of despair, and Luke cursed himself for his honesty, but she needed to know. She wouldn't find this in her text books. This was war and war was brutal. He turned on his heel and walked out leaving her sitting at the long table in the ruins of her father's hall.

"We've got to get a message through to Gloucester," he said when he found Ned on the castle wall.

"Gloucester's still besieged." Ned stated the obvious.

"It's the only place help is going to come from," Luke said.

Ned nodded.

"Send a man out through the sally port tonight." Luke drummed the stone wall with his fingers as he stared thoughtfully out at the enemy position. "I've had enough of being cooped up in here just taking what Farrington throws at us. Tomorrow at dawn, Ned, I'm going to lead a sortie. The men need some action and if we can bring in a little more food, we stand a chance of holding out for longer."

"Well, we better not eat the horses tonight," Ned remarked. He glanced over the wall at the sound of a trumpet "What a surprise. It looks like we have visitors." He pointed to a party of three men advancing on foot towards them under the white flag of truce.

Luke held up his hand to stop his own men from firing as the party came within range of the castle wall.

"Captain Collyer?" An officer stepped forward.

"I am he," Luke identified himself.

"I bring a letter from Colonel Charles Farrington to Mistress Felton and I seek an audience with the lady in order to deliver it."

"Come forward and alone. You have my word you will not be harmed," Luke replied and with a quick glance at Ned who signalled for the small door in the gate to be opened to admit Farrington's messenger, relieved to see that this time it was not Jack who carried the message.

Deliverance broke open the letter. She scanned the contents, and then read aloud.

"*Madam, as I esteem your courage in resisting the right and the might of your rightful King, I now offer you, for the last time, the opportunity to surrender Kinton Lacey Castle. Word has come to me that your food supplies have been compromised and it is unlikely you will hold out for many more weeks. Once again you have my word that you and your sister will be treated with the honor and respect due to persons of your delicacy and stature. Your household will also be allowed to depart in peace. The men of your garrison may offer their surrender and they will be conveyed to a place of confinement but otherwise unmolested. Surrender now on these terms. Yr faithful servant Chas Farrington.*"

Deliverance looked up at the circle of faces; Penitence, Melchior, Ned and Luke. She turned to the messenger and with slow deliberate care tore the paper in half and then into small pieces letting them drop at the man's feet.

"You have my answer," she said. "Sergeant Hale, see this man safely escorted to the gate."

"Ma'am!" Hale, standing guard at the door, snapped to attention.

The messenger bowed and turned on his heel. Deliverance waited until he had left the room.

"How did he know?" She looked around the faces that surrounded her, scanning each one. "How did he know our food supplies have been compromised?"

"Because the person who perpetrated the act is in contact with him," Luke answered.

"But how?"

Luke shook his head. "I don't know, but you have my word, Mistress Felton, that I will find out."

"Do you really think it is Toby Brown?" Deliverance asked.

Luke shrugged. "He is our best suspect at present. If anything else untoward happens while he is locked up then we will know he is innocent. If not..." He left Toby's possible fate unspoken. "In the meantime we have work to do. Please excuse us, ladies. Ned? Blakelocke? We need to talk. Come with me."

Ned inclined his head and hurried after his commander with Melchior following at his usual sedate pace.

Alone with her sister, Deliverance looked down at her drab, dusty, and stained gown. "I think it may be time to show my colours again, Pen. Can you help me dress?"

The red gown hung a little more on her already slender frame. Even with careful rationing, they were all looking thinner. She let down her hair and with a brave smile at Penitence, swept out of the residence.

As she climbed the steps to the curtain wall, Luke broke away from his discussions with his officers and met her at the top of the steps.

"What do you think you're doing?" he said.

"I need to have a word to Charles Farrington. Can you summon him?"

"Are you surrendering?" Luke enquired with a raised eyebrow. "If so, I think you should have discussed it with me."

"Don't be ridiculous, Captain Collyer. We haven't come this far just to surrender because some fool thought they could starve us out? Get Farrington for me. I will wait here."

Word went around the castle and a crowd gathered in the castle courtyard, eager to hear what their lady had to say.

Deliverance ignored the onlookers and at a nod from Luke, she climbed on to the box on the castle wall and looked down over the enemy camp. The bustling soldiery beyond the walls also stopped what they were doing and climbed to the top of their earthworks.

"Farrington," she called out, her voice carried well on the breeze. Charles Farrington, resplendent in a blue jacket trimmed with silver, stood with his hands on his hips on the closest earthwork. Jack Farrington, hatless and similarly uniformed stood beside his brother.

"You declined my terms, madam?" he shouted up at her.

"I wish to inform you personally, Colonel Farrington, that I shall not surrender Kinton Lacey while I have breath in my body."

From the distance she could not see his face, but the tone of his voice carried nothing but contempt as he said, "I believe you have cause to know, I do not suffer rebels lightly, Mistress Felton. When Kinton Lacey falls, as it will, no one will be spared." He swept her a low, contemptuous bow. "I bid you good day, madam."

Deliverance's stomach lurched at his last words. Everyone on the castle wall would have heard them and she felt the eyes of the garrison turned on her. A low murmur rose as the implication of what Farrington had said was passed around. They all knew the fate of the garrison at Byton.

She turned around to face her own garrison. The wind whipped her dark hair into her eyes and she pushed it back.

"You have heard the words of a fool," she said. "Kinton Lacey will not fall to him. Even now word has gone to my father at Gloucester and relief will be with us before our food runs out."

A scattered applause broke out but the faces that looked up at her had lost their confidence. They all knew their position was dire and nothing she could say or do could instil the same bravado they had once shown. They were all tired, hungry and dirty, and time was running out.

Chapter Sixteen

Deliverance could not say what woke her. She lay awake listening to the sound of steady rain beating against the boarded window of her bedchamber. Once she would have found that sound comforting. Over the rain she heard the muted sounds of men's voices and heavy boots on the wooden floorboards.

She rose and padded out into the corridor. In the courtyard shadowy figures moved in the light of covered lanterns and the low murmur of voices drifted up to her. Horses stood waiting while men saddled them, their heads tossing and breath blowing whitely in the damp, cool air.

She swallowed. Was Luke deserting her? Leaving in the dead of night?

She returned to her chamber and being carefully not to wake Penitence and the other women, grabbed some clothing, changing quickly in the corridor.

She opened the door to the residence. A tall figure in cloak and hat stood at the top of the stairs, his hands on his hips, watching the quiet activity in the courtyard below.

"Luke?"

He spun around and put a finger to his lips. "Ssh...keep your voice low."

"What are you doing?"

"We are going on a sortie."

She glanced at the horses, twelve in all. *Twelve against four hundred?*

"No!" She clutched his sleeve and shook it. "No. I absolutely forbid it."

She couldn't see his face in the dark and the shadows but beneath her hand, the muscles of his arm tightened and he shook her clinging hand free.

"Your objection is noted," he said. "But there are good reasons for taking this action, Mistress Felton. We need food and we need action."

"We can manage. We can't spare a dozen men, Luke."

"We have a plan, Deliverance. We're not just riding out there with our fingers crossed. I have given four men the task of cutting out some of the cattle from the supply Farrington has in that meadow to the south of us and Hale and I—"

"You? Surely you're not going?"

"Hale and I are going to take on the guns. If we can spike a couple of them in the time it takes the men to round up the cattle, it will be a good morning's work."

She stared at him, speechless.

He looked up at the glowering sky. "It's a good morning for it. Even those of Farrington's men officially on watch will be sheltering and the rain helps to deaden the sound of movement." He pointed at the horses. "And I've muffled the horse's hooves."

Deliverance looked at the pathetic beasts, their hooves swaddled in sacking. Inaction and poor food had taken all condition from the horses. She doubted they would carry the men far if the action got serious.

Hale appeared at the foot of the stairs. "We're ready."

Luke nodded and without another word to Deliverance strode down the stairs. The men had begun to mount, the horses shifting restlessly beneath the unaccustomed weight. Luke ran a hand down the nose of his horse, before swinging into the saddle. The horse tossed its head, prancing on its muffled hooves.

After a quick glance around to see that everyone was mounted and ready, he gave a curt nod. The portcullis rattled upwards and the great bars across the gates slid back. The gates swung open and for the first time in weeks the outside world loomed beyond the dark portal.

Deliverance stood frozen to the spot. He really was going to ride out of the gates into the teeth of Farrington's guns.

He raised his hand and the little party moved forward on silent hoofs. Only as they reached the gatehouse did Luke put his heels to the horse and it sprang forward as anxious for action as he was.

Deliverance ran to the wall, crouching down behind the ramparts as the twelve horsemen burst from the castle gate below her, like demons from hell. They made no noise, just spurred their horses on with grim determination.

The party split, the four soldiers designated with the task of rounding up the cattle turned to the south, while Luke and his seven men rode straight at the earthworks.

Deliverance cursed the dark and the rain that hid her view of the action on the earthworks. She could dimly make out the shapes of the horses, breasting the ramparts and she heard cries of alarm and the heavy clanging of steel, but no gunfire.

The rain must be their saviour, dampening match and powder and reducing the defenders to the steel-edged weapons.

Above her, their own little gun thundered from the Hawk Tower and she looked to the south seeing a small herd of lowing cattle being driven hard towards the castle. From the fortified village came the rattle of drums and scattered gunfire as horses came flying like beasts of mythology, across the earthworks.

Deliverance counted. One, two, three...eight. They were safe but even as she dared to breathe, she saw the shadows of horsemen riding out from the village and heard a bellow.

"Collyer!" In the growing grey light of dawn, Deliverance recognised Charles Farrington, bare headed and brandishing his sword.

One of the fleeing horsemen wheeled.

Don't do it, Luke, Deliverance silently pleaded.

Luke doffed his hat and swept Farrington an extravagant bow. With a whoop, he set the horse at a hard gallop for the safety of the castle, following a small herd of cattle and all eleven of his men as a hail of musket fire from the ramparts of the castle deterred Farrington from following.

The gates crashed shut and Luke drew his labouring horse to a shuddering halt. "We did it," he crowed, throwing his hat into the air.

Applause and shouts of delight went up around the castle and Luke looked up at the castle wall. Deliverance watched him with her arms folded.

She turned to the man nearest to her and said, "Tell Captain Collyer I would speak with him in the library." Without looking at Luke she returned to the residence by the curtain wall entrance.

He burst into the room without knocking. One look at his face, flushed and exultant, told her everything she needed to know even before he spoke.

"Two guns spiked and a dozen cattle, Mistress Felton."

"You disobeyed my command, Captain Collyer. I forbade the sortie."

His eyes gleamed in the early morning light as he took a step towards her. "Are you going to court-martial me, Mistress Felton?"

"I should have you whipped for your disobedience."

He stood so close to her that all she had to was reach out and touch him. His lips were curved in a smile as he looked down at her.

"You are not taking me seriously, Captain Collyer. I am seriously displeased."

She raised her hands to do what she didn't know. Slap him? Beat some sense into him?

He caught her wrists and drew her toward him, pressing his body against hers as he brought his mouth down on hers with a bruising intensity that took her breath away. She squirmed in his grasp, her protests silenced by his questing tongue.

He released her wrists and her arms found their way around his neck, drawing him even closer as he encircled her. She closed her eyes, surrendering to the moment. The scent of man and horse enveloped her, filling her senses. She started tugging at the back of his jacket and shirt, pulling material until her hands slid across the broad plane of his back, the skin silky beneath her fingers.

He did not relax his mouth, his tongue exploring her with an insatiable hunger and she responded, twining with him, as his hands ran across her shoulders, sliding the bodice down, imprisoning her arms, as he gave a tug, freeing her breasts. She knew this was wrong, the rational, sensible Deliverance was plucking at her skirts, telling her to stop now before she did something she regretted but as his hand cupped her breast, she regretted nothing. Heat flooded her body, coursing through her like a torrent. Her fingers scrabbled at the buckle of his belt. She wanted this man.

The door. It came over like a dousing with cold water. The door was unlocked. Anyone could walk in on them. She stiffened, pushing Luke away from her, struggling to restore her clothing, desire replaced with embarrassment.

He stood looking at her, panting as if he had just run a hard race, his clothing dishevelled, his hair mussed beyond redemption.

"What are you staring at?" she demanded, her voice rising on a note of hysteria. "You were the one who ended it and you were right, Luke. We have to think beyond ourselves."

"Deliverance." His voice was husky.

Her fingers shook as she relaced her bodice, her hair falling about her face, hiding the scalding tears. He put his hands on her shoulders, drawing her toward him again. If he touched her again, she would be lost. Deliverance summoned up the one weapon she had left in her armoury. She slapped him hard. He took a step back, his hand going to his cheek, as she gathered the last shreds of her dignity and walked out of the room.

Mercifully the bedchamber was deserted. Deliverance flung herself down on her bed and curled into a ball, trying not to think about the look of hurt and surprise on Luke's face as she slapped him. Tears pricked her eyes but she fought them back. She had done the right thing. If she had given in to her own base instinct, the fragile cord holding the defence of this castle together would be lost. The castle and its inhabitants came first, all else was of little importance. There would be time at the end of all this to deal with the complexities of human emotions, but for now she had to remember who she was and what needed to be done.

When...? If...?

She gave an agonised groan and rolled herself into a tighter ball to stifle the pain. Was this what was meant by a 'broken heart'?

Despite their dire circumstances, a veneer of gentility required that Penitence, Deliverance, Ned and Luke ate at least one meal together. With the shortage of rations they had been reduced to one meal a day which they ate around noon. The cooks did their best, producing a stew for the midday meal that by evening would become a weak broth, accompanied by one small hunk of bread.

Deliverance poked at the gelatinous mess on her plate, acutely conscious of her proximity to Luke. Being forced to sit and make polite conversation with him after what had passed between them that morning caused her heart to clench. She craved his touch like a drunkard craves wine.

He seemed unaffected, engaged in conversation with Ned about the possibility of another sortie. He hadn't even glanced at her, beyond the politeness required of a shared meal.

She turned her attention to Penitence, who sat staring at her plate, her hands folded on her lap, her head bowed.

"Eat up, Pen," Deliverance said with forced cheerfulness. "We all need to keep our strength up." Penitence gave a shuddering sob.

"Pen?"

Penitence's shoulders rose and fell and she pushed the plate aside, her face concealed by the curtain of hair, once bright and shining but now dull and lifeless.

"I can't go on like this," the girl said.

"What do you mean?" Deliverance stared at her sister.

Penitence looked up. "Why don't you just surrender, Liv? This house is not worth all this misery. It's just stones. People are going to die here. If Farrington doesn't kill us all first, we will die from a fever or starvation."

"We have the extra cattle..." Deliverance trailed off, swallowing hard. Penitence's words enunciated the thoughts that had been going around in her head since refusing Charles' Farrington's offer of surrender the previous day.

She forced herself to look across at Luke. She saw no sympathy in his face, only a steely resolve.

Luke pushed back his chair. "It's not just about stones, it is about principles. Principles that your father, that we," he glanced at Ned, "believe in. The King has ridden roughshod over his people for too many years. He forced this country into civil war through his own blind refusal to accept he is a man, not a king by divine providence. Enough people have suffered at his hands and if we hand over this house to him, the suffering continues."

"I don't give a fig for the king or any just cause," Penitence said, the expression on her face mutinous. "I just want this siege to be over."

Before Luke could respond, Deliverance spoke, "You know what Farrington did at Byton, do you think for a moment he will just let us go?"

"He promised you and I safe custody," Penitence said.

"But not the garrison. Not those of us who are fighting to hold this castle. These are our people, Penitence. We owe them our protection."

"You may not realise it, Penitence, but Kinton Lacey is vital to control of the southern part of this county," Luke interjected. "If the king holds it, then he can ride into Wales and the Cotswolds. We are all that is standing between him and total annihilation of the parliamentary cause in the west."

"I don't care," Penitence cried, pushing back her chair. "I just want everything to be the way it was. I want to marry Jack Farrington. I want to live out my days with children at my feet. I don't give a ha'pence for strategy."

"Or for the lives of the people within these walls?" Deliverance said.

Penitence gave her sister a look that mingled despair with defiance and ran from the Great Hall. Deliverance rose to go after her, but Luke laid his hand over hers. The touch of his calloused fingers stilled her and she sank back in her chair. He removed his hand as if it had been scorched. "Let her go, Deliverance. It's a natural reaction after weeks of a siege."

"She knows Jack is out there," Deliverance said. "Her heart is breaking."

Luke's eyes, cold and hard, met hers. "This is war, Deliverance, not a time for love and broken hearts."

The message, intended for her, jarred home with a physical pain. Deliverance gathered her dignity and stood up.

"I can only hope, for her sake, that when this war is over and the swords are hung back on the walls, there will be a time for her and Jack," she said.

"Provided he survives," Luke said, his gaze holding hers. She tried to read the smoky depths but saw only cold resolve. He had made his choice and it would never be her.

Ned, the uncomfortable witness to a conversation he didn't really understand, shifted in his seat. "Do you think it would be wrong of me to polish off Mistress Felton's meal?" he asked.

Deliverance broke her gaze and looked at the unappetising mess on Penitence's plate. "Eat it. We can't let a morsel go to waste and your need is greater than my sister's."

She went in search of Penitence and found her sister huddled in a window seat in the upstairs parlour. The damage had been roughly mended making the room vaguely habitable again, despite the boards on the broken windows. Just as Deliverance used the library, this room had always been Penitence's refuge.

"Pen..."

"Go away, Liv," Penitence responded without lifting her head. "I just want to be alone."

"Pen, if you want to leave Kinton Lacey, I won't stop you."

Penitence raised her head. "What? Walk out, just like that?"

Deliverance nodded. "Just like that. I have every confidence Jack would ensure you had safe passage to Father in Gloucester or Aunt Elizabeth in London."

Penitence looked away. "I can't leave you."

"You can. You will be quite safe. You have Jack." Deliverance tried to sound braver than she felt. "I know how you feel about him. Do you think he still feels the same way about you?"

Penitence's shoulders heaved and she laid her head on her bent knees, wrapping her arms tighter around herself. "Of course he does."

Deliverance frowned. Something about her sister's certainty made her uneasy. Apart from that fleeting moment at the start of the siege, to the best of her knowledge Penitence had no contact with Jack since the start of the war.

"How do you know?"

Penitence raised a tear-stained face, her eyes wide with fear. "I just know."

Deliverance crossed to her sister and put her arms around her. "Then if he loves you, he will wait for you."

As Penitence sobbed into her sister's shoulder, Deliverance heard her say. "You are so lucky never to have been in love, Liv."

Deliverance sighed and held Penitence closer. If her sister felt even a fraction of the agony she had experienced in the last few days she must be in real pain.

Since the scare with the miners, Luke had taken to doing a late night round of all the sentry positions. On his way to inspect the guard on the sally port, he stopped on the east wall in the shadows of the Jewel Tower, which stood in the north-eastern corner of the castle.

Deliverance had told him that the name had derived from a story that the crown jewels of the Welsh Kings had once been stored in its depths. Luke doubted the truth of the story but it made a pretty name for an otherwise utilitarian piece of architecture. He preferred the Hawk Tower with its weathered carvings of hawks in flight affixed to its ramparts.

He leaned on the wall looking down over the river. The moon glinted off its ripples as it flowed on its never changing path towards the sea. No enemy campfires lit the far side of the bank, and from this side of the castle it was almost possible to believe the world was at peace.

He turned his face to the night sky, clear and bright after the days of rain. A full moon illuminated the courtyard and above him the stars arched, timeless and unconcerned with the petty affairs of men. He straightened and turned back to his lonely patrol.

A movement, below him, caught his eye and he stiffened, stepping back into the shadows. When nothing moved he thought he had imagined it. He peered over the wall into the dark shadows thrown by the castle wall and just for a fleeting moment he caught a glimpse of a silhouette moving in a crouched position along the hidden pathway outside the castle that led to the sally port.

His hand instinctively went to his sword hilt and every nerve now attuned to potential trouble, he swivelled to look into the castle grounds. He stiffened as he saw a cloaked and hooded figure slip from the door to the Jewel Tower, also keeping to the shadows.

At first he couldn't tell if the figure was male or female until it passed below him through a patch of moonlight and he caught a glimpse of skirts.

He followed the woman's progress, briefly losing sight of her behind an outbuilding. She emerged from the shadows and he saw with grim satisfaction she was heading for the sally port.

Was this the castle traitor meeting with one of Farrington's men?

He slipped noiselessly down the stairs to ground level and worked his way along the wall until he had a good view of the sally port. He could see no sign of the man he had placed on sentry duty.

The man, Truscott, one of the Kinton Lacey men, may have stepped away to answer a call of nature or, and Luke's mouth tightened at this thought. Truscott may have been turning a blind eye to whatever liaison had been planned for the night. If that was the case the man would pay dearly for this treachery.

An owl hoot came from beyond the wall and Luke had a sudden flash of memory, recalling the long hours he and his brother had practised bird calls. The owl had been particularly satisfactory.

He heard the gentle swish of the woman's skirts, and soft footsteps on the cobbles. The woman, holding something in her right hand, passed by him without a sideways glance, her gaze fixed firmly on the sally port.

Even with the hood of her cloak pulled well up, Luke recognised the slight figure, and his heart sank. After Penitence's breakdown at their midday meal, Luke had nurtured an uneasy feeling about the girl. It was not anything she had said. Her reaction after weeks of siege warfare was perfectly understandable but the knowledge that Penitence's lover waited outside the wall gave him cause to be concerned, a misgiving that had not been misplaced it seemed.

Penitence took the large key to the door from her skirts but it dropped from her fingers hitting the cobblestones with an audible clang. The girl froze, looking up at the battlements and around her to see if the noise had disturbed anyone. Luke drew back further into the shadows.

When nothing happened, she retrieved the key and he could almost hear her desperate breathing as she fumbled again with the key in the lock. Well-oiled, the key clicked home and Penitence slipped through the door into the tunnel beyond that led down to the gate. Luke broke his cover and, well-schooled in moving silently, even in boots, he made the door in a few strides.

In her haste to reach whoever waited beyond the gate—and Luke would be willing to wager it was Jack Farrington—Penitence had left it ajar. The tunnel bent at a right angle as it neared the gate. The light of a lantern spilled over the cobbles. The lantern must have been the object she carried.

The low murmur of voices reached him. The man sounded soft and reassuring but the high tone in Penitence's voice, even speaking in a whisper, betrayed her distress. The man said something and she gave a choking sob.

Luke drew the pistol from his belt. He should get assistance but he didn't want to alarm the lovers or lose time in summoning his men. If he alerted the trysters, Jack would be gone and probably Penitence with him.

He rounded the corner and levelled the pistol into the tunnel. Illuminated by light of the small lantern, Jack held Penitence in his arms. The couple sprang apart as Luke cleared his throat. "Raise your hands where I can see them, Farrington," Luke said.

"Luke! No, you don't understand." Penitence stepped in front of her lover. "And you, Mistress Felton."

"Me?" Penitence sounded genuinely mystified. "I haven't done anything wrong."

"Both of you. Shall we proceed out into the fresh air?"

Stooping to pick up the lantern, Luke followed Jack and Penitence out of the tunnel. He shut the door to the sally port with his foot and bellowed for the traitorous guard he knew would be somewhere nearby.

"Truscott! Out here now."

He heard the man's boots on the walkway above him, coming from the direction of the Jewel Tower where he must have been sheltering.

"Sir?" He sounded breathless.

Luke would deal with Truscott later. "Sound the alarm," he ordered.

"But, sir..." Truscott began.

"Now!" Luke said in a tone that brooked no argument

The man grunted and Luke Truscott's retreating feet was followed by the clanging of a bell from the Jewel Tower. In less than a minute, the night guard led by Sergeant Hale, bristling with weaponry appeared in the courtyard.

Hale looked from Penitence to Jack and back to Luke. Luke's pistol had not wavered. Penitence began to cry, the wetness on her cheeks silvered in the moonlight. Luke regarded her without sympathy.

"We have traitors in our midst, Hale. Take Captain Farrington and Mistress Felton under guard to the Great Hall and," he jerked his head at the Tower, "put Truscott under guard in the darkest most rat-infested dungeon you can find in this place."

"Luke! For pity's sake..." Penitence sobbed but he was in no mood for pity or mercy.

He lowered his pistol as Hale accompanied by four of his men marched the prisoners away. Ned, who had come late on the scene, caught his sleeve. "Collyer, what's going on here?"

"I just caught Penitence Felton in the embrace of Jack Farrington. We've got our traitor." Luke leaned against the wall, rubbing a weary hand over his eyes.

"Penitence? Surely not. I'm sure there is an explanation."

"Of course there is," Luke snapped, "and I can't wait to hear what story our two lovebirds come up with. Now see the sally port is secured and put one of our own men on to guard it."

In the Great Hall, Jack Farrington and Penitence sat side by side at the long table with two armed men standing behind them. Standing across the table from the pair, Luke put his hands on his hips and surveyed them. Jack's hat lay on the table in front of him and the young man looked pale and drawn. Penitence, dry-eyed for the moment, had placed her hands over his and she glared at Luke.

Before he could speak, Deliverance's voice came from behind him. "What's going on? I heard the alarm," she said.

He turned. Deliverance stood at the screen, a candle in her hand, dressed in her nightgown with a loose robe flung over it.

"Meet our traitor," Luke said.

Deliverance looked at him, her gaze flicking to her sister and Jack Farrington.

"No," she said with a disbelieving laugh catching her words, "you don't mean Pen? Surely not." He fixed her with an uncompromising glance and saw her swallow.

Without taking her eyes off him, she addressed her sister, "Pen? What is he talking about?" Penitence gasped and releasing Jack's hands she sat back, her hands grasping the arms of her chair. "You don't think that I...? No! I'm not a traitor." She turned to her lover. "Jack, tell them."

Jack looked up. "I just had to see her, that's all. It was a tryst, nothing more. She's not a traitor to this castle."

Luke brought his hand down on the table with a thump that made them all jump.

"This is not the time for lover's trysts, Farrington. I don't care if you had met to play backgammon. She," he pointed to Penitence, "is a member of this garrison. You," he pointed to Jack, "are the enemy. That immediately makes her suspect. As you well have cause to know someone in this castle is in contact with your brother and right now it looks like Mistress Felton."

"No, this is wrong," Deliverance touched his arm. "Penitence would never betray us."

He rounded on her. "We are at war, Deliverance. This man," he pointed at Jack again, "has four hundred armed troops out there with no other intention but our annihilation."

Deliverance stared back at him, her eyes wide and fearful. He saw her glance at her sister. Penitence looked away.

Luke turned on Penitence. "How many times have you met?"

Her lower lip began to quiver and Jack answered for her. "This is the third time."

"And how do you arrange these assignations?"

Penitence swallowed. "I light a lantern and shine it from the window of the Jewel Tower. Three times and Jack knows it is safe."

"Safe? Is it only safe when the man, Truscott, is sentinel on the sally port?"

Penitence nodded. "He has known me all my life...I only asked him not to tell anyone..."

"Truscott is a Felton man," Deliverance said. "He is utterly honest and reliable."

"He has deliberately turned a blind eye to no less than three meetings between these two." Luke looked back at Deliverance. "That cannot go unpunished, Mistress Felton. He is as complicit in this as your sister and an example must be set." He straightened and turned to Sergeant Hale. "Tomorrow at midday, I want Truscott hanged from the Hawk Tower."

Penitence screamed.

Deliverance's hand went to her mouth. "Luke, no."

He ignored her. "Hale, take Captain Farrington to a room in the Lower Tower and provide him with a bed, water and a bucket. I would offer you food, Farrington, but alas we are a little short."

Hale hauled Jack up by the arm and pushing him before him left the room. Penitence, ashen-faced, looked up at Luke. He met her eyes without blinking.

"Mistress Felton." Luke glanced at Deliverance. "Take your sister to a bedchamber upstairs and lock her in. Bring me the key."

Deliverance went to her sister's side and put her hand on her shoulder. Penitence placed her own hand over Deliverance's.

A united front.

"Luke, she doesn't deserve this," Deliverance said.

Luke shook his head, unmoved, although the white-hot anger he had experienced on first catching the lovers together had begun to fade. "She has been caught consorting with the enemy. I cannot let her go unpunished. Rightly she should hang with Truscott on the morrow. It is only because I am merciful that she will stay locked up until this siege is ended and I will leave her to your father to deal with as he thinks fit."

Penitence gave a strangled cry and began to sob again.

Luke's anger began to ebb from him in the face of the girl's distress. In a softer tone, he said, "I'm sorry, but you must see you brought this on yourself. How did you contrive the arrangement with Farrington?"

"He...he..." she sniffed, "...he slipped me a note that first day."

"Oh, Pen," Deliverance said in a shaky voice and for a horrible moment, Luke thought she would burst into tears too.

"Deliverance, are you going to do what I asked or shall I wait for Sergeant Hale?" He kept his voice hard and unforgiving. This was not the moment for sentiment.

Deliverance straightened and put her hand under her sister's arm. "Come, Pen. I don't see we have any choice."

Luke watched the two women leave the room and sank on to the big chair at the end of the table. He would have given anything to turn back the clock. In his heart he didn't think Penitence was the traitor in their midst, but that was not the point.

He ran a hand over his eyes and cursed himself for his diligence. If he had turned for bed instead of stopping to whistle to the moon,

Penitence and Jack Farrington would have made their assignation and he would be none the wiser. Now a man would die on the morrow for no other reason except he loved his mistress too well. On the other hand he now had Jack Farrington as his prisoner and that gave him a very valuable card to play in the game.

Deliverance sat on the edge of the bed with her arm around her sobbing sister.

"I'm not a traitor, Liv. I'm not." Penitence protested her innocence through the veil of tears. "I know. But you have to understand how this looks, Pen. What were you thinking?"

"I love him," Penitence howled. "I had to see him. You would have done the same thing, Liv."

I'm not sure that I would have, Deliverance thought, no matter how much I loved him, my duty is to this castle and its inhabitants.

Penitence looked up, her face stricken. "Will he really hang Truscott?"

Deliverance thought of Luke's eyes, seeing the soft, smoky grey she had come to love replaced with the glint of bright steel.

Yes, he would hang Truscott. "Yes."

"He doesn't deserve to die," Penitence wailed. "He didn't do anything wrong."

Deliverance stared at her sister. Did Penitence really have no grasp on the seriousness of her crime?

"I will plead his case with Captain Collyer," she said. "And yours, but I am afraid Jack is now our prisoner. There is nothing I can say in his defence."

Penitence nodded and managed a watery smile. "At least I know where he is and that he is safe."

"The way the Thunderer is hammering at our walls, Pen, I'm not sure he is all that safe." Deliverance rose to her feet. "Now try and get some sleep and I am sure things will not seem quite so grim in the morning."

She returned downstairs with a heavy heart. At the entrance to the hall, she hesitated. Luke sat at the end of the table with his back to her. All she could see of him was his right hand, curled around the stem of a pewter wine goblet.

She thought of those long, hard fingers and their gentle touch on her skin, and for a moment her knees went weak. Luke, her would-be lover, her wooer was not this man. Luke Collyer, the soldier, sat at the table and that was how she had to deal with him.

She dropped the key on the table in front of him. He looked at it without moving.

"Keep it," he said. "I don't have time to be your sister's jailer. It would be better for you to take care of her."

"How long to do you intend to keep her locked up?" Deliverance enquired.

Luke looked up. The steel had gone from his eyes and in that brief unguarded moment she saw the difficult position Penitence's selfish actions had put him in. Condemning a man to death had to be the hardest decision he would ever have to make, particularly a man whose only real crime was loyalty to his mistress.

"For as long as is necessary."

"You don't really think that she was passing intelligence to Jack, do you?"

"I don't know what to think, Deliverance. She may not have been aware she was doing it. A wrong word, a whispered confidence could have been all it took."

"What about Truscott?"

His face instantly hardened. "There is no excusing Truscott. This is war, Deliverance. No quarter was given to the garrison at Byton remember. Is that what you want for Kinton Lacey?"

She lowered her eyes and shook her head.

He pushed the goblet away and ran a hand over his eyes. "Deliverance, Farrington knows everything that is going on within these walls. Someone is passing him that information. Whether it was Penitence or something she may have said to Jack without thought, lives will be lost and Truscott is as much a party to those deaths as if he had been the one who had handed over the information himself. An example has to be set."

"I see," Deliverance said with a heavy heart.

He looked up at her. "You're not going to argue with me?"

She shook her head. "No, because as awful as it sounds, you are right, Luke. Now excuse me, I am going to bed."

She left him alone in the Great Hall and crawled alone into the big bed. She had become used to sharing it with Penitence.

She lay awake thinking of her sister and her love for Jack Farrington, and felt nothing but pity. A way had to be found of making this right.

Chapter Seventeen

Luke stood back and let Hale unbolt the door of the room in the Jewel Tower where they had incarcerated Jack Farrington. He had given the prisoner six hours to consider his fate and to judge by his red-rimmed eyes and hollow cheeks, they must have been very long hours indeed.

Farrington sprang to his feet. "Is Penitence all right? What have you done to her?"

"She's fine," Luke said. "Just trimmed her wings a little. Sit down, Farrington, we need to talk." Jack subsided on to the stool and buried his head in his hands.

"She's innocent," he mumbled. "We both are."

Luke surveyed the wretched specimen of manhood. He was almost on the point of believing the pair's protestations. They were probably guilty of nothing more than stupidity but lesser men had been hanged for that crime.

"What am I to do with you?" Luke said, with a heavy sigh. "The last thing I need at the moment is a prisoner. We barely have enough to feed the garrison." He leaned against the wall with his arms crossed. "If I am to believe that you and Penitence are not the traitors, who does your brother have working for him in the Castle?"

Jack looked up, genuine surprise on his face. "I've no idea. Charles keeps his own counsel on these matters. "

So would I, thought Luke. This man seemed incapable of dissembling and Luke admitted to himself that he had to accept Jack told the truth.

"So your meetings with Penitence Felton were nothing more than lover's trysts?"

"You have my word on it," Jack said, misery written on his face and in the way his shoulders slumped.

Luke studied the younger man for a full minute without speaking. He considered the value of interrogating Jack at greater length about his brother's plans, if Jack was privy to them, which he doubted.

Jack's main worth to him was as a hostage. Even if Charles Farrington was incapable of feeling anything for anyone Charles would still have to answer to his father, and mother, about his brother's fate and that made him useful.

He wondered about Jack's relationship with his brother and it made him think of his own brother, Nicholas, whose face he dreaded seeing on a battlefield. Every time he had taken the field, he had scanned the faces of the men he faced wondering if would he even recognise Nick before it was too late.

"What are you going to do with me?" Jack ventured, rousing Luke from his reverie.

Luke straightened and turned for the door. "Nothing for the moment. Enjoy the rest but I warn you the neighbours can be a little rowdy."

As his hand touched the latch, Jack's voice came from behind him. "Collyer."

Luke turned his head to look at the young man. Jack looked up at the narrow window embrasure and sighed. "Collyer, there is something I need to talk to you about."

Luke turned back into the room and stood looking down at the younger man. "I'm listening."

An hour later, Luke left the room, shutting and locking the door behind him. He tossed the key in his hand. He couldn't spare a man to guard the room and with a Farrington agent on the loose he trusted the key to no one but himself. Back in his bedchamber he found a leather thong and hung the key around his neck.

Coming downstairs in the morning, Deliverance found herself confronted by a deputation of Kinton Lacey men. She had known them all her life and she knew why they had come. She listened to them plead the case for Truscott and promised she would do what she could to ensure he did not hang at noon.

After they had left she sat in the large chair at the long table and looked up at the portraits of her Felton forebears. What did you do when you could see both sides of an argument? She didn't think Truscott deserved to hang for being complicit in a lovers' tryst but on the other hand they had four hundred men at their gates intent on their destruction. As Luke would say, this was war, in all its brutality, and it was about setting an example. Putting her personal feelings to one side she understood that they could not afford to risk such a breach of discipline or there would be deaths, more deaths than just the life of one man. However pure his motives, Truscott had to be punished.

Her fingers tapped the table. Maybe a good flogging might have the desired effect? She had never seen a man flogged. Her guts clenched at the thought but surely it had to be better than hanging.

She rose and went in search of Luke. From the top of the stairs leading to the residence she saw him striding across the courtyard towards the Hawk Tower. She caught up with him as he entered the staircase.

"Luke."

"Good morning, Mistress Felton," he said without breaking stride. "I have to talk to you about Truscott," she said.

"You talked to me about Truscott last night. There is nothing more to be said."

His pace and her skirts made the climb up the narrow circular staircase difficult, and she was panting with the exertion, which made pleading a cause extremely difficult.

As she puffed behind him, he continued to ignore her, taking the stairs two at a time.

A light breeze fluttered the Felton pennant at the top of Hawk Tower, and Deliverance leaned against the doorway catching her breath while Luke crossed to the wall. He laid a hand on one of the weathered hawks and gazed out across the besieging forces.

Deliverance took up a place beside him. She considered going down on her knees like a true supplicant but that thought galled her and she decided to leave that measure to the last.

"Luke, please. I am asking you to show clemency for Truscott."

"Tell me again why I should do that?" he said, his gaze not moving from the enemy encampment.

"What he did was wrong but you have to understand he has known Penitence since she was born. He...any of my men...would do anything for her."

"Just because a pretty woman asks you to do something you know is wrong is no excuse, Deliverance."

"I know this is a war and I know Jack Farrington is our enemy but before that he was our friend and betrothed to Penitence. This is a *civil* war, Luke. It's not as if the Farringtons are foreign enemy. Jack has been coming to Kinton Lacey since he was a boy."

"Someone within this castle is prepared to sell all our lives to the enemy, Deliverance. I know it's not Truscott but an example has to be set."

"Surely some lesser punishment?" She swallowed. "A flogging?" Luke straightened.

"Luke—"

"This is not the time for discussion. Get down!" Luke turned, leaping at Deliverance and taking her to the ground as the Thunderer let off a mighty roar. The world exploded around them.

Deliverance hit the stonework with such force it knocked the breath from her. Instinctively she put her arms over her head as showers of dust and pieces of stone rained down around her. She knew what had happened. Hawk Tower had taken a direct hit from the Thunderer.

She lay for a long time, her eyes tightly closed, fighting for breath, incapable of moving. She drew a shaky breath and tentatively moved her fingers and toes. She felt no pain but there appeared to be a heavy weight lying across body and she couldn't move her arms or legs. She opened her eyes blinking at the brightness of the sky. Luke lay sprawled across her, pinning her to the ground.

He lay quite still with his face turned away from her and she realised he must have thrown himself across her as the cannon ball hit.

"Luke?"

When he didn't respond, she freed her pinioned arms and pushed at him but he didn't move. Dear God, he couldn't be dead...could he?

"Luke?" She touched his head and hastily removed her hand when she felt something warm and wet. She looked at her fingers, sticky with Luke's blood. The breath stopped in her throat.

No, he can't be dead...

With difficulty, she wriggled out from underneath him. Her heart hammering she knelt beside his senseless body, her hands fluttering uselessly over him. Blood matted his dark hair just above his right ear, dripping down his face and transforming the familiar features into a bloody mask.

A musket ball zinged past her ear and she looked up, seeing the place where she and Luke had been standing arguing about Truscott only moments before, was now a gaping hole as if some giant had taken a bite out of the tower. Bits of rock and dust lay scattered across the full width of the remaining platform of the tower. Nothing stood between her and a long fall to the ground and she was completely exposed to the enemy lines. Musketeers lined the nearest earthwork, intent on only one thing.

Her death.

She stood up and seizing Luke by the collar, dragged him towards the stairwell. She had no idea an unconscious man could weigh so much and without help she'd never get him down to safety. Another musket ball whistled over her head, crashing into the wall behind her.

In the shelter of the doorway, she crouched down. At least they were now out of sight of the musketeers and she could see to Luke.

She gathered herself together and forced herself to look down at his slack, blood spattered face. "You're not dead," she told him. "You can't be dead."

She tugged at his collar and her shaking fingers searched for and found the pulse in his neck, beating slow and steady. She realised she had been holding her breath and let out a sigh of relief. Having established he was still alive she turned her attention to the wound in his hairline. It had bled profusely but on close inspection did not look like much more than a deep cut.

"Luke, wake up!" She patted his cheek with some force. He stirred and moaned but did not open his eyes.

Hearing footsteps on the stairs she looked up as Ned and two men appeared around the corner. Ned's eyes travelled from the gaping hole in the tower to Luke's unconscious face.

"He's alive," Deliverance said in answer to the unspoken question on Ned's face.

Relief flooded Ned's face. "And you? Are you all right?"

Deliverance nodded concealing her shaking hands in the folds of her skirt. Now she started to think about it, her legs had begun to feel most peculiar too. She sat back against the wall.

"Just a little wobbly."

Luke...she wanted to say Luke had saved her life but couldn't find the words.

Ned knelt down beside his friend and slapped his face with considerably more force than Deliverance had used.

The action provoked a groan from Luke and his eyes flickered open. "What...? Ouch." He closed his eyes again with a grimace.

"You've had a knock on the head, Collyer. Lots of blood but I doubt there's any real damage. You were always blessed with a thick skull."

"Go away... my head hurts," Luke mumbled.

Ned stood up dusting his breeches and gestured to the two soldiers waiting in the stairwell. "Get him to his chamber. I'll see to Mistress Felton."

After the two soldiers had none-too-gently hefted Luke by his shoulders and legs and begun the tortuous descent down the narrow winding stairs, Ned put his hand out for Deliverance. She rose up on shaking legs and did not demur at the strong male arm that circled her shoulders, helping her down the stairs and across the courtyard to the sanctuary of her own bedchamber and the care of her women.

Deliverance sat on the stool in her bed chamber looking down at the blood on her hands. Luke's blood. At the thought of how close they had both come to death and how he had saved her life, she began to cry. What if he had died? What would she do without him?

Meg put an arm around her mistress. "There, there, ma'am," she said. "You've had a nasty fright. I'll go and fetch a nice posset for ye."

"I'd prefer brandy," Deliverance said. She fumbled at her belt and handed her keys to the maid. "It's in the locked cupboard in my father's library and" she looked up at Meg, "can you release my sister and send her to me."

"Aye, mistress. Right away," Meg said.

As her maid reached the door, Deliverance added, "and give Lieutenant Barrett an order from me. I am repreiving Truscott's sentence of death."

Meg's eyes widened slightly but she bobbed a neat curtsey and left without comment.

Alone, Deliverance wrapped her arms around herself, rocking back and forth as the tears poured down her dusty cheeks. She didn't even hear the door open, or her sister enter the room until she felt Penitence's arms around her.

"Oh, Liv, thank the Lord you are safe," Penitence said. "I heard the explosion. Meg says you and Collyer were on Hawk Tower when the round hit."

Deliverance sobbed into her sister's shoulder. "He saved my life, Pen."

"Who?"

"Luke and now he's hurt. What if he dies?"

Penitence hushed her as if she were a child as Meg reappeared with the brandy and water. Together the two women washed the worst of the dust and dirt from Deliverance's face and hands but when they suggested she take to her bed to rest, she refused. Instead she took a hefty gulp of brandy and rose unsteadily to her feet.

"I'm fine. Don't fuss," she lied.

"Liv, you've had a nasty shock. I really think you should rest."

"I need to see if Luke is all right."

"I'll go," Penitence offered.

Deliverance shook her head. "No. I must see for myself."

At the door she stopped. "Pen, you must give me your word, you won't try and see Jack?"

Penitence's mouth drooped and she nodded. "You have my parole. Just please don't lock me up again."

With Toby still incarcerated, Deliverance found his sister in attendance in Luke's bed chamber.

Lovedie looked up from winding clean bandages as Deliverance entered. She stood and dropped a curtsey.

Deliverance waved a hand at the door. "You can leave."

Lovedie didn't move.

"You should rest, Mistress Felton," Lovedie said. "You've had a bad fright today."

"I'm fine. I'll sit with Captain Collyer for a little while. Please fetch me a little broth."

Lovedie's mouth compressed in a tight line and she gave Deliverance another small bob curtsey before leaving the room.

Deliverance waited until the door shut behind the girl before moving across to the bed. She stood for a moment looking down into Luke's ashen face, made paler by the neat bandage tied around his head. A slight starring of crimson on the white linen marked where the wound had bled but it did not seem to be spreading. Deliverance sat down on the end of Luke's bed, pulling her feet up beneath her. She wrapped her arms around her knees, watching the gentle rise and fall of his chest as she remembered the argument that had preceded the missile thrown up by the Thunderer. If those had been the last words they had exchanged...

He stirred and grimaced, life flooding back into his face. His eyes opened and he looked up at the panelled ceiling of Sir John Felton's best bed.

"How do you feel?" Deliverance asked.

He raised his head slightly to see where the voice had come from and fell back on the pillows with a curse. "I've got a headache to rival the worst excesses of drink," he said closing his eyes. He beckoned her with his right hand, patting the bed next to him. "Move closer...can't see you down there."

Deliverance obliged, perching on the side of the bed next to him. He looked up at her and smiled. "How are you?"

"I'm fine...thanks to you. You saved my life," Deliverance said, her fingers closing over his hand that lay on the outside of the covers.

"Anything to silence you." He closed his eyes and grimaced. "What were we arguing about?"

"Nothing of importance," Deliverance said.

Not now she had taken command and rescinded the execution order. Luke didn't need to be bothered with such things right now.

"That bloody gun," Luke muttered. "It will beat us into submission."

"I know," Deliverance said and instinctively shut her eyes as another shot from the Thunderer crashed into the Hawk Tower, rattling her teeth. The gunners had their aim now. The tower would be gone by nightfall.

When she opened her eyes she saw Luke looking at her. He raised a hand and his finger lightly brushed her cheek.

"I do love you, you know," he said.

She stared at him. "Don't be silly. You are feverish," she said, as her heart cried out *'Tell him you love him too. Now before it is too late.'*

"Could never...Didn't mean..." His eyelids flickered and closed, his hand falling to the bedcovers. For a horrible moment, Deliverance thought he had died but the gentle rise and fall of his chest assured her he had only fallen asleep.

She sat looking at him, her heart swelling with his words. He had said he loved her.

Why couldn't she have brought herself to repeat the words back to him?

She put out her hand and with the back of her forefinger stroked his cheek, feeling the rough bristle beneath her skin. His eyelids fluttered before he muttered something and sank back into sleep.

"I love you, Luke Collyer," Deliverance whispered, voicing the words at last.

She bent down and kissed him gently on the mouth. His lips were soft and unresponsive beneath her touch. She picked up his hand and pressed it to her cheek as cold fingers clawed at her heart. She had come so close to losing him and she couldn't bear the thought of living without him.

If he died...

She gave a strangled sob, biting it back as the door opened and Lovedie re-entered the room, carrying a tray with a bowl of the weak broth that would be their main meal for the day. Deliverance restored Luke's hand and hastily stood up making a show of straightening the bed clothes.

"Mistress Felton?" Lovedie asked. "Are you alright?

"I'm fine," Deliverance said. "Just a little tired."

Lovedie bent over the man in the bed and smoothed his pillow, fiery curls falling around her face from beneath her cap.

"You've had a bad shock today. I'd go and get some rest," Lovedie said without looking up.

The green demon of jealousy gripped Deliverance as Lovedie stroked Luke's cheek. Had she missed something? Was Lovedie the reason Luke had pulled away from her? She had no doubt in normal times Lovedie Brown would be exactly the sort of girl, Luke Collyer would have pursued.

She hated leaving Luke with the girl but being around Luke Collyer seemed to turn her reasoning power to gruel and she needed to think.

Deliverance strode from the room. She reached the library and shut the door.

Chapter Eighteen

As dark descended on Kinton Lacey, the Thunderer finally fell silent. Deliverance left her father's library where she had spent the day, trying to distract herself from the destruction of the Hawk Tower with an illicit copy of Shakespeare's plays she had purchased on a long ago visit to her bookseller in Ludlow. Her restless wandering took her to the East wall. As the moon rose, she leaned on the wall looking down at the dark ribbon of the river beneath her.

Behind her the castle inhabitants, subdued by the pounding of the Thunderer, were inspecting the damage. Sergeant Hale's booming voice reached her as he supervised the clearing of the rubble and she knew if she turned around she would see the ruins of the Hawk Tower rising like a broken tooth above the wall. The once mighty tower where she and Luke had argued only that morning had been reduced to rubble.

She didn't want to look. She wanted to be down there, beside the river, away from the stench of the castle. After several weeks the effect of one hundred human beings living in close proximity along with assorted livestock, had begun to overpower the castle and the smell from the midden they had created in the ditch outside the south wall of the tower was overpowering.

She thought of the cool, peaceful pond. Never before had the need to talk to James been so strong.

It would be so easy to slip through the sally port and ... She dismissed the thought. To leave the castle would be utter madness.

"There you are."

At the sound of her sister's voice, Deliverance turned her head.

"What are you doing out here?" Penitence enquired and shivered, wrapping her arms around her. "It's cold, come inside, Liv."

Deliverance leaned on the wall, her head in her hands. "I can't think any more, Pen." "It's the effect of that gun," Penitence said. "My ears are ringing."

Deliverance shook her head. "No, it's more than that. I'm so tired."

Penitence put her hand on her sister's arm. "Have something to eat and an early night. You will feel better."

Deliverance let her sister lead her away but Penitence overestimated the restorative power of the weak broth that constituted their supper and even after they had gone to bed, Deliverance lay awake staring at the panelling of the bed above her.

When the castle finally fell silent, she rose, dressing in an anteroom. She crept through the residence, pausing outside Luke's door. Candle light shone through the half-open door and she entered, grateful to find him alone and unattended. He had slept through the day and now lay sprawled across the big bed, still asleep.

She looked down at his face, peaceful in the candlelight and her heart swelled. She drew up a stool to the bed so her face would be on a level with his and stroked his unshaven cheek. They couldn't go on like this, not when people she cared about were getting hurt.

If only I could clear my head, she thought in despair.

She picked up Luke's hand, pressing his fingers to her lips.

So tired... She laid her head on the bed, her fingers still meshed in Luke's.

Behind her the door clicked open. At the sound of skirts she sighed. Lovedie had returned.

She shook herself awake, releasing Luke's hand and straightening

"It's all right, Lovedie. I'll sit with him," she said without looking around.

"'Tis good you're here, Mistress," Lovedie said. "You've made it so much easier for me."

The girl moved behind her. Deliverance's nose twitched at the scent of raw perspiration and something else, indefinable and acrid. From the corner of her eye, Deliverance caught the cold glint of steel and a knife bit into her throat. She squeaked in alarm, prompting Lovedie to press the knife harder. The knife pressed harder and a trickle of blood left a warm trail down her neck.

"Don't make any sudden moves, Mistress Felton," Lovedie whispered in her ear.

"Make no mistake, Mistress Felton, one move and you will be dead. Now stand up slowly."

Deliverance complied, rising on shaking legs. She swallowed, feeling the sharp blade of the knife against the thin flesh of her throat. One slip and she would be dead. Her gaze dropped to Luke as she wondered how she could wake him.

Lovedie gave a low, unpleasant laugh. "Don't you be looking to him for help. I've given him a sleeping draught that will keep him quiet till morning."

She saw the whole situation with biting clarity and cursed herself for a fool for not guessing sooner.

Everything pointed to Lovedie. "You're Farrington's agent?"

"Time to talk later, my lady. You're coming with me."

The knife withdrew from her throat but if Deliverance had any thoughts of escape, they dissipated as she felt the sharp point against her ribs. Lovedie jerked the knife, pushing her towards the door.

"After you," Lovedie said, her tone calm. The very calmness of her tone, made Deliverance's skin prickle with fear.

To a casual observer, they would have appeared to be two women walking side-by-side but they encountered no one as they slipped out of the side door of the residence and crossed the short distance to the Jewel Tower. Deliverance scanned the wall looking for the sentry but the wall was dark and still.

Lovedie pushed her inside the door and up the stairs to the room where Jack Farrington was imprisoned. At the door, Lovedie stopped. She held out a key on a leather thong.

"Unlock the door," she ordered.

With shaking fingers, Deliverance complied, stumbling as Lovedie pushed her across the threshold.

Jack Farrington sat up on the cot, pushing hair from his eyes. "Deliverance? What's happening?"

"No time for polite chatter, Captain Farrington," Lovedie said. "You're coming with us. Yer brother is waiting."

"You're his agent?" Jack sounded shocked, but even as he spoke he was reaching for his jacket and boots.

"Deliverance, I'm sorry..." Jack stood.

Lovedie gave a hiss of exasperation. "She's coming with us. Now hurry up."

They stumbled out of the Jewel Tower and keeping to the shadows, crept along the wall to the sally port. Deliverance cast around for a sign of the sentry but it was only as they stepped into the dark recess of the gate that she saw the still form slumped against the wall.

She turned to the woman behind her. "What have you done to him?"

Lovedie's answer was to press the knife harder against her ribs. She tossed a key to Jack, and Deliverance was in no doubt that it would be the same key that Luke had taken off Penitence. Lovedie had been through Luke's possessions.

Jack unlocked the gate and they slipped through into the corridor, carved in the rock, that led out on to the narrow path. Jack relocked the gate behind him.

Deliverance knew this path well but even though Lovedie relaxed her grip, there was no chance of escape and her disappearance would not be noticed for hours yet. With Jack in front and Lovedie behind with the knife still at her back, she had nowhere to go.

They made the riverside path and once again, Lovedie took Deliverance's arm, pressing the knife into her ribs.

"Not a sound," she whispered, pushing Deliverance ahead of her towards the woods.

Once they gained the shelter of the trees, they stopped. Deliverance scanned the dark trees and the breath in her throat stopped as five dark shapes stepped out of the shadow, men in dark clothes with their shapeless felt hats pulled down well over their faces so she wouldn't see the glow of white faces.

Four muskets and a pistol were levelled at her.

"Now then, Mistress Felton, it's late to be taking a stroll by the river," the man holding the pistol spoke. She didn't recognise his voice. How did he know who he was addressing?

"Come along with us. The Colonel is waiting for you."

The clergyman's house in the village had been commandeered as the Farrington headquarters and it struck Deliverance as strange to be standing on such a familiar doorstep as the commander of her guard knocked on the door.

Leaving the four common soldiers on the doorstep, accompanied by the young officer, Deliverance, Jack and Lovedie were shown into the parlour.

Charles Farrington stood by the fireplace, a glass of wine in one hand. To judge by his unshaven chin and crooked shirt collar, he had been roused from his bed but there was nothing soporific about his eyes. They gleamed with malevolent delight and he held out his hand to Lovedie.

She went to him and he drew her in to him, kissing her on the mouth. "You've done well," he said.

He put his arm around the girl's waist and turned to face Deliverance. "Mistress Felton, welcome to my humble abode. I have a pleasant bedchamber prepared for you. As for you," he turned to his brother, "what in God's name were you playing at, trysting with Penitence Felton. You deserved to be caught."

The young man flushed beetroot red under his brother's withering condemnation. Deliverance almost felt sorry for him. It had never been easy for Jack, living in his brother's shadow.

"Sorry, Charles. It was stupid of me."

"Stupid," Charles expostulated. "You could have ruined everything. It was just fortunate that we managed to bring Collyer down. Is he going to live?" He asked Lovedie.

She pulled a face. "Aye. He'll be up and around in the morning."

"Pity you didn't think to dispatch him before you left."

Lovedie glared at Deliverance. "I would have but I found this one in his chamber."

Deliverance's heart jolted. If she hadn't been there, would she have been the one to find Luke in the morning with his throat cut or would Lovedie have come in search of her after dispatching Luke?

Charles shrugged. "It makes no difference. One way or another, Collyer will be dead by sunset tomorrow."

Chapter Nineteen

Deliverance passed a sleepless night on a hard, narrow cot in a small room at the top of the stairs. She lay awake staring at the small patch of black sky through the high window. When exhaustion eventually claimed her, she dreamed of explosions, and Luke lying dead with blood around his head. She woke in a cold sweat.

A grey light now filtered in through the window. The endless night had passed and daylight was not far off. A day that could only end in death. Hers? Luke's? How many of her garrison?

As she lay with her hands clenched together, , planning how best to deal with Charles Farrington the next time she saw him, she heard the key turn in the lock. She sat up, swinging her feet to the floor as the door opened.

The smell of fresh baked bread made her traitorous stomach growl but she lost her appetite when she saw who carried the tray.

"Lovedie." The name fell from her lips, dripping with venom. "You treacherous harlot. I'll see you hang."

"Now, now, Mistress Felton, that's no way to talk to me," Lovedie responded, setting the tray down on the floor. She straightened and surveyed Deliverance's dishevelled appearance with her hands on her hips. "Not such a fine lady now, are you...ma'am?"

Deliverance rose to her feet with what shreds of dignity she could muster and faced the girl.

Lovedie's long tresses were no longer confined in a modest cap, but hung in glowing waves around her shoulders, displayed for view in an indecorous and inappropriate gown of green satin. She looked like the slattern she had proved herself to be.

"How long have you and Farrington, been...been..."

The girl gave her a cool, appraising look. "Lovers?" Lovedie shut the door and leaned against it, crossing her arms. "That day you and Collyer came to Byton, I could see how things would be if I stayed, so as soon as Charles and his father were on the horizon, I offered my services to Charles."

"And did you play agent in Byton?"

Lovedie gave a snort of derision. "Curtis was fool enough to be his own destruction but I might have helped a little."

"But your own brother was in Byton. You must have known what would befall it."

She had hit a nerve. Lovedie straightened and sniffed. "Toby's old enough to know his own mind."

"Does he know about you?"

"Toby? Don't be a fool, of course he doesn't." Lovedie took a step forward. "I want you to know, Mistress Felton, that Toby had no knowledge of," she paused as if searching for the word, "my business."

"Your 'business'?" Deliverance drew herself up to her full height, failing to overtop Lovedie. "It was you who destroyed the food?"

Lovedie nodded. "Of course. It was a simple matter to copy your key."

"And did my sister or Jack Farrington, have any part of this?"

Lovedie laughed. "Jack Farrington hasn't got the stomach for war. He's a quarter of the man his brother is but once the plan changed I had to get him out of the castle. Couldn't leave him there for Collyer to bargain with."

Deliverance shivered. "The plan changed? What did you intend?"

She shrugged. "I was to seduce Collyer and then see to him one night." She drew a finger across her throat and Deliverance shivered. "Without Collyer you'd have had to surrender." She frowned. "But he wouldn't have any part of that. Him being wounded was a godsend. I knew all I had to do was finish him off, take the key and release Jack and you'd have nothing to bargain with."

Deliverance blinked trying to digest everything Lovedie had just said. Traitorously the only thing that came to mind was the revelation that Lovedie had tried to seduce Luke and failed. That thought made her feel oddly happy.

But she didn't have long to process the implication as Lovedie stepped aside to let Charles Farrington into the room.

He stood in the doorway, his legs apart and his hands on his hips.

"Lovedie, my dear, you talk too much. The solution to your current difficulty must be clear to you. If Collyer wants you kept in one piece, my dear Deliverance, he will hand over Kinton Lacey to me this morning."

Deliverance whirled around to face him, trying to muster her last ounce of defiance and courage. Jack Farrington stood behind his brother. The younger man looked grey with fatigue. "And what would you do with me if he doesn't agree?"

Farrington appeared to consider that point. "That's a good question. Probably hang you in sight of the castle. That would be amusing."

Deliverance flew at Charles, her fingers clawed and reaching for his face. She managed to drag her nails down one side before Lovedie and Jack pulled her off.

Charles mopped the blood from his face, his eyes blazing. "You'll pay for that, you little cat." He advanced on her with an upraised hand.

Jack twisted her out of his reach. "Leave her, Charles. You wouldn't dare hang her and you know it."

To her surprise Farrington lowered his hand and reached out and clasped her chin, twisting her face up to look at him. "No, that would be too easy. There are other ways of dealing with you, Deliverance. You need to learn a little humility and that you are only a woman who should stop playing a man's game." His eyes narrowed. "There is only one good use for a woman, and trust me, that would give me great pleasure. I might be generous enough to share you with some of my men in plain sight of the castle walls." The obscene tilting of his hips made his meaning clear.

Jack gave a sharp intake of breath but said nothing.

A wave of nausea enveloped Deliverance. There were worse things than death for a woman caught in the middle of a war. Although she hoped that even Charles Farrington would not resort to public rape and humiliation, she would not put it past him.

Charles flung her back at Lovedie. "Shut her up again. We'll give Collyer time to realise his precious Deliverance is missing and then surprise him."

Luke woke at first light with a thudding headache. He lay still for a long time trying to recall the events of the previous day. Deliverance. That damned woman. There'd been some argument and then...nothing. He frowned and put a hand to his head, feeling his way around the bandage until he reached a recognisable lump of padding. He gingerly pressed it producing lightning bolts of pain.

Penitence appeared in the doorway with a tray of breakfast.

"Oh, good. You're awake," she said, setting the tray down on the table.

Luke grunted a response and was about to swing his bare feet on to the floor when he realised he was naked. He pulled the sheet up to his chest.

"Pass me my breeches." He pointed to the chair where his clothes had been hung.

Penitence put her hands on her hips and regarded him. "You shouldn't be out of bed. You need to rest..."

"Bloody nonsense," Luke swore. "Breeches, woman."

With a snort, Penitence threw the garments at him, and he managed to pull them on beneath the bedclothes.

He rose gingerly, and the room tilted and swum alarmingly for a moment or two before righting itself. Penitence helped him with the rest of his clothes and he swallowed down most of the meagre breakfast, hoping he would manage to keep it down. He needed his strength to deal with Deliverance.

Penitence sat across from him as he ate, her hands folded in her lap. He looked at her, frowning as shreds of memory started to come back into his fuzzy mind. "What are you doing here? Didn't I have you locked up?"

Penitence flushed and lowered her eyes. "I gave Deliverance my parole," she said.

Deliverance. Trust her to countermand his orders. No doubt that man, Truscott, had been reprieved as well. The list of matters he needed to discuss with her was growing by the minute.

"Where is Deliverance?" he demanded. "I have to talk to her."

Penitence's lips tightened and she swallowed. "I don't know. She disappeared in the night without leaving a note or any sign as to where she has gone. Ned is searching the castle."

Penitence's hands twisted in her lap. "There's more... Lovedie's gone as well, and Jack Farrington." Luke's hand flew to his neck. The key to Farrington's cell was missing. He rose to his feet as Ned flung the door open and stood in the doorway, flushed with the exertion of running.

"Collyer, thank God you're up. The man we put on the sally port last night—he's dead."

That news came as no surprise. The sally port may as well have been High Holborn with all the people coming and going through it. Luke went to run his hand through his hair and then remembered his injury.

"How?"

"Knife through the ribs. Neat job."

And easy for an attractive woman, Luke thought, seeing the plot unfold. Lovedie had taken the key, released Jack and made their escape. A cold tremor of fear ran through him.

What about Deliverance?

He leaned on the table to gather his thoughts. "I think we can assume that our enemy agent was Lovedie Brown. She's made good her escape with Farrington and," he paused, hardly daring to voice the thought, "and possibly Deliverance."

Penitence gave a sharp intake of breath, her hand rising to her throat. "If Farrington has her..."

Luke turned his gaze on her. "One thing at a time, Penitence. We don't know that. Ned, bring me the Brown boy. I'll be in the Great Hall."

Two burly soldiers, accompanied by Sergeant Hale and Melchior Blakelocke, escorted the boy into the hall, depositing Toby at Luke's feet where the boy huddled, close to tears.

Luke looked down at the boy with little sympathy. "Your sister's gone taking Jack Farrington with her. What do you know about your traitorous sister's activities, Toby?"

Toby looked back at him with large, frightened eyes. "Lovedie? What's she done?"

Luke crossed to him and grasped him by the front of his shirt, pulling him to his feet. "Where's your sister?"

"She'll have gone back to Farrington," the boy blurted out. "I told her he was no good." Luke stared at him. "Gone back to Farrington? What do you mean?"

"She was with him at Byton but I thought when I saw her here that she had..." the boy's brow creased and tears filled his eyes."Oh sir, I don't know what I thought."

"Did you know your sister was the traitor in these walls?" Luke demanded.

The boy shook his head, his eyes large with fear and disbelief, and this time Luke believed him. Toby crumpled to the ground at his feet.

"I'm your man, Cap'n Collyer. I'd no part in her wicked ways." Toby snivelled. Luke looked at the faces of his officers. No further explanation was necessary. "Do you think she's taken Deliverance?" Penitence ventured.

"I'm sure of it," Luke replied. "But just to be sure, I want another search of the castle..."

He got no further as one of the men came charging into the hall. "Captain Collyer. Come quickly, you're wanted on the wall."

"It can wait." Luke rounded on the man.

"It's Colonel Farrington and he's got Mistress Felton with him," the man said, his breath coming in short gasps from his haste.

Deliverance...in the hands of a man who had murdered a garrison in cold blood.

Ignoring the pain that rapid movement caused to his throbbing head, he ran out into the courtyard and up the steps to the curtain wall beside the gatehouse.

Farrington stood just out of range of the muskets, surrounded by his own men. His left hand held Deliverance's upper arm and his right hand a pistol, its muzzle resting just above her right ear.

He scanned Deliverance's face looking for signs of violence. Even at the distance, she looked dishevelled but otherwise unhurt.

"Collyer," Farrington shouted, his voice carrying well in the still air. "I think the time has come to discuss surrender."

"What are your terms?" Luke responded.

Farrington laughed. "I don't think we need to discuss terms do we? The terms are simple, your unconditional surrender for the life of this girl."

Surrender or Deliverance dies? What choice did he have?

"What are you going to do?" Ned asked, tight-lipped. "He wouldn't really kill her would he?"

"You saw what he did at Byton? He's capable of anything, Ned. He may not kill her but by all that is infernal, there are other things he can do."

Ned paled beneath his freckles. "God help us all."

Luke turned back and looked down at Farrington.

"I will give you an answer in an hour, Colonel," he said.

"An hour? It would seem to me that your answer is fairly clear, Collyer." "I must consult with the lady's family," Luke said.

"Very well. An hour, Collyer."

"Who is there to consult?" Ned said in a low voice. Luke looked at Penitence. "Well?"

Penitence turned despairing eyes on him. "Save her!"

Luke turned his eyes heavenwards. "We need a distraction."

Chapter Twenty

Deliverance sat on a stool in the corner of the clergyman's parlour, sunk in despondency. An hour glass stood on the table in front of Charles Farrington and he leaned back in his chair watching the sand trickle through it. Lovedie had draped herself across the back of his chair and was occupied in curling his hair in her fingers.

"What will you do to the garrison?" Deliverance ventured.

Charles tore his gaze away from the glass and looked at her. "What do you think I will do?" "Byton?" She spat the name out.

He stared at the ceiling. "Probably not all the garrison. Father would not like that and it wouldn't be necessary. Collyer and the other officers will suffice. I think I will hang them from the gatehouse. That will serve as a pleasant warning."

Deliverance suppressed the sob that rose to her throat.

"Oh, look at her," Lovedie said. "She's sweet on Collyer, you know?"

Charles caught Lovedie's hand and kissed it. "Is she indeed? So, Deliverance Felton, it will pain you to watch Collyer die?"

Deliverance did not respond.

"I will think of something drawn out and gruesome for your lover," Charles said with a smirk. "And I will make you and the whole of the Kinton Lacey garrison watch him die in agony."

"Charles," Jack protested.

"Oh, don't be so soft, brother. These rebels need to be taught a lesson."

The last grains of sand trickled through the glass and Charles jerked to his feet, dislodging Lovedie. He handed one of his pistols to Jack.

"You bring Mistress Felton and if she makes one wrong move, kill her."

He laughed as he saw the look of horror on Jack's face. He picked up the second pistol, pointing it directly at Deliverance. "If you don't, I will."

Jack's fingers closed on Deliverance's arm as he pulled her to her feet. She searched his face for a spark of sympathy but saw only the cold gleam of utter commitment. Whatever Jack's feelings for Penitence, his loyalty to his father and brother appeared to be absolute.

She blinked in the bright daylight of a beautiful day. Jack pushed her before him and she saw the faces of Farrington's garrison, watching them with interest as they passed. A few made lewd gestures, indicating that rumours of Charles' intended punishment had gone around the camp. Regardless of the castle's surrender, she would not escape that fate, of that she was certain. Nausea rose in her throat and for a moment she thought she would cry.

Gathering her courage she tilted her chin and straightened her shoulders. She was Deliverance Felton and she was damned if she would let these men see her snivelling like a feeble-minded child.

They stopped just out of musket range of the castle defenders. Deliverance looked up at the castle walls and saw the faces of her garrison ranged across the curtain wall. She ran her eye along the wall, doing a mental count of heads until she reached Melchior Blakelocke's unmistakable figure and beside him, no doubt standing on the box that she had stood on, her fair hair blowing in the wind and wearing the same red dress Deliverance had worn to issue her defiance, Penitence.

Jack's fingers tightened on Deliverance's arm. He had seen Penitence. She glanced around at him seeing for a brief moment the utter misery on his face.

"Jack, it doesn't have to be—" she began but he pressed the pistol to her neck.

"Not a word, Deliverance," he said in a voice that sounded so unlike Jack that all she could do was nod.

"Well, well, that milksop of a girl you were so keen on, Jack. Mistress Penitence Felton. I wouldn't have thought she had it in her," Charles remarked. He raised his voice. "Mistress Felton? Do you have an answer for me?"

Penitence's voice, clear in the still, soft air drifted across towards them.

"You have my surrender," she said. Deliverance's heart sank.

No, Penitence, you don't know what you've done. It will be for nothing. You have condemned Luke to death and me.

She glanced at Charles and shuddered.

"Excellent," Farrington responded, "Now send out Collyer, unarmed and I want to see the hands of every man on the wall."

It seemed a long moment before Penitence replied. "Very well."

As she spoke the gates opened wide and Luke walked through them, alone. Above him the men on the walls raised their hands above their heads.

Luke wore his mulberry-coloured jacket and his hat with a curling feather that swept around the crown. He wore no baldric or sword and carried no weapon but he walked with a quiet confidence as if this were nothing more than a pleasant stroll.

Deliverance's heart beat faster. She wanted to scream at him to go back but the words stuck in her throat.

Farrington gave a snort of satisfaction as Luke stopped within twenty feet of Farrington. Farrington gestured to two of his men. "Secure him."

Luke didn't move as the two men stepped forward, one on each side, holding his arms in a secure vice. They brought him forward until Luke stood within a few feet of Farrington. He kept his eyes fixed on Farrington's face, not even glancing at Deliverance.

A choked sob escaped her and for the first time, his gaze slid towards her.

Charles Farrington seized Deliverance's arm, jerking her away from Jack and thrust her at Luke. "Say your goodbyes, Deliverance. By sundown your precious Captain will be dead."

Deliverance fell against Luke's chest. She wrapped her arms around his waist and laid her head against his chest, not caring who saw or what they thought. His body felt hard and reassuring, the beat of his heart steady. If Charles Farrington were to have his way, by nightfall that good heart would be still.

"I'm sorry," she mumbled. "This is all my fault."

Luke, too securely held to touch her, bent his head and lips brushed her hair.

"No it's not. Just trust me, Deliverance," he whispered too softly for the two thugs who held him to hear properly.

She looked up at him and he smiled. "Jack, secure the Felton woman."

Jack pulled her away from Luke as Charles turned once again to address the woman on the wall. "Now the garrison, Mistress Felton."

Deliverance looked up. All the men had gone from the castle walls. Only Penitence, resplendent in her red dress, her fair curls tossed lightly in the breeze remained a sole sentinel by the Gatehouse tower. She looked magnificent.

From within the castle came the slow beat of a drum. Behind Farrington, the besiegers gathered to watch the humiliation of this stubborn little castle and Deliverance heard the murmuring, as if they held their collective breath.

Thrmm...thrmm...

A solitary figure appeared at the castle gate, holding the Felton standard and behind him the drummer. They walked forward slowly until they reached the end of the bridge.

"Toby," Deliverance said in a quiet voice.

As if on cue, the beat of the drum suddenly changed. Deliverance had lived with soldiers long enough now to recognise the call to arms. Above the standard and the drummer, the wall bristled with the gleam of weapons and from the ditch came a bloodcurdling battle cry.

"For Felton!"

At that command, a line of men sprang from the ditch in front of the castle and charged toward the onlookers. Ned Barrett led the charge, bareheaded, looking like a wild warrior from stories of the Celts.

Farrington's men had left their posts and their weapons to watch the tableau of the surrender and were not prepared for any attack, by however pathetic a force. Now shouted orders and the sound of general confusion enveloped her as the royalists scattered to their positions.

A smattering of musket fire came from the royalist lines but the Kinton Lacey men came onwards unhindered. As they approached a nauseating stench of human and animal excrement wafted towards the royalist lines and Deliverance saw that the men were mired to the waist. She gagged.

Farrington's eyes widened and he gestured to Deliverance. "Jack, kill her, kill her now..." Deliverance closed her eyes, steeling herself for the pistol ball. Instead the grip on her arm relaxed.

"I don't think so, Charles," Jack Farrington said in a quiet voice.

Deliverance caught her breath and opened her eyes as Jack Farrington caught his brother's neck in his arm and pressed the pistol that had been pressed to Deliverance's neck against his brother's temple.

"What are you doing?" Farrington's eyes bulged with surprise and rage.

"I think I'm turning my cloak," Jack replied calmly. "Get your men to lay down their weapons. Make no mistake, Charles, I will kill you for what you did at Byton."

The Kinton Lacey assault came to a halt and a line of muskets faced the royalist troops. A pathetically small number against the hundreds of men they faced.

"Do what he says!" Farrington screamed. "Lay down your weapons."

A mutter ran through the lines of his men and one by one they complied. "Good. Now release Collyer," Jack gestured to the two men holding Luke.

They let him go, and Luke brushed his sleeve as if removing an annoying piece of lint. "Thank you, Jack," he said and swept Deliverance a bow.

"Mistress Felton, shall we return to Kinton Lacey? Captain Farrington, your prisoner will accompany us."

Holding Charles securely by one arm with his pistol still pressed to his brother's neck, Jack moved forward, Luke and Deliverance fell into line beside him and they walked abreast back towards the line of Kinton Lacey men who parted to allow them through and then turned and followed, making a dignified, if smelly, procession back inside the castle.

Toby and the drummer, once again beating a slow march, followed and the gate shut on Kinton Lacey with all the defenders and their hostage safely within its walls.

A cheer went up as the gate swung shut with a resounding thud. Relief flooded through Luke as the portcullis chain rattled. For a brief moment he thought his legs would give way, had it not been for Deliverance.

She nestled beneath the curve of his arm, her own arm around his waist. She looked up at him. Dark rings of exhaustion circled her eyes. He bent his head and kissed her forehead as a whooping crowd of the delighted, and unharmed, garrison celebrated around them.

Charles Farrington, his face purple with rage pushed himself free of his brother and turned to face him.

"You bloody traitor. You'll hang for this," he screamed at Jack, his eyes bulging with rage. Jack looked down at the pistol in his hand.

"Not a decision made lightly, Charles," he responded. "But I couldn't in all conscience go on serving under you. Not after what you did at Byton."

"They were rebels. We needed to set an example." He swept his hand around the assembled garrison. "So these bastards knew what to expect."

"There are some rules to war, Farrington," Luke said. "And what you did will see you hanged. You are my prisoner and I intend to see you stand trial for the coldblooded murder of the Byton garrison."

He gestured to Sergeant Hale and another of his men. "Lock him up."

"I'll see you all hang first," Farrington shouted over his shoulder as he was led away, spittle flying from his mouth. "Wait till my father gets word of this impudence."

"Jack!" Penitence emerged from the door of the gatehouse and ran through the crowd to reach her lover. He swung her into his arms and another roar of approval went up from the garrison.

Luke shook his head. Young lovers were more trouble than they were worth. Love was more trouble... but perhaps it was worth it.

He held Deliverance closer. "You need to get some rest," he whispered.

She nodded. "Later but first tell me how did the men get into the ditch without being seen?"

Ned grinned. "Can't you guess?"

Deliverance put a hand to her nose. "You came through the south ditch?"

Ned nodded. "Oddly Farrington didn't seem to pay the south ditch much attention, but I think we would all be grateful if the water and soap could be spared to allow us the dignity of a good wash."

Deliverance nodded. "Immediately," she said.

"Capn' Sir!" One of the men on the curtain called down. "Come and see."

Luke released Deliverance and bounded up the stairs to join the man on the wall. "Look!"

"What's happening?" Deliverance stood at his side.

"They're pulling out," Luke said as he scanned the distant movement of men and wagons.

"Is it over?" Deliverance asked, her voice cracked with emotion.

"It will be by tonight."

She looked up at him, all exhaustion banished. "We did it! Oh, Luke, we did it!"

Her arms circled his neck and all modesty and decorum abandoned, they kissed to an accompaniment of whoops and catcalls.

Luke looked down at the courtyard. "That's enough cheek from you lot. They've not gone yet, so to your posts all of you and you, my lady, need to go and get some rest before you fall over. Go!"

He watched as she descended back into the courtyard and crossed over to the residence, a small, defiant figure. She had caused him to take the biggest risk of his life and he would do it again, and gladly.

A clean and perfumed Ned found Luke in the library where Toby had brought him a tray of something unidentifiable that the cook had described as 'dinner'.

Ned sat down with a heartfelt sigh. "I think you owe me an explanation."

"I do," Luke agreed. "What do you suppose this is?" He held up a piece of unidentifiable matter. "A turnip?" Ned suggested.

Luke wrinkled his nose and pushed the plate to one side. Tonight they would eat properly. "What do you want to know?"

"Jack Farrington?"

"That night we took Jack Farrington prisoner I had a long talk to him. He was wavering in his loyalty to his brother so I just let him talk. By the end he had convinced himself to turn his cloak. I didn't do anything."

"And you didn't think to tell me?" Ned looked aggrieved. "In fairness, Ned, events rather got ahead of us."

Ned sat back with his hands behind his head and looked up at the ceiling. "Not an easy decision for Jack. It wasn't just about Penitence then?"

Luke shook his head. "A man can be ruled by the contents of his breeches but I think he was genuinely appalled by his brother's handiwork at Byton. Jack Farrington is a man of conscience and honor, and while it is not an easy matter to turn against your own family, Charles' own actions forced him to it."

"I suppose you would know," Ned observed.

The old pain turned like a knife in Luke's heart as he thought about his own brother, Nick, but Nick was no Charles Farrington. In that talk with Jack, he deemed it prudent to confide his own family story as a way of drawing Jack to the decision to turncoat. He had no doubt that Jack would be incapable of keeping the story from Penitence and Penitence in her turn would tell Deliverance.

The time had come. He needed to get to Deliverance first.

"Mercifully my brother is an honourable man," Luke said. "He would never do what Charles did at Byton."

"But how did you know Jack would turn the pistol on his brother?" Ned enquired. "I didn't. I just had to trust him to rise to the occasion."

"If he hadn't?"

"Then you would have had to carry through the attack and hope they were startled enough, or repelled by your smell, to let us get away without too many casualties."

Ned shook his head. "You took a gamble."

"A huge gamble," Luke agreed. He gestured at the window with its broken glass, beyond which they could hear the sound of the departing royalists. "But it paid off. My guess is they are heading back to Ludlow to report to Sir Richard and lick their wounds."

"The older Farrington will be back though."

Luke shook his head. "Not while I'm holding his son." He drew a deep breath. "We need to get Charles Farrington to Gloucester for trial."

"A problem for the morning." Ned rose to his feet and clapped his friend on the shoulder. "But for the time being, I think a celebration is called for."

Luke nodded. "We'll kill some of the cattle and send out a patrol to see what our besiegers have left. I think there is still a cask of Sir John's wine that is unbroached."

"Leave it to me." Ned saluted and left the room.

Luke, suddenly exhausted, leaned back in Sir John's chair and studied the severe face that glared down at him from the wall.

"Well, Sir John," he said aloud. "I think you can be proud of your daughter."

Chapter Twenty-One

Deliverance woke to someone shaking her shoulder. She buried her face deeper into the bolster. "Wake up," Luke's voice whispered in her ear. "I think you might want to see this."

"Go away," she mumbled.

A finger lightly traced a line down the back of her neck. Lips followed lightly touching the nape of her neck, sending shivers down her spine.

Deliverance rolled over and looked up blearily into Luke's smiling face.

"See what?"

He gave a low-throated growl. "You look lovely when you are only half-awake."

"So do you," she murmured, remembering the words spoken aloud while he was under the influence of Lovedie's sleeping draught.

He put his arms either side of her, pinning her to the bed. His lips curled and his eyes gleamed with mischief.

"Why did you wake me?" she asked as he lifted his right hand and tugged at the lace of her chemise.

"Hmm, now you mention it there's no hurry," he murmured as he slid the garment away from her shoulders.

He kissed the soft spot at the base of her throat and drew back, touching the place where Lovedie's knife had drawn blood.

"Oh, Deliverance," he said with a shake of his head. He pulled her chemise back into place and stood. "Time for that later. Get dressed. I want to show you something."

She pulled herself up on one elbow, running the other hand through her hair. The soft golden glow of late afternoon wove its way in to the room around the roughly-nailed boards. After the drama of the morning, she had barely made it to her bed, falling asleep in her clothes. Someone, Penitence probably had taken off her boots and loosened her bodice. She must look a fright. "What time is it?"

"About five in the afternoon," he said.

"I've been asleep for hours."

"You needed the rest. Now up, my lady, and come with me." He pulled her toward him and kissed her first on the forehead, then the nose and finally the mouth. When they stopped to draw breath, he spoke in a hoarse tone. "You are a terrible distraction."

Releasing her, he waited outside the room while Meg helped her dress.

"I would love to have a wash," she grumbled as she joined him.

"Plenty of time for that." He took her hand, pulling her toward the stairs. "Hurry."

For a moment she had to stop and think what was different. Light from the lowering sun flooded through the open gates into the courtyard and the garrison and household were streaming out across the bridge.

She squeezed the hand that held hers and he answered her unspoken question. "They've gone but they left us a present."

They followed the crowd across the empty area between the castle and the village to the abandoned fortifications. Deliverance stopped in her tracks and gasped. "They left the Thunderer!"

"Evidently decided it was too cumbersome to bother with. Sir

Richard will rue the loss of this beast even more than that of his sons," Luke said.

As they neared the great gun. Sergeant Hale, bared to the waist, jumped up on the steps behind the gun that enabled the gun crew to light the fuse. He carried a massive mallet and he held this aloft to the cheers of the crowd.

In his other hand he raised a long, iron spike. With deliberate theatricality he placed the spike over the firing hole in the gun and crowd began to chant.

"Spike! Spike!"

He raised the mallet and brought it down with a mighty crash against the head of the spike driving it into the hole. He repeated this only two more times before the spike went home and the Thunderer would fire no more.

A mighty cheer went up to see the great gun that had brought them so much misery over the last few weeks reduced to an impotent lump of iron.

The sisters squabbled about who would wear the red dress to the celebration. To have such a petty, normal quarrel after all the weeks of tension made them both stop and fall on the bed laughing. In the end Penitence insisted Deliverance should wear it and Penitence, who would look like a princess in sack cloth and ashes had to content herself with her blue satin.

"You might have told me about Luke," Penitence grumbled as she attempted, not with any great success, to coax Deliverance's straight hair into more fashionable curls.

"I still don't believe it myself. What does a man like Luke Collyer see in me?"

"Men are strange creatures," Penitence, woman of the world, mused.

Deliverance caught her sister's hand and kissed it. "Well, your Jack certainly surprised me. I never thought he had it in him. Luke and I both owe him our lives."

Penitence returned to Deliverance's hair. "Surely, Father can have no objection to our marriage now?"

"Even if Jack is cut off by his father?"

"I would live in a hovel with him,' Penitence said, her face serious."And I think you need to ask your Luke about divided families."

Deliverance swivelled on the stool and looked up at her sister. "What do you know about Luke's family?"

When Penitence didn't reply, Deliverance continued. "He told me his family has taken the King's part."

"Yes but he hasn't told you who his family is, has he?"

Deliverance shook her head, sending a shower of pins to the floor.

"I give up." Penitence threw her hands in the air. "He'll just have to take you as you are."

She combed out the freshly washed hair so it fell in dark, straight, silken sheets across Deliverance's shoulders. "Love has made you truly beautiful, Liv," she said, dropping a kiss on her sister's head. "And you, Pen." Deliverance looked up at her sister and smiled.

Penitence straightened and looked at the door. She turned back to her sister, her eyes shining. "I can hear music, shall we go down?"

She took Deliverance by the hand and like a pair of young girls, they ran down the stairs, stopping at the screen door to make their entrance.

Deliverance had rarely seen the Great Hall so crowded. As well as the garrison and the household, some of the local men had retrieved their families. Trestles lined both sides of the hall and every available surface had been decorated with greenery and summer flowers. A makeshift group of musicians had installed themselves in one corner and a fiddler, Deliverance recognised as one of Luke's men, played a cheerful jig. Sergeant Hale standing near the door, saw the two women first.

"Silence!" he bellowed and all eyes turned to the door. "Mistress Deliverance Felton and Mistress Penitence Felton."

A roar went up and a round of applause that nearly lifted the much-patched roof off the hall. The crowd parted as the two women entered, allowing them their first glimpse of the officers of the garrison: Luke, Ned, Melchior Blakelocke and Jack Farrington. A high table had been set across the end to form a U and they stood beside it, applauding, all clean, and shaved, and wearing whatever passed for their best clothes.

Deliverance had eyes only for Luke. He wore the mulberry-coloured jacket and like the others sported a barbered chin. His hair stuck up on one side where he had been struck by the rock and washing and combing would have been painful but otherwise she had never seen him looking so handsome. Her insides turned to water. Whatever would happen from now, they would have tonight.

He held out his hand and she took it. He bowed and she curtsied, and the crowd went wild, whooping and thumping the tables. Luke's shoulders shook as he laughed, pulling her in beside him.

With one arm around her shoulders he raised his other hand calling for silence.

"We are here to celebrate a victory," he said. "In the great scheme of things it is a small victory but all of us here will remember how one little garrison held out against a mighty force." This was met by another round of cheering. Luke continued. "However we should also remember our comrades who fell in the gallant defence of Kinton Lacey and give due thanks to God for our liberation. Sergeant Hale will lead us in prayers of thanksgiving."

Hale puffed out his bear like chest and began. As Deliverance had expected the prayers were fulsome and lengthy. When he eventually finished to a resounding amen, Luke raised his hand, indicating for the food to be brought in and the celebration to begin.

The table groaned with roast beef and freshly baked bread. Deliverance breathed in the smell as Luke poured red wine from a jug into the Felton's best glassware. "Where did you find all this?" she asked Luke.

Ned replied. "Farrington's men left the private stores. Charles liked to live well."

"And what is he eating tonight?" Penitence asked.

Luke grinned. "Our leftover stew from yesterday washed down with water."

"What will you do with him?"

"Get him to Gloucester to stand trial as soon as possible. I could try him here and trust me nothing would give me greater pleasure than to hang him but..." He cast a quick glance towards Jack. "I think it better that he meets his maker at the hands of someone else." He curled a strand of Deliverance's hair and smiled. "Enough gloomy talk. Do you dance, Mistress Felton?"

A lively country jig had struck up and the couples were taking to the floor between the tables. Even those members of the garrison without female partners were stomping around with each other. Luke stood up and with one hand correctly placed behind his back, he offered Deliverance his hand.

Deliverance rose to her feet.

"Do you know how to dance?" she enquired.

Luke shot her an aggrieved glance. "I was not always a rough soldier," he said. "My education covered all the rudiments of a gentleman's upbringing."

He led her out on to the floor with a flourish. Luke's gentlemanly accomplishments put Deliverance to shame. She had never had much time for the finer things of a gentlewoman's upbringing and music and dancing had been left to Penitence.

As Luke caught her by the waist, he bent to whisper in her ear. "My dear Deliverance, I fear you may entirely lack any sense of rhythm."

Heat rose to her cheeks. "You're right," she mumbled as they parted to allow the lead couple to skip down the line of dancers.

Despite Deliverance's very evident lack of rhythm, they danced the next three sets. Out of the corner of her eye, Deliverance saw Toby sitting at the end of one of the benches, dejectedly poking his knife around the scraps of food remaining on his plate. Deliverance excused herself to Luke who had no shortage of partners. She subsided with an exhausted sigh on to the bench beside the boy.

"I am not a very good dancer," she said.

"No, you're not," Toby agreed. His eyes widened. "Oh mistress, I didn't mean that..."

Deliverance laughed. "It's all right, Toby, I know my weaknesses."

"You're very good at other things," Toby said. "You kept us all alive."

"Thank you," Deliverance said.

"What you did yesterday was so brave," the boy continued.

Deliverance looked away. "And you were brave too," she said. "Coming out with the drum like that."

"I saw Lovedie with that man," Toby said. "Is it true what everyone's saying, that she was a traitor?"

Deliverance nodded. "I'm sorry, Toby. Did you really have no idea?"

He shook his head. "Lovedie's looked after me all my life. When she left Byton, I thought she'd gone to get help. Didn't know she'd gone over to...to...him. She left me in that castle to die, Mistress Felton. I'll never forget that."

The hurt and anger in his face was so acute, Deliverance put an arm around his stiff, proud, young shoulders.

"I'm sure she had her own reasons, Toby."

"And they say she killed Tom Watts. Is that true?"

"I think so."

"Tom was always good to me. He didn't deserve to die like that," Toby said. "I'll never forgive her, Mistress Felton, never!"

Deliverance wondered where Lovedie had ended the day. She must have fled with the royalists but had she gone with them to

Ludlow or struck out for new pastures? She had a feeling Lovedie was more than capable of making her own fortune.

"What about you, Toby? Will you stay here? You're more than welcome."

Toby shook his head and his eyes sought out Luke on the dance floor. "I'm Cap'n Collyer's man now, Mistress Felton. Where he goes, I go too."

"I'm glad. He needs someone to look after him," Deliverance said. "Will you dance with me, Toby? I promise not to tread too hard on your toes."

The boy smiled. "Me? Dance with you?"

"No one else will," Deliverance said and rose to her feet.

Chapter Twenty-Two

As dusk closed in on the castle, Luke and Deliverance stood on the east wall looking down over the river.

Luke drew Deliverance towards him. She fitted into the shelter of his arm as if she had always belonged there.

"Last night I stood here and I thought that the end had come. Now I can just walk out of the sally port and there will be no one to stop me. I can't believe it is all over," she said.

Luke sighed. "It's far from over, Deliverance. There is still a brutal war to be fought and there is no guarantee that Farrington won't be back. He wants Kinton Lacey."

Her shoulders sagged beneath his touch. "I suppose you're right."

"This county is loyal to the King and if he prevails in the fight, your father stands to lose everything." She turned her face to look up at him. "Are you always such a realist?"

He nodded. "I've learned to be but I have also learned that moments of happiness are not to be wasted, so just for tonight we are at peace once more and this lovely evening belongs to us."

He turned her so she faced him and put his hands on her shoulders.

"Deliverance Felton, you are the most irritating, strong-minded, difficult female I have ever had to deal with in my life which is why I am going to say something to you that I have said to no woman in my life."

Deliverance's eyes widened.

"I love you," he said.

She reached up and put her hands on his shoulders. "Luke Collyer, you are the most arrogant, enigmatic, frustrating man I have ever met and I love you with you all my heart."

A slow smile lifted the corners of his mouth and the grey eyes twinkled in the last of the daylight. "Good, I am glad we have settled that. Now, what are we going to do about it?"

"What do you mean?"

He put a finger under her chin and tilted it up, searching her eyes. "I want you, Deliverance, all of you. Not just your heart."

Deliverance's legs trembled as he bent his head, his lips seeking hers. He pressed her to him, his tongue plundering her mouth with the pent-up passion of weeks of close confinement. She responded in kind, pressing her body against him, while her fingers raked the back of his neck.

They broke apart, panting for breath. "Mistress Felton, will you trust me?"

She nodded and he took her by the hand, leading her back into the residence. The festivities continued in the Great Hall and no one noticed them creep up the stairs to Sir John's fine bedchamber. Deliverance stood in the centre of the room and her arms wrapped around herself.

"What about Ned?" she ventured, scarcely believing what she was about to do. The thought scared her. She would be giving herself wholly to one man. There could never be another and yet there was no one and never would be anyone but Luke Collyer.

"Ned knows when to make himself scarce." Luke crossed to a small table where a flint and candles stood, lighting the candles. Their light bathed the room in a soft glow.

He stood looking at Deliverance for a long moment before he crossed the floor toward her, stopping an arm's breadth distant.

She shivered. "Are you cold?"

He stepped forward, folding her in his arms, his face resting on the top of her head. "No," she murmured. "Not now."

He brushed the dark hair away from her face, allowing the silken strands to play through his fingers. "You smell of summer," he mused.

"We washed our hair with herbs," Deliverance replied.

"Deliverance I want you to know that—"

"Stop talking," Deliverance said with a laugh. "I've waited too long for this night for you to squander it on words."

She pulled at his jacket and he shrugged it off letting it fall to the dusty floor as she unlaced his shirt and ran her hands through the hair on his chest. She kissed the naked flesh.

"Mmmm...you smell of lye soap," she said.

It was his turn. She wore no collar and her shoulders were bare. He bent his head and kissed the sensitive spot at the base of her throat, and she threw her head back as shivers of delight ran down her spine. Supporting her with one hand, he let his fingers trail across her chest, running lightly across the top of her bodice. The laces were at the back of the bodice and tied in a simple knot that came away with one practiced tug.

The bodice fell away revealing a simple white chemise.

"You are beautiful," Luke murmured, cupping her firm, full breasts in his hands through the fine material.

She gasped as his thumbs slowly circled her nipples, her own hands tearing at his shirt, running her fingers across his chest, sculpted to hardness by his years of soldiering.

He undid the laces on her chemise, exposing her breasts and bent his head to each one in turn. Deliverance thought she would die from the sheer pleasure. She fumbled with the lacings of the petticoats and they fell around her ankles in a cloud of red satin. Luke slid the bodice down over her hips and she stepped free of her gown wearing nothing but her chemise.

Luke stepped back and putting both hands to the sleeves of the chemise gave it a tug. It slithered down her body joining the gown and Deliverance stood before him, naked and glowing in the candle-light. She made no attempt to cover herself.

"You are beautiful," he said, and she knew he meant it. She could see herself reflected in his gaze...the small, pointed face to narrow waist and the full womanly breasts and hips. A little thinner than she had been, but still a woman, Luke's woman.

He unbuckled his belt and stepped clear of his own clothes. Her eyes raked his long, hard body, resting on the erect penis. Apart from that one fleeting glance in a dark stable, she had never seen a man in full arousal before and the sight both scared and fascinated her.

"And so are you," she responded.

He stepped forward and lifted her in his arms, depositing her on to Sir John's magnificent bed. Deliverance ran her fingers down the line of dark hair from his chest, her fingers brushing the magnificent erection that would be all hers. Her fingers stroked the silky skin on the head of his penis.

"For a virgin," Luke muttered. "You are acting in a manner most unbecoming."

Deliverance stopped what she was doing and looked at him. "Luke," she whispered. "It's true, I'm a...I've never...except with you..."

He folded her in his arms and hugged her close. "Oh, Deliverance, you do make me laugh. I know your history and I want to teach you. I want you to remember this night for the rest of your life."

He released her and slid down beside her, propping himself up on elbow. He teased her nipples with his tongue, lips and teeth until her body arched. Her eyes shut and her lips parted as she surrendered herself to the sensations he created in her.

His calloused fingers traced the curves of her body, followed by his lips as he kissed and caressed every inch of her body. When those questing fingers slid between her legs, Deliverance welcomed them.

"You are ready," he whispered.

A little of the other Deliverance wormed its way into her consciousness and her legs snapped shut and she stiffened in his arms, her eyes springing open, her frantic gaze raking his face. "Luke, I..."

"Ssh...trust me, Deliverance." His eyes looked hazy in the candle-light as he hushed her and kissed her.

She relaxed again, closing her eyes and he eased himself on top of her. As he met with resistance, a moment of panic seized her. She took a sharp breath and he withdrew, looking down at her anxiously. "Did I hurt you?"

"No," she said in an uncertain voice. "Don't stop."

He dropped down, cradling her head in his arms and kissing her gently as he pushed past until he was completely inside her. He rested for a moment, allowing her to become accustomed to the myriad of sensations that flooded her mind.

She took a breath and began to move against him, raising her hips to meet his. He moved inside her and she wondered for a moment if it were possible for two people to be any closer. Two had become one. Thoughts vanished as she surrendered herself to sensation.

"Deliverance," he whispered, as he came in a shuddering gasp, collapsing against her. She circled his body with her arms, drawing him closer, with a fierce desire never to let him go again. She had never thought it possible for her heart to be so full.

"You're crying," he said. "I'm sorry. I tried not to hurt you."

She shook her head, temporarily bereft of words. "That's not why I'm crying. I've never been so utterly happy in my entire life."

He rolled off her and lay beside her, his face so close to her that their noses touched. "We're not done yet. Just lie still..." His fingers slid down between her legs again and gently began to rub her.

She began to ask him what he was doing, but he silenced her question with a kiss. "Close your eyes," he whispered.

A wave of pleasure ran through her body, such as she had never known before. Others followed and her body arched. She heard someone cry out. Her—it had to be her. She came to a shuddering halt, breathing hard as she fell back in his arms. She just wanted to sleep.

The last thing she remembered was the touch of his lips on her hair and a whispered voice.

"Deliverance Felton, I love you. I am never going to let you go."

Deliverance woke with a cramp in her leg. A heavy weight lay across her and she tried to wriggle out from underneath it. She gave a squeak of alarm as she realised she was completely naked and there seemed to be another body in her bed. The other body mumbled and turned over and Deliverance lay back, allowing herself a silent laugh as she remembered where she was, why she was naked, who the man in the bed was and, more importantly, what they were doing there.

She closed her eyes and smiled as she remembered also the place where Luke's skilled fingers had taken her. Who could ever have imagined such a glorious sensation existed. Just thinking about it, made a warm glow spread through her body and she realised she wanted to do it again...and again. She propped herself up on one elbow and kissed Luke's ear, the only part of him she could reach. She let her hand run down his body until her fingers closed on his penis, quietly slumbering. She nibbled his earlobe until he stirred, rolling on to his back and pulling her over on top of him

"What do you want?" he teased.

"You," she said. "All of you."

"Deliverance, you will probably burn in the eternal fires of hell, for your wanton behaviour."

"I don't care. I've faced death too many times in the last few weeks to concern myself with my eternal soul."

It was too dark to see his face so her fingers traced the curve of his lips, sensing the smile.

"You are an extraordinary woman, Deliverance," he said

"Stop talking and kiss me."

They made love again. This time she knew what to expect and she allowed herself to savour every moment, the feel of him inside her. She had never thought it possible that two people could become one. Now she understood and she knew that whatever happened she did not ever want to be parted from Luke Collyer.

He brought her to climax and this time, her animal soul let fly with a howl of pure pleasure.

"You will have the whole garrison in here," Luke said, his lips silencing her moans of desire. "I'm sure no one is under any illusions about what we are about tonight."

"I don't care," she muttered. "You said tonight was just for us."

"And so it is, but tomorrow we have to face the world."

She lay in his arms, not wanting to sleep and not wanting to talk about the future. He was a soldier, they were at war and he would be gone within a few days, a few weeks...it didn't matter. She just wanted to enjoy what time she had with him.

They talked about trivial matters, small snatches of childhood memories of happier times. When she pressed him to talk about his family, he silenced her with a kiss. Eventually he stretched and pulled himself away from her, swinging his feet on to the cold stone floor.

"Where are you going?" she asked.

He looked down at her. "I think you should go back to your own bed. While I am sure no one in this castle is in the slightest doubt about the nature of our relationship, I think we should at least maintain an appearance of respectability."

Deliverance groaned. "I don't want to face the day."

He bent over and kissed her. "You must. We both have responsibilities."

He tossed her chemise at her and she reluctantly complied. She slipped into the dark corridor, every floorboard creaking as she crept back up to her room. Meg didn't stir and Deliverance slipped into bed beside Penitence, putting her cold feet on her sister.

Penitence grumbled. "Where have you been?" She turned over. "Don't tell me, I don't want to know."

Deliverance stared up at the dark alcove of the bed and whispered, "Pen, have you and Jack...?"

Penitence's eyes widened. "No."

"Why not?"

"Because we're not wed." Penitence sat bolt upright. "Deliverance what if he gets you with child?"

"I don't care," Deliverance said. "He could be killed in battle tomorrow. Isn't it better to have known total happiness with the man you love? And if there is a child, well at least there will be a part of something you had together."

"Oh, Liv," Penitence sighed, sliding back under the covers. "We are so different."

"That's why I love you, Pen."

Deliverance put her arms around her sister and kissed her.

Chapter Twenty-Three

L uke leaned against the castle wall, ostensibly watching the repair work to the roof of the residence, but his mind kept drifting to the night in Sir John Felton's bed. He longed to repeat the experience but the circumstances were conspiring against them.

When he next saw Sir John, he would ask for her hand. As he ruminated on what exactly he would say, Ned's elbow in his ribs brought him back to earth.

"Collyer!" His friend looked at him with knowing eyes and shook his head. "You have got a bad case, my friend," he said.

Luke sighed and ran his hand across his eyes.

"The quicker we get our orders to move on, the better," Ned grumbled. "I was just saying that I've received this list of demands for reparation to the villagers and farmers who suffered losses."

Luke took the paper Ned brandished and ran his eye down the list of figures amounting to a considerable amount of money. "Not much I can do about it. I haven't even got coin to pay the soldiers."

"Captain Collyer!"

Luke sprang to full alertness as one of the scouts he'd sent out that morning, came riding across the drawbridge at a full canter. He threw himself off his lathered horse and came running up to where Luke and Ned were standing. "What is it?"

"Farrington..." The man puffed as if he had been the one doing the galloping. Weeks of siege did nothing for the fitness of man or beast. "An armed force with Farrington's standard coming from Ludlow. About an hour away at the pace he's going."

Luke swore. "I didn't expect him back. Ned, sound the alarm and get everyone back inside the castle walls."

With Hawk Tower destroyed the highest vantage was afforded by the Gatehouse tower and by the time Farrington's standard came into view, the officers of the garrison and Deliverance waited for him there.

Luke leaned on the wall, watching the progress of the standard. He straightened. "It's not a large force," he said. "One hundred men at the most. No guns."

Even as he watched, a single horse detached itself from the main body and rode slowly towards the castle. The rider carried the white flag of parlay.

Recognising the magnificent chestnut stallion and the rider as Sir Richard Farrington himself, Luke gathered the officers and took the stairs down to the castle wall.

Farrington stopped within musket range and looked up at the wall. Luke addressed him. "My lord, what can we do for you?"

Farrington shifted his grip on the flag pole. "I have come to speak with my son."

"Which son?"

Farrington's gaze travelled across the row of faces, stopped at Jack and then moved back to Luke. "I have only one son," he said. "And you are holding him captive."

Luke heard the hiss of breath from Jack and out of the corner of his eyes saw Ned clap him on the shoulder.

"Colonel Charles Farrington is to be sent to Gloucester to face trial for his crimes," Luke replied. "What is your business with him?"

Farrington's shoulders stiffened. "A father's wish to speak with his son. Nothing more."

Luke turned and gave a nod to the soldiers on the gate. The door opened. Farrington dismounted, laid the flag down on the ground, unbuckled his sword and placed it carefully on the ground before crossing the bridge.

Luke waited for him in the courtyard with an escort of four armed soldiers. At his insistence, Deliverance waited in the Great Hall to receive her visitor. Farrington looked from one to the other and across at the Thunderer. Luke's men had dragged the great gun inside the castle and it now stood as an impotent testament to their survival.

"I honour your flag," Luke said, indicating the escort. "This is just a precaution. I'll take you to the prisoner."

"Before you do, I would speak with you and Mistress Felton," Sir Richard said. Luke nodded and, indicated for Farrington to follow him.

In the Great Hall, Farrington looked up at the ceiling where Luke's men had been patching the holes. "Is it true?" Farrington asked.

"Is what true?" Luke asked

"The stories I have had relayed to me about the fate of the Byton garrison?"

Luke nodded. "The garrison had surrendered. Your son ordered them to be tied them in pairs and their throats to be slit. I saw the bodies."

Farrington looked away.

Luke gestured at Deliverance. "His crimes don't end there. He threatened to strip and rape Mistress Felton. Do you want me to continue?"

Sir Richard shook his head. All his confidence and swagger had gone from him. He looked old and tired.

"You still have one son," Deliverance said.

The older man stiffened. "Jack is lost to me. I can never forgive his treachery."

"Even after you have seen everything Charles is capable of?" Deliverance said. "Would you rather hold on to a cold-hearted murderer or have a man of honor and integrity?"

"Jack has betrayed his family. That is the worst betrayal. Now take me to my son. My only son."

"Sir Richard, please, if ever you were a friend of ours, what Charles did was the act of a monster," Deliverance persisted.

Sir Richard ignored her and turned towards the door.

Luke caught Deliverance's stricken look. He shook his head, trying to convey to her that this was civil war and the Farringtons and the Feltons would forever stand on either side of a line that could not be crossed.

Luke allowed father and son to meet in private but he waited outside the door with the armed escort. The Kinton Lacey garrison watched Farrington's men from the walls, their weapons primed, for the first sign of trouble from the royalist force outside the gate.

Whatever passed between Sir Richard Farrington and his son was concluded in less than fifteen minutes. Luke locked the door behind him and with the escort saw Sir Richard to the gate.

At the gate Farrington stopped. "Thank you, Captain Collyer. You have proved yourself an honourable adversary."

"We are all subject to the dictates of our consciences, Sir Richard."

Farrington stroked his moustache. "Maybe. I bid you good day."

Luke watched by the gate as the man picked up his sword and flag and remounted the horse. He rode away at a gentle trot, rejoining his troops. The whole body wheeled and rode away.

Luke left his men at the ready but Farrington had gone and Luke doubted he would return. The campaigning season ended in a few short months and the New Year would bring new challenges and maybe another force to the gates of Kinton Lacey, but he doubted he would be there to see them.

Deliverance lay awake watching Luke sleeping in the thin light of early morning. She had shared a bed with her sister for many years but a man was different. She smiled. She didn't mind that he slept on his stomach, sprawled across the bed, leaving her with only a narrow strip on the edge. She liked the comfort of his even breathing, the gentle rise and fall of his back.

She flicked the covers back revealing the whole, long, beautiful length of him from his broad shoulders to his narrow hips, firm buttocks and long, lean rider's legs and sighed deeply. It still astonished her that this beautiful man seemed to love her.

She let her finger glide down the length of his spine. She followed her finger with gentle kisses and when he still didn't wake, she slapped his rump. He groaned and swore, rolling over to look up at her.

"What did you do that for?"

"It's time for me to go," she said.

They had received the message yesterday. Gloucester had been relieved and her father was on his way home. This would be their last opportunity of a night together before Sir John returned.

"We both need to be at our best today," she said.

Luke sighed. "Toby has been polishing my breastplate for the last two days. I hope your father is impressed."

Deliverance laid her head on his chest. Luke stroked her face. "He should be very proud of his daughter."

Deliverance turned her head to smile at him. "And his garrison commander."

She sat up, her hair tumbling around her shoulders. Luke curled a strand in his finger. "Are you in a hurry?" he wheedled.

Deliverance rolled on top of him and kissed his nose, his chin and his mouth. "I'm sure a few more minutes won't matter."

A sharp rap on the door startled them both into wakefulness. Bright daylight and the sounds of a castle at work told them they had slept too long.

"Sorry to bother you." Ned's voice came from behind the stout oak door. "But Sir John Felton has been sighted. He's only a mile away."

Deliverance shot a desperate look at Luke. "He must have been on the road since break of day. Oh no, this isn't how I meant to meet my father."

No flitting back to her room in the cold light of dawn. She groped for her clothes. She needed to look properly dressed and as if she had been up for hours.

Luke made a poor lady's maid. He seemed to be much more adept at getting her out of her clothes then back into them.

As he tied the lace on her bodice he said, "You look fine, Deliverance."

Deliverance threw back the bolt on the door and shot past Ned Barrett. She didn't have time for

pleasantries.

From beyond the walls, she heard a trumpet and drumbeats and a mighty cheer from the garrison, no doubt lining the castle walls. Her father had arrived and she felt like a strumpet who had just climbed out of her lover's bed.

She was a strumpet who had just climbed out of her lover's bed.

In her bedchamber she found Penitence, immaculately dressed in a sober gown of grey wool. Penitence looked at her sister and gasped, "Oh, Liv. You can't meet Father looking like that. Quick,

Meg, fetch some water."

Her plans of greeting her father from the gatehouse abandoned,

Deliverance took a deep breath and composed herself. Clad in a gown of dark blue wool trimmed only with plain collar and cuffs, her hair shoved into a neat white matronly cap, she descended with dignity to the Great Hall, her heart beating wildly beneath her bodice.

Did she have strumpet tattooed on her forehead?

The room seemed full of men in armour and uniform. Her father stood with his back to them, talking to Luke, who looked, annoyingly calm and unflustered and perfectly attired. Deliverance wondered when he had found the time to draw a razor over his chin. Luke said something and Sir John turned. A smile

spread across his face and he held out his arms, in a curiously uncharacteristic, paternal gesture. "Here, they are. My beautiful daughters. Come here and greet your father!"

The two women came forward. Deliverance gave her father a dutiful kiss on the cheek and stepped back when he made no move to embrace her. Penitence he folded in his arms and hugged her.

Deliverance saw Luke's quick glance in her direction. Nothing had changed. Penitence would always be her father's darling.

Sir John released his younger daughter and looked from one to the other with a fond smile.

"Girls, I know we have much news to exchange but run along. I have men's business to discuss. I

will see you in the parlour shortly."

"But, Father..." Deliverance stared at her father in disbelief. After all she had done, she was to be dismissed out of hand?

He waved at the door. "I will see you in the parlour."

Luke looked at Deliverance and gave her a barely perceptible shrug and a sympathetic smile, as Sir John turned back to the officers of the garrison. "Now, Collyer, a full account of what has transpired here, please."

Fuming, Deliverance paced the parlour floor. "Dismissed, like a pair of brainless ninnies," she said for the fourth time.

"Liv, please stop your pacing, you are making me quite ill. You know what Father is like. I'm sure

Luke will explain it all to him," Penitence said.

It was an hour before Sir John appeared at the door. He entered the room and sat down in his familiar chair, crossing his legs. He steepled his fingers and regarded his daughters.

"I hear nothing but good things about the way you two have conducted yourselves over the last few months," he said. "I am very proud of both of you."

"Thank you, Father," Deliverance said. "We could not have done it without Captain Collyer."

Sir John nodded and fingered his moustache. "I have to say I had my doubts about sending him here but he was causing nothing but trouble in Gloucester. I've given him orders to escort Charles Farrington to London to stand trial. Collyer is best placed to give the evidence needed to see the man swing."

"You're sending him away?" Deliverance stared at her father in disbelief. "He will return here—after

London?"

"Return here? Don't be silly, girl."

Panic gripped Deliverance. A world without Luke in it was unimaginable. "But what if Sir Richard tries again?"

"If he does, I have every confidence in my new garrison commander." He patted the arm of his chair. "Penitence, dear child, come here."

Penitence glanced at her sister and like an obedient young girl, perched on the arm of her father's

chair.

"Penitence, I have given my consent for Jack Farrington to marry you. I have no doubts about the

boy's loyalty to you and that his commitment is to the cause of Parliament." "Oh, Father, that is wonderful!"

Penitence kissed her father and jumped up, running over to Deliverance who hugged her fondly.

"The wedding will be conducted as soon as the banns are called and as my son-in-law, I have no hesitation in leaving Kinton Lacey in his hands."

"What?" Deliverance released her sister and stood staring at her father. "Jack is your new garrison commander? Father, no. That's not fair."

He met her outburst with surprise on his face. "Deliverance? Are you questioning my judgement?"

"Father, you don't understand..." she struggled to find the words to explain what Kinton Lacey meant to her. Words failing her, she ran from the room.

Luke, busy with Sir John's demands did not see Deliverance until supper. He took his place next to her, pressing his knee against hers. When she did not respond, he glanced at her, seeing the downward cast of her mouth.

The reason for her despondency became apparent when Sir John rose to his feet and announced that his daughter Penitence would marry Jack Farrington. Everyone stood to applaud the news. Amidst the cheers, Sir John held up his hand.

"Of course, now I am blessed with a son-in-law to take the worry of Kinton Lacey from my shoulders, I shall be leaving the castle in Jack's capable hands."

Luke's fingers clenched as he looked at Deliverance's stiff shoulders and bowed head. She rose to kiss her sister and offer public congratulations to the happy couple, but he knew her heart would be breaking.

He seemed to be alone in understanding what Kinton Lacey meant to Deliverance and his hands by his side clenched into fists at Sir John's blindness to everything his daughter had done. As she sat down again his fingers sought hers under the table and he squeezed them in silent sympathy.

Sir John set down his glass and turned to Luke. "Collyer, I quite forgot. A letter came for you in

Gloucester just after you left. I have it about me, somewhere. Oh, here we are."

He handed Luke a much creased and stained square of folded paper. Luke turned it over. He read the words written on the outside, recognising the writing and for a moment the world tilted on its access.

How had she found him?

There could be no good news to be imparted in this missive. He stowed the letter inside his jacket without breaking the seal.

"Luke?" Deliverance looked at him with an enquiring lift of her eyebrow. He smiled at her. "Nothing of any importance."

His heart hammered at the lie. Whatever the letter contained, it was not something to be read in public. It could wait until later when he was alone.

The paper burned in his jacket all through the interminable meal but as soon as Sir John dismissed them, Luke retired to his room.

With Sir John's return, Luke and Ned had found other quarters in the upper floor of the residence, in a room badly damaged by shot. It had begun to rain and the roof leaked abominably.

Luke found a dry corner, lit a candle and with shaking fingers pulled out the paper. He traced Elizabeth's bold hand *"Msr Luke Collyer, officer of Gloucester garrison."* His sister had always been tenacious. Somehow she had tracked him down.

He broke the seal, swallowed and read the short epistle three times before the import of the words sank home. He sat down heavily on the one chair in the bare room, balling the paper in his fist.

A gentle knock on the door roused him from his reverie as he recognised the coded knock as being Deliverance.

At his quick '*Come in*', she pushed open the door and slipped inside. When he didn't rise to take her

in his arms, she crossed over to him and knelt at his feet. "Luke, what is it? You look as if you've seen a ghost?" "In a way I have," he said.

"Who was the letter from?" Deliverance asked.

He lifted his hand and Deliverance took the crumpled paper, smoothing it on the table.

"Who is Beth?" she asked, having only glanced at the signature. He heard the suspicion in her voice and smiled.

"My sister," he said.

"She has terrible writing," Deliverance said. "I can barely read it. Oh, it's dated over five months

ago."

"Read it," he said.

"*Dearest Luke,*" Deliverance began, "*It is only by sheer chance that I have had reports of you being seen in*

Gloucester so I am sending this there, even though it is in enemy hands, in the hope that somehow it will reach you. They tell me you go by the name of

Collyer so I have addressed this accordingly. I write with sad news of great import to you. Our father was wounded in a minor skirmish in March. He came home to recuperate but the wound turned gangrenous and he died in great agony. During his last illness he spoke your name and clutched at my sleeve, beseeching me to find you and to tell you that in his heart you are forgiven. He did not, despite all his threats, change his will and you remain the heir to the estates in Yorkshire. The rest, of course, have passed to Nicholas and he is now Viscount Harcourt. I fear he remains obdurate and unforgiving. He will not hear your name mentioned in his presence. So we remain a house divided but, despite Nick's injunctions, I wished you to know that father's last thoughts were of you and that while Nick is away from home, dear brother, you are always welcome in this house. I long to see you. Your loving sister Beth."

Deliverance set the letter down on the table and rose to her feet. "Who are you, Luke?"

Luke swallowed. "I am the disappointing younger son of the late Viscount Harcourt of Chirton in

Warwickshire. My brother, Nicholas, who fights for the King, has, as you have read taken my father's title

and estates. My sister Beth stands between us both, as she always has done. The good news is that I

apparently now own quite considerable estates in Yorkshire, which were my mother's."

Deliverance stared at him. She shook her head, opened her mouth and shut it again. For the first time in all of their acquaintance, Deliverance had been struck dumb.

He took her hand and pressed it to his lips. "Here, with you, I am plain Captain Luke Collyer. Collyer was my mother's name. The person referred to in that letter no longer exists. I have been estranged from my family since two years before this accursed war."

"Tell me again what did you do?"

Luke looked away, propping his elbow on the table and leaning his head on his hand. He took no pride in the cause of the family estrangement. "I...I cuckolded my brother," he said. "Nick entered

King Charles' service when he was still a boy and spent most of his time at court. He advanced rapidly and was betrothed to marry one of the Queen's ladies." He took a breath, feeling the heat of embarrassment burning

his face. "I'm not proud of what I did but I only went where she led." He brought his gaze back to face Deliverance and swallowed. He may as well confess all. "Nick found us in bed. There was a terrible row and father banished me from England. When I returned our political differences put a greater divide between us. I'm sorry to deceive you, Deliverance. I thought it a life I had put behind me."

She looked at him for a long moment before she said. "None of that matters to me. You are Luke

Collyer, soldier of fortune and the man I love."

He caught her in his arms and kissed her. As they broke apart, he drew her in closer, wrapping his arms around her. "And I am trying to summon the courage to ask your father for your hand in marriage. Will

you marry me, Deliverance Felton?"

Her arms tightened around him. "I think that would be a terrible idea," she said. "But if you're the best offer I'm ever likely to get, then yes"

He laughed and looked down at her strong face with the beautiful eyes and sharp, determined chin. "Yes, I'm afraid you are stuck with me," he murmured as he bent to kiss her.

And maybe, when all of this is over, you will be Deliverance Harcourt, mistress of a beautiful house in Yorkshire, that will bring you solace for the loss of Kinton Lacey, he thought.

Chapter Twenty-Four

L uke stood outside the library, which had been turned back to its rightful owner, staring at the blackened studs in the old oak door. By his side, Deliverance fidgeted. He had never seen her so nervous and in truth riding into the teeth of enemy musket fire seemed less daunting than facing Sir John Felton. He squeezed her hand and knocked.

At Sir John's abrupt '*Enter*', Deliverance put her hand to her chest and flattened herself against the wall.

They had agreed, after some argument, that Luke would face Sir John on his own so he turned the handle and stepped into the familiar room, shutting the door behind him. He had every confidence that Deliverance would have her ear to the keyhole.

Sir John sat at the table, now cleared of Deliverance's books and Luke's papers. A bottle of wine stood at his elbow and he appeared to be engrossed in writing a report. Above him, the man's portrait glowered at Luke as if sensing what business Luke had come about.

He looked up. "What is it, Collyer?"

Luke decided to come straight to the point. Sir John was not a man for idle chatter. "Sir, I would like to request your daughter's hand in marriage," he said.

Sir John straightened in the chair, his face taking on the forbidding cast of his portrait above him. "Which daughter?"

Luke stared at the man. *Which daughter?* Penitence was betrothed. As far as he knew that left only one other.

"Deliverance," he replied.

Sir John turned an interesting shade of puce. "Don't be ridiculous, Collyer. What on earth makes you think that I would let you marry my daughter, a man with your reputation?"

Luke swallowed. He had played this over in his mind and in every iteration, Sir John had stood and grasped him by the hand and wished him well.

"Sir, I assure you—"

Sir John rose to his feet, with a finger pointed at Luke's chest "I sent you here against my better judgment. I know all about your little escapade to Ludlow and how you deliberately endangered my daughter's life. If you think for one moment that I would hand her over to you...in marriage. Marriage! My daughter marry a scapegrace such as you?" Spittle formed at the corners of Sir John's mouth as he spoke.

"I—" Luke got no further.

"First you get her shot and then you send her out as bait for that bastard, Farrington to have his way with. She could have been killed, or worse. I was prepared to turn a blind eye to your lack of judgment but if I thought for a minute that you...you... if you have compromised my daughter's honor, Collyer. I warned you what would happen."

Luke stared at Sir John. His mind had gone completely blank and he could think of nothing to say in his defence.

The door burst open and Deliverance raced in, her anger matching her father's. "That wasn't how it was, Father. Luke saved my life."

"Be quiet, Deliverance." Her father roared her. "This man has

236

taken advantage of your innocence and placed you in grave danger on more than one occasion. He is an irresponsible, womanising—"

"I want to marry him." Deliverance's voice rose, choked with emotion. "You are letting Penitence marry Jack Farrington."

"That is an entirely different case. They have been betrothed for years and Jack is a thoroughly respectable young man whereas this," Felton waved a hand at Luke, "wastrel and whoremonger." He straightened and ran his hands down his coat as if the gesture would erase his anger. In a more moderate tone, he said, "In the circumstance, Collyer I cannot permit you to spend another night under this roof.

Barrett will take Farrington on to London. You can take the rest of your men and find service with the Earl of Essex. I never want to see your face again. I want you out of my home and away from my daughter by sundown tonight."

"Luke! Do something." Deliverance turned to him.

He knew what she wanted him to say but the words stuck in his throat. If he tried to speak the white anger that burned in his heart at the injustices just meted out to him would cause him to act intemperately. Memories of the arguments with his father flooded back, with their equally disastrous consequences. He needed to clear his head before he spoke another word.

He turned on his heel and strode out of the room.

"Deliverance Felton, do not move!" Sir John said before the door slammed shut.

In the corridor he stopped and leaned his head against the cold stone of the castle wall. This was what was meant by the old proverb 'as you make your bed, so shall you lie in it'. Womanising and drink had for so long sustained him, masking the bitterness, anger and pain of his family's rejection.

In Deliverance he had found not only his equal but a friend, a soul mate. He straightened, hearing the sound of Sir John's wrath echoing down the corridor.

A man fought for one's friends, gave his life for your friends, you didn't just walk away. For a lover you fought to the death. He threw open the door.

Deliverance stood facing her father alone, tears tracking scalding courses down her face.

"I made a grave error sending that man here," he said. "And it grieves me that he has seduced and ruined you, daughter, but you were always of an independent mind, not biddable like your sister. It seems I must beat that sense into you that you so lack."

Her father moved out from behind the desk, undoing the buckle of his belt. She stared at him. Surely he didn't intend to beat her? A grown woman?

She backed away, putting out her hand as he advanced her. "I am a grown woman with my own mind, father. You cannot beat me," she said, surprised at how calm her voice sounded. Her father's sword and baldric hung slung over the nearest chair, well within her reach.

She looked at her father's face, still purple with rage, as he folded the belt, preparatory to beating her. She remembered these beatings from her childhood. She had tried so hard to please him, to be more like Penitence, but it was never enough.

In one swift movement she drew the sword from its scabbard. It came out with a slight hiss. Well- schooled in swordsmanship, she assumed a stance that Sir John would know only too well. *En garde.*

"I will not be beaten like a recalcitrant child," she said.

Sir John took a step back. "You dare draw a weapon on your father?"

"In self defence, yes," she replied.

The door crashed open.

"I can see you seem to have the situation under control, Deliverance," Luke's voice came from behind her.

The point of the sword wavered. "Luke, tell him."

"Put that sword down, Deliverance," Luke said. "It's never a good idea to draw a weapon on your father. I speak from experience."

Deliverance laid the sword on the table and moved to Luke's side. Her father appeared to be frozen, staring at her. The colour had drained from his face and she wondered if perhaps she had really scared him.

"Where did you learn to handle a sword?" Sir John finally spoke.

"Did you think I spent the last six months mending sheets and doing fine embroidery, Father?"

"She's a fair shot as well," Luke put in.

She glanced at him. "Father, please can we talk," Deliverance said.

She swallowed and opened her mouth but Luke laid a hand on her arm as Sir John restored his belt to his breeches.

"Sir John. I know my reputation but believe me when I say my intentions towards your daughter are entirely honourable."

Luke put his arm around Deliverance drawing her into him, giving her courage.

"Father, I am over twenty-one. I do not need your consent to wed. If Luke leaves this castle today then I go with him."

The last sparks of defiance burned in Sir John's eyes. "If you go with him, you will be no daughter of mine. I shall disinherit you."

Deliverance glanced up at Luke. "Father, you have already made it quite clear that you intend for Jack and Penitence to have Kinton Lacey. That is...was the only thing in the world I cared about. You have already disinherited me."

Sir John pointed at Luke. "Collyer. Why do you fight for the cause of parliament?"

Luke considered the question. "Because I believe the King has brought this country to ruin through his own stubbornness and refusal to listen to the voice of the people."

"What manner of man are you?"

Deliverance held her breath. Would Luke tell her father the truth of his birth?

"Sir, I come from a family divided in this war. It would grieve me to see a wedge placed between you and your daughter. There is enough enmity in the world without that." He paused. "My brother is Viscount Harcourt. I hold lands in my own right in Yorkshire. Grant your consent for Deliverance to wed me and you have my word I shall see her bestowed in a manner worthy of her station in life.

"Harcourt, you say?" Sir John stroked his moustache. "And you daughter," he addressed Deliverance. "Are you determined on this course of action?"

"I am, Father."

Sir John sat down heavily and picked up the bottle of wine. He poured a glass and took a drink. "No." He held up his hand at the squeak of protest that came from Deliverance. "Hear me out. I need time to think on this, daughter, and I do not take kindly to the sort of wilful disobedience you have shown me here today. Collyer... Harcourt...whatever your name is, take Farrington to London as ordered and return here. Then we will talk."

"Very good, sir."

Deliverance started forward but Luke caught her arm. "Deliverance, your father has spoken."

He propelled her out of the door, shutting it firmly behind him

As Deliverance opened her mouth to protest, he laid his finger on her lips. As she glared at him, he smiled. "Trust me, Deliverance?"

Chapter Twenty-Five

L uke paraded his men in the courtyard. Breast plates and helmets gleamed in the winter sunlight, faces were clean-shaven and even the faded coats looked fresh.

Under his orders, they had taken particular care to look their very best and managed to transform themselves once again from the raggle taggle band of defenders to a smart, fighting force. Beneath the gleaming breast plate, Luke pondered his future with a heavy heart. He couldn't bear the thought that he was leaving Deliverance but he had his orders. Charles Farrington, manacled, and looking far from his sartorial best, would ride in a covered wagon. Keeping him safe until London would be a dangerous mission and his men had orders to shoot Charles at the first sign of attack.

Luke's horse tossed its head in anticipation of being away from this terrible place where they had been confined to stables for weeks and threatened with being turned into food. Luke held the bridle and waited as Sir John Felton appeared on the stairs with Penitence and Jack beside him.

Sir John had given him letters to deliver and he had no doubt that the one addressed to the Earl of Essex contained orders for Luke to join the Earl's force. Felton did not want him returning to Kinton Lacey.

Luke scanned the castle windows for Deliverance. They had decided to say their farewells in private.

Deliverance had, as he expected, been sharp tongued but he had seen the brimming eyes as she turned away.

Whatever means Felton employed to keep them apart, he would return and claim Deliverance. "Collyer. Your men are well turned out," Sir John commented.

"Thank you, sir," Luke replied without warmth.

"Once again, I wish to thank you all for the gallant defence of this castle," Sir John said, hypocritically, Luke thought. "Had Kinton Lacey fallen, our cause in this county would have been lost. God speed and keep you safe."

Luke saluted and swung himself into the saddle. He doffed his hat, still bearing the neat round hole of Deliverance's greeting, in salute to Sir John Felton to the applause of the household and resident garrison. "God speed, Collyer," Sir John said.

Luke nodded to Sergeant Hale and the man gave the order to the men to form into file. With their two drummers beating the march, the men wheeled but before they had advanced a step, a voice came from the residence.

"Wait!"

Luke wheeled his horse at the sound of Deliverance's voice. She came running out of the house, one hand holding her hat on her head and the other clutching a leather satchel. Luke threw back his head and laughed as his beloved Deliverance, dressed in her men's breeches and wearing a baldric and sword, paused to plant a kiss on her father's cheek.

Before the astonished man could react, Deliverance had run down the stairs and stood at Luke's stirrup. He took the satchel from her and extended his hand. She looked up into his eyes and smiled as she grasped his hand and he swung her up behind him. A resounding cheer from his soldiers and the Kinton Lacey garrison echoed around the courtyard.

"Deliverance!" Sir John had found his voice. "What do you think you're doing? Get down immediately. You look ridiculous. Come down off that horse and behave in a more decorous manner."

Deliverance hooked her hands into Luke's belt and her body pressed against his, warm and familiar, as if they belonged together. He twisted to look into Deliverance's eyes.

"You? Decorous?" he said.

Deliverance looked back at her father. "I'm afraid my mind is made up, Father. I am going to follow the drum. Wherever Luke goes, I do too."

Her father raised his hand. "Deliverance, get down now."

"Luke has his orders, Father. Farewell. I will write."

A resounding cheer went up and Luke turned his horse back to take his place at the head of the column.

"Collyer," Sir John Felton roared.

Luke turned his horse back. "Sir John?"

"By God, you'd better take good care of her."

Luke smiled. "One thing I have learned, Sir John, is that she is quite capable of taking care of herself."

"Father, I will be a far better camp follower than I would ever be a housewife," Deliverance said. "Please give us your blessing?"

Sir John Felton looked around the courtyard. The unsmiling faces of the garrison glared back at him. He cleared his throat.

"It seems I have little choice," he said. "You will go with or without my blessing?"

"Father, please," Penitence added her entreaty to her Father.

Sir John shook his head. "Then God speed and God bless," he said, raising his right hand. "And for His sake, if not mine, marry her, Collyer."

"At the first preacher I can find, Sir John," Luke said with a grin.

Luke nodded to Hale and, with Luke at their head, the defenders of Kinton Lacey marched out for the last time. As they passed under the gatehouse, Deliverance twisted to look back.

"Not too late to change your mind," he said.

Her arms slid around his waist. "You know me. When I make my mind up, it takes a lot to change it. I love you, Luke Collyer."

Luke smiled. Whatever lay ahead of them would not be easy but no one could ever say it would be dull.

Author's Note

While Kinton Lacey Castle and its inhabitants are fictional, this story was inspired by the extraordinary bravery of two women, Brilliana Harley, who held her husband's castle (Brampton Bryan in the county of Herefordshire) against a besieging force for many months. Sadly her story did not have a happy ever after as she died of pneumonia shortly after the end of the siege. The second woman was Charlotte, Countess of Derby, nicknamed "Babylon" by the besieging force. The Countess of Derby held Lathom House in Lancashire for her royalist husband against the forces of parliament. Lathom House eventually fell and, like Brampton Bryan, was slighted.

The fate of the garrison at the fictional Byton Castle is based on the very real fate of another Herefordshire Castle, Hopton Castle.

Cover Photographs: Reproduced under license from Hot Damn Stock and Barry Wilson

Acknowledgments

There are always so many people to thank. Books just don't write themselves and I could not have written this story without the ongoing input and support of my wonderful writer's group, The Saturday Ladies' Bridge Club. From frantic pleas not to eat the horses through to suggestions for titles, this group has been with this book from the beginning. I am particularly grateful to those who agreed to "beta read" the draft. Their input was invaluable.

My professional production support team: editor Annie Seaton, cover designer, Megan, Merry Bond of Anessa Books who does my formatting and my patient mother-in-law (and second copy editor) PJB.

And of course, my wonderful husband... to whom I dedicate this story... who is more than happy to discuss the characteristics of siege guns with me.

About the Author

Alison Stuart is an award winning Australian writer of cross genre historicals with heart. Whether dueling with dashing cavaliers or wayward ghosts, her books provide a reader with a meaty plot and characters who have to strive against adversity, always with the promise of happiness together. Alison is a lapsed lawyer who has worked in the military and fire service, which may explain a predisposition to soldier heroes. She lives with her own personal hero and two needy cats and likes nothing more than a stiff gin and tonic and a walk along the sea front of her home town.

Connect with Alison online and join her readers' group for a free book, exclusive content, contests and more at
www.alisonstuart.com
alison@alisonstuart.com

OTHER TITLES by Alison Stuart

Historical Romance

And Then Mine Enemy

Guardians of the Crown Series

By The Sword (Book 1)

The King's Man (Book 2)

Exile's Return (Book 3)

Paranormal Historical Romance

Gather The Bones

Secrets In Time

Prologue – By The Sword

Devon 1646

"Thrrm. Thrrm."

The beat of the drum, as steady and relentless as the rain was the only sound in the village square as the wretched group of men staggered out of the church. Dirty, unshaven and reeking, they still wore the tattered vestiges of a once proud blue uniform; the shabby remnants of the King's Army. Blinking in the light and oblivious to the rain, they stared in bewilderment and disbelief at the five hastily erected gibbets that faced them.

The stony faced drummer continued his steady cadence as the prisoners shuffled into line. Watching from his vantage point beside his drummer, Captain Stephen Prescott, resplendent in the scarlet uniform of the New Model Army, scanned the line of men, seeking out the face of his nemesis.

Little distinguished Jonathan Thornton from his men, except his height. He staggered forward with his head bowed. Only as the trooper behind him, pushed him to the end of the row, did he lift his head and Prescott smiled with vicious satisfaction at the sight of the bruised and battered face, the legacy of the savage beating his prisoner had received the night before.

Prescott's eyes flicked away from Jonathan Thornton to the fresh-faced boy, barely old enough to grow a beard, who stood beside him. Despite a defiant expression on his face, the boy's hands shook with more than just the cold and the rain. Prescott summarily scanned the rest of the line and gave a curt nod of his head. The drummer rested his sticks on his drum and stared straight ahead, his face expressionless.

A trooper stepped forward. In his hand he held pieces of straw which he fanned out. A restless murmur of dissent rose from the prisoners. The fragile pieces of straw were all that stood between them and the gibbets.

The trooper moved slowly along the line of prisoners. The first two prisoners were lucky but their quiet self-congratulation was short lived as the third drew his straw. He gave a strangled cry but the trooper had moved on, slowly down the line. Four short straws were drawn. He reached the young cornet, one straw left in his hand. Jonathan Thornton would not have to draw.

The boy hesitated, turning frightened eyes on the tall figure of his captain beside him. Jonathan looked up at Stephen Prescott, disbelief in his eyes.

"Surely not the boy?" he said.

Prescott stared back at him, his face inscrutable. "Draw," he commanded the trembling boy. Jonathan stepped in front of his cornet.

"Not the boy!"

Two burly troopers moved forward and seized Jonathan, roughly pulling him away. Prescott's cold blue eyes fixed on the boy.

"Draw!"

Cornet Williams stared in vacant disbelief, first at Stephen Prescott and then at Jonathan. With a shaking hand he reached out, knowing even before he drew it that it would be his death. He stared at the fragile piece of straw in his fingers and began to weep, not out loud but silent tears that ran down his face, leaving tracks in the dirt.

The drum began its pitiless beat again. "Thrrm, thrrm…"

The onlookers expected the five chosen men to go to the gibbet, screaming and protesting, but the absolute silence was more chilling. The men stood quietly while their hands were bound and they were forced up onto the stools, brought out from the inn, to serve this grim purpose. The lips of a couple of the condemned men moved in silent prayer as the ropes were placed around their necks.

Cornet Williams turned one last despairing glance towards Jonathan, who stood, firmly held in the grip of two troopers. Jonathan met his eyes and held them. To turn away would have been cowardice. The Cornet's gaze did not flinch as one by one his companions' stools were kicked away from underneath them. He was the last.

As the five innocent men danced their last, macabre dance of death, Jonathan Thornton stood motionless forcing himself to take in every last dreadful detail, fixing it in his memory forever.

Only when it was over, did he turn again to look at Stephen Prescott whose eyes had not left him through the whole ordeal. The Roundhead officer smiled a grim humorless smile of triumph. Prescott gave a nod and the troopers released their grip. Jonathan dropped to his knees in the mud and wept for the five innocent lives that his own actions had bought so dearly.

CPSIA information can be obtained
at www.ICGtesting.com
Printed in the USA
LVHW111401050921
697034LV00014B/357